D0482246

Praise for *Jean Harley Was Here*
Finalist for the Readings Prize
for New Australian Fiction

"*Jean Harley Was Here* performs the work of which only the best fiction is capable: it reminds the reader of the precious value of life, of the responsibility we have in caring for one another as best we can, and of the beauty that can result from these efforts. I laughed and cried and loved these characters, each and every one, without reserve. You'll be so glad to be a part of Jean Harley's world."
—Kayla Rae Whitaker, author of *The Animators*

"Heather Taylor-Johnson has a poet's understanding of the world: her exploration of the way in which our lives intertwine—for better or for worse—is nuanced and poignant. A book to savor."
—Hannah Kent, bestselling author of *Burial Rites* and *The Good People*

"Warm and insightful."
—Christos Tsiolkas, author of *The Slap*

"I loved the book. . . . It's really beautifully done and extremely well-written."
—Jennifer Byrne, ABC First Tuesday Book Club

"Full of heart and soul, this book is one of the year's best."
—*Readings*, "The Best Fiction Books of 2017"

"I just couldn't put it down. I was engrossed immediately and tearing up by page two; it felt so real. This is a moving portrayal of the power of love and of friendship and it's wonderful."
—*Readings e-News*, "Books That Made Us Cry in 2017"

"Accomplished . . . moves freely between the poetic and commercial, creating a compelling rhythm."

—*Australian Book Review*

"Taylor-Johnson's interweaving of her characters and management of chronology is particularly impressive."

—*Sydney Morning Herald*

"I loved this book and highly recommend it."

—The Big Book Club

"Contemplative and hopeful."

—*Good Reading*

"A pleasure to read about the life of someone special to those who loved her."

—*Australian Women's Weekly*

"It's a clever novel which somehow manages to avoid being overly emotional despite the premise. This said, the story did make me laugh and cry, and reminded me of people I know."

—*Readings Online*

"But Taylor-Johnson has somehow created a character who is imagined, remembered and grieved-over through the intricate overlapping of her life with the lives of the people she connected with, and it is so beautiful that I fought back tears more than once."

—*OddFeather*

"It is filled with lilting language and a pulsing beat."

—*Avid Reader Blog*

JEAN
HARLEY
WAS
HERE

JEAN HARLEY WAS HERE

A Novel

HEATHER TAYLOR-JOHNSON

Arcade Publishing • New York

First North American Edition 2018

This is a work of fiction. Names, characters, places, and incidents are either the products of the author's imagination or used fictitiously.

First published in Australia in 2017 by University of Queensland Press

Quote from *You Are My I Love You* © 2001 by Maryann K. Cusimano. used by permission of Philomel, an imprint of Penguin Young Readers Group, a division of Penguin Random House LLC.

Arcade Publishing books may be purchased in bulk at special discounts for sales promotion, corporate gifts, fund-raising, or educational purposes. Special editions can also be created to specifications. For details, contact the Special Sales Department, Arcade Publishing, 307 West 36th Street, 11th Floor, New York, NY 10018 or arcade@skyhorsepublishing.com.

Arcade Publishing® is a registered trademark of Skyhorse Publishing, Inc.®, a Delaware corporation.

Visit our website at www.arcadepub.com.

10 9 8 7 6 5 4 3 2 1

Library of Congress Cataloging-in-Publication Data

Names: Taylor Johnson, Heather, author.
Title: Jean Harley was here : a novel / Heather Taylor-Johnson.
Description: First North American edition. | New York : Arcade Publishing, 2018.
Identifiers: LCCN 2018017372 (print) | LCCN 2018020521 (ebook) | ISBN 9781628729603 (ebook) | ISBN 9781628729597 (hardcover : alk. paper)
Classification: LCC PR9619.4.T3985 (ebook) | LCC PR9619.4.T3985 J43 2018 (print) | DDC 823/.92—dc23
LC record available at https://lccn.loc.gov/2018017372

Cover design by Erin Seaward-Hiatt
Cover photo courtesy of iStockphoto

Printed in the United States of America

To Deb Martin
Your death cut our friendship short
and yet our friendship still endures

JEAN
HARLEY
WAS
HERE

PART
1

A Moment before the Moment

Jean Harley was here. Ask her mother, who will say it had been a difficult labor but raising the child was like a picnic: sometimes the wind picked up and sometimes the clouds rolled in, bringing chill or rain, but mostly there was sun. Ask her husband, who hates sleeping alone but will not take a new lover. Ask her son, who will need photographs to remember her face as the years forge ahead. Ask the professor she was assisting with research. They'd only had one day left together in their office before the university closed for holidays. "Bloody hell," he'd said that day. More than once. Ask someone from her bank. Ask the Australian Department of Immigration. Ask the three birds that flew from the tree when her bicycle hit the ground.

Some people say "she never saw it coming," but there was a moment, before the moment, which made her heart jump. It was a pinpoint, as if everything she had ever done was about to culminate in the very next moment, and she knew this. She saw it inside of herself and then it was over. The moment had passed. Cars rolled on.

Ask the onlookers who saw its carnage and will remember the scene in great detail: the police lights blurry in the early morning rain; cars resting off to the side of the black road, crushing the wet grass, almost lost, almost confused; two police officers; an ambulance; a burly man who looked to have a foul taste in his mouth; a hysterical woman holding a small baby; the baby getting wet, but it wasn't a heavy rain and it wasn't a cold rain so at least there was that; witches hats guarding the tragedy; the banged-up bicycle; the crumpled cyclist being attended to.

Ask her closest friends. They will say that Jean Harley, the energetic woman who could dance without break for four hours straight but couldn't hold her pee in if she laughed too hard, the shortest woman in the room who had the largest self-esteem but never, ever was she big-headed, they will say that, yes, Jean Harley was here. They will say to each other for a very long time that they do not understand, that it makes no sense. Ask the paramedic who worked on her in the ambulance; his morning had proved to be quite busy. Ask the attendant at the nurses' station who had to phone her husband. Ask Charley, who had only wanted to mail a letter.

PART
2

Waiting for Betelgeuse to Die

Stan and Jean were destined to be lovers. It was painted on the walls of prehistoric mountains and sung by the fish in the southern seas; *Stan and Jean* were written in the stars.

As children, on opposite sides of the world, they took notice of the heavens. They each saw Orion's Belt as upright and natural. They weren't to know that in time they would both see it upside down and filled with possibilities, their bodies almost touching.

When Stan was twenty-three, he inherited thousands of dollars from his grandfather and left Kangaroo Island to spend six weeks skiing in the French Alps and six weeks mountain biking in the American Rockies. Only hours before he first met Jean, he was thrashing his bike over fallen wood and leaves. A canopy of aspens surrounded him while the incline of the earth tested his agility. His focus on the trail consumed him, which is why he hadn't seen the deer—he'd heard it first, then hit it. Stan would later say the deer ran into him, but his front tire hit the deer's left side, so it was certainly he who ran into it. "I never saw it coming," he would later tell the story. "Never knew they were so big."

Naturally he fell off his bike, banging and scraping his shoulder and leg. There was no pain at first, his body so full of adrenaline.

He was stunned, even thought momentarily about death. "I didn't know they were so strong." One cannot simply go back to camp and settle in after such an experience with a deer. One needs a large meal and a few pints.

"Oh my god!" the girl outside the Corner House Grill blurted out, no doubt seeing the hundreds of dots of blood seeping through the skin of Stan's shin.

"It hurts," he laughed, limping carefully. "I hope this place has beer."

The girl stopped walking. Stan stopped too.

"What did you do to yourself?"

"I ran into a deer."

"A deer!" Her mouth hung open. Was she shivering from imagining his pain or was it the chill from the fading light, from the breezes born off the San Miguel River, off the walls of Bear Creek Canyon, where Stan had met his deer?

He liked her surprise. Her reaction to the wound and its cause made him want to tell her the story. He had to tell someone. And there were other stories to share. The hailstorm he hit while cycling in Southwestern Utah and the shenanigans at the crazy little pub in Salida, Colorado.

"Where are you from?"

"Place called Kangaroo Island."

"No shit," she laughed.

"Yeah, Kangaroo Island, South Australia."

Her eyes grew wide, her smile seemingly caught midstream of disbelief and fascination. "What's that like?"

"It's small. Full of beaches with fast waves. Good bushland."

Bushland, he could see her thinking, as if summing up every-thing as "other," yet "simple" too.

"Are there lots of kangaroos?" she asked.

The same question every time and still he loved it. "Heaps, but I've never crashed my bike into one before."

"Wow."

Wow—such an American reaction, somehow so innocent and big, and Stan thought it mixed perfectly with the bigness of her thick hair and fullness of her breasts, and her eyes too, blue and *big*. It was then that Stan jumped somewhere inside himself. It was only a moment, but it would stay with him forever.

After the girl marveled at his leg for a bit, Stan showed her his shoulder.

"Oh my god!" This time she almost jumped backwards.

"I know. Big rock." He was beginning to feel quite manly, impressing even himself. "Took a good chunk out, didn't it?"

"Sure did."

There was a pause. A silence not quite awkward, not quite comfortable.

"I'm Stan." He held out his hand with his good arm.

"Jean." She happily shook it.

"Have you had dinner yet, Jean?"

"No." She appeared taken aback, as if sensing he was about to ask her to join him for dinner and not at all sure why a boy like him might do that.

"Can I buy you dinner tonight?"

Jean laughed, looked around Fir Street and said, "Yeah!" nodding her head. "Yeah!"

Stan ordered a bison burger. He had just run into a deer and was starving for meat, though Jean recommended the veggie burger because she was vegetarian. She said the veggie burgers were the most popular burgers on the menu, and she knew this because she worked there, in Telluride's Corner House Grill: her first big gig away from home. Stan translated this as "an explorative year between *girl* and *woman*." Felt he was doing the same bloody thing, only it was his year between *boy* and *man*. Technically he was a man. When he got home, he was going to move into a shared house on the mainland with some mates, so he'd be well and truly untangled from his mother's apron strings. He was enrolled in uni to become a teacher, following an ancestral pull. He would miss Kangaroo Island, though (and his mum). The four-wheel-drive tracks round every corner. The fishing. The Arctic wind.

They compared KI to Jean's home in Missouri, where dampness could thicken a summer sky, make it steamy, get a person restless. They compared the flatness and the hills that made up both of their homes, though one swam in saltwater and the other in the purity of Little Sugar Creek. When they closed their eyes, one said he saw golden and the other said she saw green. She told him she was homesick and blue, having found out only hours earlier her first boyfriend had died, drunken and drowned. The boy had been fifteen when they'd dated. She thought it might have been his birthday tomorrow and that he would have been twenty if he'd lived through the night. She told Stan that when she got off work she wanted nothing but to go back to the house she rented with Macy from Illinois and Lacy from New Mexico and watch a movie, something to make her cry, because she hadn't yet cried about James, but she needed to: such a terrible waste of a human life. She mentioned James's parents to Stan, his poor parents, and then she cried. Then followed discussions of a philosophical and spiritual nature, which all came back to Stan affirming that one must seize the day, while Jean wondered if she was doing the right thing living in Colorado. Did her parents and her brother and all of her old friends miss her as much as she did them? Did the Little Sugar Creek miss the feel of her feet? By the time the restaurant began to close, they'd told things to one another they hadn't even realized needed telling.

~

10

Later, outside the Corner House Grill, Stan and Jean were silhou-
ettes against the moon for any small insect looking up at them.

"I have to make my way to Denver in the morning." It was a
313-mile bike ride and his plane left for Australia in three days.
He wanted to kiss her and could feel she wanted to kiss him too.
Together they settled on looking at the stars.

"Orion's upside down here," he told her.

"Are you serious?"

"Shit yeah."

"That's amazing. To know you're really on the other side of the
planet, not because a map shows you but because the world does."

They stared at Orion a little longer.

"It's such a big world," she said.

"It's not so big." He looked at her, hoping she'd look back. And
when she did, the contact lingered too long, but not quite long
enough.

"See you." And when he walked away, he was already feeling
nostalgic.

"Careful of the bears," she called to him. "They're much bigger than the deer!"

★

In the sixteen months that passed, the earth had tilted and spun
in its foolish little way and jostled them ever closer. In the end it
was determined that no land could separate Stan and Jean, no
ocean could deter them, and the stars could not exist without
their love.

Dinner was served from five to eight, and at seven, with a full
dining room, the waves of Bass Strait reached three metres high.
The ferry was doing its best to leap from the water into the heavens, moving from one form of darkness to another. People took

their time walking from the bains-marie to their tables, stumbling while carrying their trays of roasted meats and vegetables. Bread rolls jumped. Hokkien noodles splattered on the floor. Red wine splashed onto tablecloths. There was plenty of noise, all the *oh*s and *whoa*s of the diners trying to carry on conversations. It was sensory overload for Stan, and the cheesy broccoli wasn't doing him any favors. The oil from the cheese coated his throat and his stomach felt pregnant with dead curd. The fact that the woman next to him told her husband she was going to be sick didn't help either. The woman's face turned rotting-apple green and, for thirty intense seconds, she stifled umlauted sounds while puffing up her cheeks, so Stan wasn't surprised when the woman threw up. What did surprise him was when the teenage boy nearby took one look at the woman with vomit dripping from her chin and he threw up too. The woman was crying, her husband asking neighboring diners for napkins, the boy's brother laughing and yelling, "Gross! That's so gross!," every diner watching, so when Stan stood up to leave, everybody saw him. Including Jean.

She caught him as he was about to exit. Among passengers queuing for dinner—utterly unaware of how dinner might turn on them—Jean grabbed Stan's arm.

"Stan!"

When he turned and saw her, that was it. He would later tell the story that that was the moment he knew he was in love with Jean Harley.

Beyond retreating thunder clouds, clear sky was beginning to take shape. Perhaps the waves were calming down. Perhaps it was an illusion due to their distraction.

"What are you doing in Australia?"

"Going to Tasmania!" Jean laughed, her body leaning backward and her hair blowing forward. "I'm going to cycle around it. I got the idea from meeting you. Been on lots of cycling trips now. What are you doing?"

"Going to Tasmania," he countered. "A mate's wedding. My girlfriend and I are going over for the week." His stomach turned and it wasn't the waves or the cheesy broccoli; it was the word "girlfriend" and the instantaneous knowledge that he and Jean would not kiss. "She's sick," he said, looking to the sea and making a sweeping motion of all that came with it.

"I saw those people next to you get sick. That's how I saw you."

"Can you believe that?" He rolled his eyes incredulously, laughing at the memory that would never disappear.

"Totally charming."

Stan thought *Jean* was totally charming.

"Why are you in Australia?" he asked again, stunned at the coincidence and already wondering if it was more than a coincidence. Stunned by the blue of her eyes, amazed he had somehow forgotten them.

"After you left I started thinking about traveling. I figured if I went to college in some other country, then I could live there for a few years on a student visa. So I go to Flinders Uni and I'm on break now."

"Cycling round Tasmania."

"Cycling around Tasmania."

They both looked out at the sea, as if they might be able to see the lights of Devonport together.

"I wanted to go to Kangaroo Island when I first moved here," she said. "I thought I might find you."

"Why didn't you?"

"Too much like a silly romance movie."

"And here we are now." When Stan looked back at Jean, his heart rose in his chest and tried to touch her cheek. He wondered if she could feel its vibration. It scared him that he wanted to spend the rest of the ferry ride with Jean. That he couldn't scared him more.

They talked until nearly midnight, when it seemed most of the passengers had gone to bed. Stan said he should go check on Grier. *Grier.* Saying it aloud convinced him the relationship could not last. Grier was wonderful, a great girl and sexy as, but she was nothing like Jean.

"Orion." He pointed to the hunter in the sky.

"Upside down," she said.

Jean sent Stan a postcard from Bicheno, a laid-back seaside town on the eastern coast of Tasmania. Stan kept it on his dresser. He thought of Jean every morning while he went for his jocks and socks, every night when he turned on his bedside lamp just to reread her words: *Sometimes I daydream about where we'll meet next.*

He stayed with Grier for another two weeks. It could have lasted longer, but Grier knew something was wrong and didn't let it sit.

"I'm not in love with you." It was the worst thing he could say, but it was the most honest.

"Does it matter?" she asked, and he felt humiliated by the way she seemed to feign the strength of a woman who also did not love her lover, although he knew she was more than smitten. Yes, to Stan it did matter.

"It's been almost four months, Grier. I just don't think it's going to happen. It doesn't seem fair to either of us."

"You don't *think*?"

Stan crouched into himself, sitting on the beanbag across from Grier, who sat on her hands on the sofa. They were miles apart. "I know it. I know I can't fall in love with you."

Grier sobbed. They made love one last time and kissed good-bye in the morning. Stan sent a postcard to Jean's address in Adelaide that evening on his way home from work.

Did you know that Betelgeuse is Orion's second-brightest star? It's also nearing the end of its life. When it finally dies, it will explode, and it will be seen at all times, even in the day. Maybe someday we'll be able to look at a small part of Orion together over breakfast.

Years later Jean told Stan that she'd taken the postcard to be a very good sign.

★

In sixteen years a lot can happen. Stars are born and stars die; people too. The wet waves of first love become as jagged as a coral reef on bare feet but then, somehow, at some point, they smooth out into a sandbar and, before you know it, you're swimming in waves of love again. It's a cycle, though not as regular as the moon.

Sixteen years after Stan and Jean had come together over the riotous waves of the Bass Straits, all the odds were against them conceiving—the statistics, the doctors, the dysfunctional uterine bleeding. She'd been told that 70 percent of women suffering from DUB don't produce an egg during menstruation and therefore can't conceive. "Stuff 'em," she'd told Stan. "I want a baby." Orion was born thirteen months later and the galaxy grew larger.

A ridiculous morning already at only a quarter to seven. Stan spilled the cereal all over the table and floor. It was impossible. Jean hadn't torn the plastic bag properly along the perforated edge. She never did. She had the most annoying habit of tearing the bag so it ripped vertically and the cereal couldn't possibly find a straight path to the bowl. He swore. His son said, "Dad," in an admonishing tone because, even at four (and the little guy would add "almost five" given the chance), Orion knew these two things: "fucking hell" was a bad thing to say, and his father was not a bad man.

"Sorry, mate," he told his son, wiping some cornflakes into his hand. "Don't tell Mum." He winked at Orion. Orion winked back the best he could. Many wrinkles around his nose formed with the effort.

"Where is Mom?" Stan's heart almost dropped hearing the way Orion said "Mom" like a little American, just the way Jean had taught him without even trying.

"She's sleeping, mate." No, nothing felt right about lying to his son, but for now it seemed to be the sane thing to do. He'd told himself to let the accident sit for twenty-four hours; then, when he had a better idea of how things really stood with Jean, he'd take Orion to see her. But for now he said, "She's got a big day ahead of her today, so we're not gonna wake her up, OK?" The twenty-four hours was almost up. Stan ruffled Orion's hair, trying to appear happy for his son's presence on this hollow summer morning.

It was unseasonably cold and damp outside. For the second day in a row, washing hung on the line, now soaking from last night's rain. Stan had only gotten home from the hospital at five-thirty in the morning because he wanted to see Orion, ensure everything seemed normal, and the little sleep he managed to get in the chair in Jean's ward had been interrupted by the sound of rain loud on the roof and the dark roads. Alongside his fear and his anger at the injustice of it all, he was spent.

She's the strongest person I know; she can survive this. It had become his mantra since he first got the call yesterday morning.

16

Stan and Orion ate their cornflakes in silence, Orion concentrating on satisfying his hunger, Stan concentrating on his love for his son. He had Jean's thick hair and his own brown eyes. He was adventurous, like his mum, yet gentle in his own way. Stan knew that if the worst were to happen, Orion would get through his mother's death, but he would spend a lifetime crying in quiet places.

Stan heard a rustle from the study, which acted as a spare bedroom. He got up from his cereal and began gathering the fruit and yogurt his mother brought when she came to spend the night. Bananas, strawberries and frozen blueberries; the woman loved her smoothies, part of her daily routine since a scary bout of cancer, and at her age she should be able to keep routines even in extreme circumstances. Stan making the smoothie for her was only a small gesture toward thanking her for sleeping over last night, only a minor thing he could do, and for the past twenty hours, helplessness seemed to rule his world.

The blender was whirring when Stan's mother hugged him from behind. "Good morning, my love."

Stan was unable to say "good morning." What could possibly be good about this morning? In less than an hour he would be at the hospital staring at his wife with tubes coming out of her face and arms. He hadn't gotten The Call while he'd been home these few hours, so that was good. *That* was good. "Morning, Mum."

Record-breaking rain in December, and all through the day it rained: while Stan's mother cried with controlled dignity when she hugged him goodbye; during the slow drive to hospital and the blinking of construction arrows; through all the merging of cars. With each new face it rained: the receptionists, the nurses, the doctor who'd told him there had been no change. It rained as he held her hand and held her hand and held her hand and it rained when his mum brought Orion to hospital. Not an easy scene. It rained on the drive home, with the windshield wipers getting noisier and quieter and noisier and quieter with the fluctuation of each new speed zone, and no words were spoken because the passenger seat was empty. It rained as Stan pulled into their garage and closed the door, as if trying to shut it all out, as if the rain were a memory of something he wanted to forget. Still, it rained on the tin roof, a constant echo throughout the house.

He'd come home to have dinner with Orion and his mum, the plan being to return after Orion was settled for bed. Somehow Stan thought it might ease Orion's fears if he was with him for a couple of hours in their own safe environment, but he was eager to get back to Jean. He didn't know if he was hiding his anxiety well, but Orion seemed relaxed and happy, as a four-year-old should. His boy laughed in the bathroom as Stan helped to brush his teeth.

"I'll read to him," his mother said. "You go."

He accepted her wish to help in this way, at this time, so he kissed his son and told him that he loved him more than any other star in the sky—"I love you too, Dad"—then he went to the kitchen and filled up the sink with suds that smelled of grapefruit and dropped the plates in to soak. He would leave the dishes, as he did the bedtime reading, to his mother. She would do that for him, and so much more. He poured two glasses of wine so they could have a quiet chat about Jean and how the next twenty-four hours would run before he headed back to hospital—if his mother didn't want one, he would drink them both. Stan walked outside. Finally, the rain had fucking stopped.

"Digger," he called out to the dog, and the feisty kelpie–staffy came running. Clouds flew in small bundles across the sky, the wind pushing the day away, as if making room for the crisp scent of something new. The sky opened before him, Orion's Belt enormous, always the first constellation he saw. "It must be because it's the brightest constellation up there," he'd once told Jean in the Flinders Ranges. They were still new to their relationship then, only two months officially, but they'd felt confirmed. As fixed as the constellation itself.

"It's the first one we see because our eyes instinctively move to it. And Betelgeuse is our star."

He wanted to share tonight's sky with Jean.

Inside, he listened for noise, heard a muffled voice in his son's room. As he stood in the doorway, he watched his mother read to Orion and tried to remember her reading to him as a boy. He couldn't. He couldn't remember so he closed his eyes and imagined it was Jean reading—Jean with her singsong words, shifting from high to low tones as she told stories to their son. Later, Orion would tell the story to Stan that it was he, his father, who had taught him the riffs of his guitar but it was his mother, Jean, who had taught him rhythm.

Stan watched until his glass was empty and his mother and Orion had both fallen asleep. He picked up the book and put it back on the shelf, pulled the covers up close to their chins, kissed both of their temples, stared those twenty seconds longer and turned out the light.

As he walked back to the kitchen, eyeing the second glass of wine then going for the car keys instead, he heard the rain again, this time banging on the tin roof, pummeling the living earth.

But There Were Three of Them

The night before Jean Harley's bicycle went down, the slightly famous, very sexy Keith Lincoln had passed Viv on the street. She'd recognized the slump of his lean body and the layers of his shaggy brown hair. The Cheats. Of course. It had to be the guitar player. She felt energy rise from her toes straight up to her nose, where she breathed in hard to keep the gasp from coming out of her mouth, and she felt nineteen again—all in an instant. She saw his eyes move from her knee-high boots to the furry collar of her sleeveless top, then linger on her lashes. Perhaps he was taken by the length of them because he himself often wore mascara. (He was, in fact, wearing mascara at that very moment.) His attention made Viv feel slightly famous too. But she didn't dawdle. She was loath to be a minute later to meet Jean and Neddy, who'd been waiting for almost an hour, so she smiled and walked into the pub, and Keith carried on his ambling way.

The Cellar, as always, was quiet, which was why the girls had chosen to make it their regular. Four men with gray hair in gray suits sat by the corner window, laughing and drinking their beers and wine. The one facing the door gave a welcoming smile to Viv as she came inside. Another table was occupied by a group of five who looked as though they could be rowdy, given a different venue. No lone drunks sat at the bar keeping the French bartender company. This wasn't one of those places. The Cellar was for mature boozers only. There was no music playing, only a lot of hardwood flooring, a few polished tables, the colors of red and gold.

Jean waved at Viv when she came through the door.

"I just ran into that guy from The Cheats!" Viv was whispering, though she wasn't sure why. She was eager, awaiting signs of incredulity. But Neddy looked at her blankly. Jean gave an awkward smile. "You know, *Yesterday you were in my car / and I can't get you out of my head. Yesterday you were la la la . . .*" It wasn't much of a mainstream song but it was big in the indie rock world, and even though Neddy loved her earthy female artists and Jean was a world-music listener with a penchant for banjo, Viv saw no reason why they wouldn't know The Cheats.

"Was he hot?" Neddy asked, stone-faced. Viv knew straightaway: it had been a rough day for Ned; she probably didn't have much patience.

Viv placed her bag on the floor and sat down at the table. "May I?" She poured herself a glass from the bottle, had a quick mouthful, rolled her eyes and said, "So hot."

"Is that the band with the drummer who's dating that model?"

"Yes." She pointed a finger at Jean. "Totally." Viv had been back from California for more than three months now and still hadn't rid herself of "totally." She'd picked it up with furious gusto and threw it around whenever she felt the need for emphasis. She especially liked saying it when talking to Jean, her best American friend. "Nice wine."

"Nice top," Neddy said, pouring herself a second glass.

"Recognize it, do you?"

"Looks better on you." Neddy had raised her glass to Viv. "You've got bigger boobs."

"Not while you're breastfeeding, I don't. Cheers. Cheers, Jean." Viv simulated a kiss to Jean.

Jean topped up her glass only to find slightly more than a dribble was left. "We need another bottle." The way she said it was definitive. It would be a lengthy girls' night out at the Cellar and they would be the last patrons left in this civilized drinking hole.

Jean walked around the table to kiss Viv's cheek, then went to the bar to order a second bottle of the spotlight wine: a deep and moody Riverland shiraz, something to counter the surprising chill in the summer air.

Last week had been a riesling from Eden Valley. The week before a sav blanc from McLaren Vale. If Viv had saved every spotlight bottle from all of their Thursdays at the Cellar, not only would she have had a collection of impressive labels, but a timeline of memories as well.

"I got the best gig today. A gorgeous house in Tennyson, right on the beach. Lleyton Hewitt used to own it. *Big* money. Floor-to-ceiling windows. I can hear it screaming low couches, bold-striped beanbags, lots of space." And this was Viv, entering a situation and taking right over. She never planned on being at the center of attention but it was inevitable. Things happened to her—*totally amazing* things—and people became rapt. And because their interest fueled her, incidentals grew lavish. Her eyes became exclamation points. Her hands conducted symphonies. "The client's fabulous. Giving me so much room to really run. And it's great it's in Adelaide. I need a rest from traveling, you know?"

"No, I wouldn't," Neddy said, shaking her head, most likely feeling that pinch of stay-at-home-mum syndrome she occasionally complained about. "You've got the best job." Last month it was: "Where is the art in random toys in the middle of the hallway?"

"Sounds like an installation to me," Viv had answered, and she figured she could make a joke because she knew Neddy like a sister and knew that Ned loved her life and, most of all, loved her children. Still, they had all been artists of some form or another when they had met at uni, and Viv knew it pained Neddy that she was the only one no longer using her creativity. Viv could see this in her friend's slanted smile, yet she couldn't help her playfulness and said, "I know. I love it."

There was talk of films they'd seen or wanted to see, the book one of the films was based on, other books that particular author had written, what they were reading at the moment, the fantastic thrift shop Viv had just discovered and how happy she was when she found the lovely teal reading lamp embroidered with purple beads. When the discussion turned to family life, Viv had nothing to offer. Willow's teething (etcetera); Orion got a stiffy in the bath last night and got really scared (laughter and the obligatory *awww*); Rodd got a stiffy in bed last night and Neddy got really scared (more laughter and a mental pat on the back for not being married with children); but he was a good man, Rodd, and Neddy was sorry she hated sex right now and clearly there was tension, clearly he was frustrated (once Viv had dreamed that she was having sex with Rodd and she woke up wet and guilty); Rodd's dad was falling deeper into his dementia; Jean's dad had had dementia for the last two years of his life; Jean missed her dad.

"Of course you miss him, lovey. He only died, what, a year or two ago?"

And then, as if "segue" were flashing over Jean's head: "So we're moving to America."

"Holy fuck!" (Neddy.)

"Jean!" (Viv.)

"Not for good. Just a year. I got that fellowship I applied for at Indiana State. On Native American dance." Jean puffed up, eager for their replies.

"Wait!" Viv looked over her shoulder and called out, "Simone! Is it too late for another bottle of wine?"

"It is after ten." The bartender looked exasperated, though Viv knew it to be an exaggeration because Simone had been serving the girls for years and they joked with her all the time. "And you have already had two bottles," she reminded them, shaking her finger.

"But there are three of us!" yelled Neddy, and they all laughed. "Shit," she said, turning back to her friends. "I'll be doing some serious expressing tonight."

Viv held up the last of her glass to cheers. Simone brought over another bottle of the wine and, after pouring each of them a glass, left the bottle on the table. "After that, I close."

The girls were giddy, thanking Simone, clapping their hands. Goodness knows there'd be work tomorrow for Jean and Viv, and Neddy's house got going so early, but this had become a celebration.

There were only two other customers in the Cellar at this point and one of them kept sneaking glances at the girls. Not quite as hot as Keith Lincoln and definitely sans mascara, but Viv'd noticed him noticing them and geared up for the game. She caught his eye. Younger than her. He smiled. More conservative too. She smiled back.

"What are you doing?" Neddy knew exactly what Viv was doing because Viv did it a lot, so it wasn't as much a question as it was an accusation.

"Him?" asked Jean. "He's so young."

"Not too young, you think?"

Neddy leaned back in her chair as if resigned. "What's too young?"

"Go for it, Viv. Egg him on." Because Jean herself loved egging on Viv.

Viv accepted the challenge, aware of her every gesture and how it might work to her advantage. "Jean, that's great news, but don't go. What will *we* do?" She said this with a pout, sensing his gaze. Inviting it. Even as she listed the ways in which she depended on Jean—and there were many—she was performing. "Who will I ring when I can't remember the name of some actor?" But what she really wanted to say was, "Who will I ring when I'm lonely?" Because there had been many of those phone calls over the years, Viv knowing that no matter what, Jean would answer, often making room in the day or night, any day or night, to meet up.

When they'd been at uni, because neither of them had family nearby, the two would often celebrate holidays together, like Christmas and Jean's American Thanksgiving, but smaller ones too, like the Queen's Birthday or Presidents' Day. At first this meant a lavish feast for two, but as life expanded for them, growing more complex and somehow containing fewer hours in a day, the two girls, in keeping up a semblance of tradition, eventually settled for the more practical option of a single shared piece of cake at a favorite café.

Can you miss what you don't have? At first Viv hadn't thought so, but she'd always been lonely, always known that something or some*one* was missing from her life. It was only after she'd started seeing her therapist that she'd realized it was her family and that, yes, you certainly can miss what you don't have.

"She thinks it's my parents' fault I can't commit. They rejected me, so now I'm afraid of rejection from anyone." A banana and caramel cake. Two forks. Two hot chocolates on the side.

"What do you think?" Jean: forever speaking with her mouth full.

"The theory is floatable, but I have to say that the older I get, the happier I am being single."

"Really?" Jean hadn't appeared convinced but she was the most open-minded and non-judgemental friend Viv had, so she was the best friend to say this to when wanting to hide from the truth. Neddy would have called bullshit, then taken the last bite of cake.

"Yes, really. Sex is always better when it's new, right? So I can tick that box because I never have a man long enough for it to get old. And with my job I get to travel, so not having a long-term partner means I don't have to feel guilty about that or, worse, I don't have to *stop* traveling. And I like my space, you know? I like to read in bed till three in the morning if I so choose. I like to spread out when I sleep."

"Are you going to keep going?"

"I could."

"Because it sounds like you're trying to convince me and you don't need to do that. I believe you, Viv."

"You do?"

"Yeah, I totally do. I also believe that one day someone's going to come along and change your mind."

"Really?"

"One day. And I can't wait to meet him." Jean's eyes grew wide and her hand flew to her mouth.

"What?"

"What if we already know him? Oh my god, what if he's right under our noses and it's just not the right time for you two yet?"

The girls had giggled away, naming names and pointing to the occasional pedestrian through the café window. Who knew—maybe it would be the guy from the Cellar who now couldn't stop looking at Viv?

Eventually the guy came over to the girls' table with his friend, said they were from out of town for work, would they take them to a more happening place?

Viv looked at her friends. "There's Casablabla?"

Neddy raised her hands. "I've got a baby at home. I'm out. You girls go but no texts about hangovers tomorrow, please, because I'll be dealing with poo and will have no sympathy. *No sympathy.*"

"Jean?"

Jean thought for a few seconds and Viv knew she had her.

"OK, OK, I'll go," said Jean because Jean was a dancer and Casablabla was the only place around with dancing aside from the gay bar and the club with all the uni students. It's why Viv had mentioned it, Casablabla being Jean's weakness.

On their way out the door, Viv put her arm around Jean's shoulder. "See? Whatever will I do without you?"

"Oh, I'm sure you'll get by. You always do."

Viv looked at her friend and it was then that she briefly froze time and etched a picture of Jean into her mind: buoyant and rambunctious sparks coming out the ever-so-slight gap between her front teeth; each freckle on her childish face dotted with an aged fidelity; her smile a bigger spotlight than all three bottles of wine blended into one.

The club had a Spanish/hip-hop/reggae groove and the ladies knew how to work it. The men danced too and kept the drinks coming. Viv and Jean were well and truly tanked by the time the DJ called it quits.

"I'm screwed tomorrow. Professor Ironed Pants is going to smell the booze on my breath. I'm going to stink."

"Oh, never mind. He'll be wildly jealous that it wasn't him out drinking with you."

"Who's ever been jealous of a hangover?"

"Just tell him your news and he'll think you're brilliant, no matter how hungover you are."

"Oh, yeah! I'm going to America!" Jean hugged Viv instantly and the two rocked back and forth in each other's arms.

The four of them ran out to the taxi rank in a steady drizzle of rain. Reece, the fairer of the two men, opened the door for Jean and gave the taxi driver a twenty-dollar bill to get her home safely. Unlucky to be paired with the happily married mother-of-one, he'd still been a gentleman. The darker man, coincidentally named Keith, asked Viv if she wanted to share a ride. With a sultry slur Viv told him, "You know, I think I was destined to meet a Keith tonight so we should probably share a taxi, yes."

"Is that right?"

"I do believe."

Reece slipped away unnoticed as Keith said to the happily unmarried mother-of-none, "I've always wanted to be someone's destiny."

"Are you glad you're mine for the night?"

"The night, huh?"

"The night" sounded perfect because this Keith would not be the man who would one day change Viv's life and make her want to commit. This Keith was like a little boy and Viv was only interested in being his toy.

When he kissed her in the back seat of the taxi on the way to her place, Viv forgot about the frozen picture of Jean in her head, but it would resurface the next day, after she had dealt with the wake-up sex; after the coffee and the crumpets with butter and honey; after the exchange of phone numbers and email addresses; after she had kissed Keith goodbye, letting her terry-towelling dressing gown fall from her shoulders and reveal her breasts; after he'd pressed his body to her own and she'd smelled his skin all over again; after the phone call had interrupted what would've been their third round of romp-festivities in less than eight hours; after telling Keith he didn't need to come to the hospital, then accepting his offer to share a taxi. It would resurface after the hospital and the quick in-and-out to and from her office, and after she'd gone back to the hospital, then left it again, had taken a bus in the rain, closed the door to her apartment and stripped on the way to the bathroom. It would resurface during the much-needed shower. When the hot water washed the hot tears from her cheeks and down the drain. When the news of Jean Harley's accident no longer felt like a dream.

Emotional Fishing

Charley sat as far back as he could, feeling out of place, though that was nothing new. His bald head shone under the fluoro lights and the back of his neck itched—an eczema problem that flared up when he was nervous. He kept smoothing his long beard to a point—another nervous tic. One might think he was made of tougher stuff because if this was an eye-for-an-eye world, here was a man who'd seen things that should've blinded him, a man who'd done the sorts of things people don't talk about at the dinner table but read about in newspapers over breakfast, a man who'd spent a quarter of his life behind bars. But he'd repented; Charley had done his time.

Leaning forward, elbows on knees, he eavesdropped on a man who was probably in his forties, a good ten years younger than Charley. The man called people, told people it was Stan, then said things like, "It's not good," and "still no change." Charley knew he should say something, but what? *I was there. I'm to blame.*

Charley got up and moved like a great bear just out of hibernation and asked the man at the reception desk if he could have a pen and paper.

"Excuse me?"

Charley was a mumbler. "A pen and paper, thanks." It was almost distressing.

When he got what he'd come for, he let his shoulders rest. He turned to walk back and got a good look at Stan from the front. Shortish. Fit. His hair a bit windswept. Charley noticed hair, admired hair, wished he had some.

He pressed himself uncomfortably into the chair and stared at the blank sheet of paper long and hard before he closed his eyes and took three deep breaths through his nose. This is how he always composed: first, in his mind.

Dear Lisa—You probably just sat down with a coffee on your veranda. I remember you wrote that once so I always picture you reading there. He opened his eyes as if to snap himself out of some daydream. What was he doing? This isn't how he wanted to begin. If he started like this, he wouldn't be able to slide into the horrible truth. Better he start with the meat of the beast.

Dear Lisa—I might've killed a woman. What a crazy way to start a letter. Most people probably start with the weather or something. Well, it's been pissing down. A real summer storm. What the bloody hell was he talking about the weather for? He mentally erased the words to start again, keeping only the salutation.

Dear Lisa—I want to tell you about the cars at the accident. I didn't think they'd ever stop coming at us. They just kept coming and they were moving so slow. The headlights in the rain were like torches searching me out because I did something wrong.

Charley opened his eyes, checked to see if anyone was staring at him. It wasn't his norm, composing in public. He liked to do it over an ashtray full of cigarettes and some coffee or whiskey, or both.

He wrote down what he'd composed about the accident, slowly. He thought carefully about how to spell certain words: *accident, lights, searching*. When he finished he knew some of the usual suspects looked wrong, but couldn't work out what to do with them: *would, something, because.* He left them misspelled. At the end he wrote that he knew the cyclist's name: Jean Harley. And after spending fifteen minutes writing those five sentences, he needed a break.

Looking around the room, he decided there was nothing good about the place. There were magazines he could read if he wanted to take the time, but they'd be a waste because they were complete crap. Dr. Phil was on the television and had Charley thinking, *Bugger that man and his guest with anorexia. Who cares if it's not normally a bloke's thing? He reckons he's too embarrassed to leave his house but he can come on bloody TV!* Charley never watched TV, didn't own a set, but still he knew that Dr. Phil would fix his guest's problem by offering the best help money could buy and the skinny guy would cry and the rich audience would cry and everyone would fucking cry and the next show would come on. TV was bullshit and so was Dr. Phil.

Charley stared at the sheet of paper once again—long and hard like he always did—then closed his eyes and took three deep breaths through his nose.

The coppers gave me a good questioning after but they let me go because they said they couldn't keep me. There will be an investigation and I can't say I blame them, guy like me. Of course I'm nervous. I don't ever want to go back to prison. You know what it was like. Well, not really.

Charley looked up as Stan hugged a woman struggling with a baby in one arm and a little girl hanging off her skirt. The woman was OK at first, but then she sat down and put her head in her hands and started crying. Stan started to cry too. The woman said it wasn't fair because Jean was supposed to be going back home, as if a homecoming was reason enough to not get run over by a van. Charley watched them, though he pretended not to watch because their grief was private, even in this public space. *NOTHING SEEMS REAL*, he wrote, then transcribed his dealings with the cops. He felt so on-display, hunched over his paper and holding his pen the incorrect way, that he began to sweat. He not only scratched the back of his neck but his armpits too. It all felt like a nightmare, and Charley knew about those. Now he'd have to dream about the bicycle going down in front of his bumper and him not being able to stop. The heavy bounce of his van lumping itself over Jean's body. The brokenness of her bike. Of her body. The paramedics doing their job. The cops taking notes and eyeing him. All those fucking cars. One more nightmare among so many others.

Closing his eyes, trying to keep everything together going round in his mind, he calmed himself and started composing again. *The other person with me was a woman named Sam. She was hysterical. She kept talking about late nights and early mornings with her baby and saying, "I can't handle this I can't handle this" so many times she couldn't hardly breathe. What happened was she opened her car door and knocked poor Jean into the traffic. Lisa, I was the traffic.*

He liked the emphasis on her name because Lisa was his savior and confessor. How ironic that right before the accident he was a quarter mile away from the big red mailbox where he would've posted the last letter he'd written to her. How ironic that he'd almost gotten into a second accident on the way to the hospital this morning because the letter was still on the seat next to him and, when he'd noticed, he became so distracted he had to brake hard when the car in front of him stopped for a red light. Then he tore it up because everything in it was now a lie. After the accident, nothing in the letter mattered.

Charley needed a smoke. He tried not to make eye contact on his way out of the ICU waiting room, but the little girl was running around and almost ran into him. She stopped and stared up, up, all the way up to the top of Charley's body and into his eyes, where shame was pouring out.

When the smoke hit, it hit the back of his throat and filled his lungs like angry relief, and he went in for more. The sign said no smoking within 150 feet of the building, so Charley walked as far as he could from the door, squinting in the white light of cloud cover and the sheen of solid rain. By the time he'd reached his destination, he'd finished his smoke, so he lit another. His doctor had told him he needed to quit and lose fifty pounds, for a start. His health wouldn't be on his side when he needed it most if he continued in this way. He'd have maybe ten years at the most. Charley thought living to the age of sixty-six sounded more than fair. Hell, he was amazed he'd made it this far. If the manual labor he did at work wasn't enough to help him lose the weight, Charley didn't know what would do the trick. And as for the smoking, fuck it.

He threw the butt down, twisting the sole of his shoe over the smoldering remains. An old woman holding a little boy's hand passed him and gave him a disapproving look; he'd done worse things in his life than litter, and some habits are hard to break. He followed them all the way to the waiting area, and when they got there, Stan picked up the boy. No doubt he was his son. Jean Harley's son. They hugged for a very long time.

Charley went directly to his chair and read what he'd written so far. It seemed he'd been writing for hours and there wasn't much on the page. Always the way. A person needed patience with tasks like this, yet he wrote to Lisa religiously. Vigorously. Gratefully. It was like emotional fishing: he'd release, then wait. Release his tormented thoughts, then wait for a reply.

Stan kept coming and going. Each time he came back into the waiting room, he looked sick. Charley thought Jean must look awful. Old Doc at the prison would've told him to find a way to make peace. Charley reckoned "making peace" meant telling Stan, who sat only steps away, sorry. But every time he thought about it, his body froze. *Surely* they didn't need his apology now. *Surely* now all they needed was each other. Charley marveled at them glumly, wondering if this had happened to him, if he were in such bad shape, who would be waiting for him to recover? Seriously, who would the hospital call? How would Lisa find out if he couldn't write her a letter to tell her he'd been mowed down? No, he didn't want to apologize. All he wanted was to hear the next update, then get the hell out of there. Go home and crash and dream about it all over again.

It's been two days, he said in his head, *and it's all I can think about. It hurts. One thing I'm learning, Lisa, is that pain doesn't disappear. You think I've done my time and I've forgiven myself but pain lives on. I have nightmares and in the morning I wake up and all I want to do is start my day like a normal person but it hurts. The accident and everything else.*

Lisa was normal. Did she start her days in pain? It's something Charley wondered often, how many people around him began their mornings in pain. The years before prison were hard and he'd never been proud of what he'd done, but at least he wasn't ashamed. He was sane when he killed that puny shit. Even though it happened really fast, he knew he was in control. He knew his hands were smashing the man's life to pieces. He saw the life leave the fucker, saw his face let it go. They were Charley's hands that did it and Charley felt each punch. He had complete control over what he'd done and he was not, nor would he ever be, ashamed.

Not everyone deserves to live.

Charley opened his eyes quickly, knowing he wouldn't transcribe any of that. He was getting ahead of himself. Or behind, thinking of the past. His eyes moved to the little boy. He had freckles. He played with a LEGO airplane. His father took his hand and they both walked up to the reception desk, then disappeared around the corner where Charley knew Jean Harley was.

At least the little boy had a dad to help him through. At least the man had the little boy.

Charley closed his eyes again to focus, thinking it was about time to finish the letter and get the hell out of this miserable place. *I'm at the hospital. I wanted to see if she was OK because the guilt was driving me crazy. I'm really worried because she's in a coma. I think she might die. I remember at the accident there was a bus that passed by and a person on it looked right at me and it seemed like ages but it must've only been a second but I swear he was shaming me.*

Transcribing, he only got three sentences in before he lumbered out of his chair. He had good penmanship but he wrote big. He had to ask a woman at the reception desk if he could have more paper. Please.

"I'm sorry?" Granted it wasn't the same person he'd asked for the paper in the first place, but this was always the case. Mumbler or no mumbler, of course they could hear him. It's just that people don't give you their immediate full attention unless you make an immediate full *impression*. One would think Charley made quite the impression, but as big as he was, he was also very small, and often people didn't see him. Twenty years ago the case had been otherwise because he'd had a different look in his eyes. Now he hid his eyes as much as he could, afraid someone might look into them.

"Did you say paper?"

"Please."

When she returned with three sheets of blank paper, Charley managed a "ta" and walked back, trying to avoid the eyes of the mother and her children and the old woman, but not being able to look away. The mother looked tired, the old woman looked tired, and when Stan returned with the little boy, he, most of all, looked tired.

Charley squeezed himself into the chair again, pinching his hips and legs between the armrest and seat. Again he closed his eyes and took a deep breath. This time he took more than three breaths because there was a lot to clear out before he could write. And when he finished, all he wanted was another smoke.

Giving Back

On day one Marion noticed the windowsill and its ledge hadn't been wiped down for ages, maybe not even once in the seven years Stan and Jean had lived in the house, and there was mildew around the sink taps and building up on the silver of the drain. She'd been brushing her teeth, fighting the temptation to swivel around for fear of finding the bathtub. She knew she'd have to help bathe Orion at some point over the next few days and surely there'd be dirty water rings. Who knew how long she'd be staying at her son's house? *Well, maybe I'll clean it—somebody has to,* she thought, because Jean had never been a good housekeeper. Marion would be the first to say that Jean was a good mother and a good wife to her son, but didn't both of those somehow entail keeping a clean house? Hadn't it for Marion? It was the one thing her ex-husband, Donald, had demanded of her on the few occasions he was around, and it was the one thing she'd taken with her when she and Stan had left him: this obsession for cleanliness.

Leaving Donald hadn't been as hard as her friends said it would be. When she'd told him over cigarettes and cask wine at the kitchen table, he'd said, "Fair enough," and when she'd asked him for some money to get them started, he'd said, "How much?"

He'd told her he never did think he'd be a good husband and he was surprised they'd lasted this long.

"You weren't so bad all the time, just most of it."

They were both looking at their glasses or the table or the rings on their fingers.

"My heart wasn't in it for long, I guess."

"Nor was mine."

"So what'll you do?"

"Get a job, I suppose."

"You can't get a job. You can't even clean the house properly."

Her parents took her and Stan in. "Come and stay with us for a spell. It's quiet here. You'll love the birds." And she did. She spent hours bird watching while her son fished on the little island south of Adelaide named for kangaroos, where her parents had retired. Her father was a former school teacher who'd taken to making cheese. Her mother cared for injured roos and painted lovely landscapes. Marion felt guilty about the free accommodation, she being in her forties with a child of her own. Felt she should've been able to take care of herself and Stan without anyone's help, yet what could she do? "I'll keep your house clean in return for room and board." They'd said it wasn't necessary, but with all of the baby joeys in and out of the place, it was.

Eventually she got a job at the regional school, desperate as it was for teachers. She struggled with teaching math and science, but loved teaching history and literature. Every year she taught *Julius Caesar*; Shakespeare made her weep.

It was hard when her father died. He'd taken a piece of Marion to the grave and she knew this because she no longer felt whole. Her mother stopped talking, clung tighter to the roos, and Stan left to travel the world. Marion discovered the plays of Chekhov that year and cleaned like mad, because cleanliness wasn't so much about appearances or sanitization, but more about telling Donald, telling her parents, telling the world, "See, I can work, parent and keep a clean home, and I can handle anything else you damn well throw at me." She'd been guilty of being passive aggressive with Jean in the past, saying things like, "Yes, it's wonderful you had the ceiling fans put in, but the problem is now someone has to dust them."

So on that first morning of her indefinite stay at her son's house, Marion had rinsed her mouth and spat, stared hard at the drain, then took her toothbrush and scrubbed at the mildew, swearing silently because now she'd have to buy a new toothbrush to replace the one she'd just thrown across the bathroom, the plastic bouncing hard off the glass of the shower wall. Of course the flying toothbrush had nothing to do with the state of the drain. Marion had been thinking about Jean's coma.

It was on day two that she got the check for a play she'd written fifteen years earlier. London had revived it, garnering reviews of "it's a classic" and "another Australian icon," so there she sat, holding the gutsy sum, not knowing what to make of it. *Mortality and existentialism*, she thought; it could be the title of a stellar tragedy if it hadn't been so close to the goddamn truth.

Already she'd fed Orion, gotten him dressed for bed, read to him and kissed him goodnight and then phoned Stan at the hospital to tell him all was fine—at least in his house, considering—and already she'd called Jean's brother in America to give him an update on the sad state of his sister's condition. Nothing had changed and, in this case, no news was bad news. John Harley had asked if he should come. She hadn't known how to answer. He'd said things were difficult with him moving out of his home, a marriage break-up, a fragile daughter—what more could life throw at him now? Marion hadn't known how to handle the delayed response of the telephone line, let alone this stranger's tears, because he was, indeed, "losing it." So when everything she'd taken on had been ticked off and filed away under More Awful Jobs for Another Awful Day, including wiping down the kitchen cupboards, she took the check out of her purse and held it in the silence of her son's lounge room, Digger the dog an apostrophe next to her, giving her the kind of comfort money could never buy. She petted him lovingly, which woke him up and then he fell back to sleep, leaving Marion staring beyond the check. She was seventy-seven. She had enough money to see her through until the end, and she could still provide for Stan and Jean's future (if Jean lived through the night) and that of her grandson too. Whatever could the money mean?

It was Jean and her two friends who had introduced Marion to the Fringe Festival when they'd staged a performance about menstruation. Given the subject matter, Marion hadn't had high hopes for the girls' theatrical piece—clearly it wouldn't be the Shakespeare that made her weep—but she was going with Stan, who was introducing her to Jean, his new American girlfriend. *Well, it can't last*, she'd thought. *She'll have to go home eventually.* How was Marion to know that this Jean would one day give birth to her only grandchild, her brightest star Orion? How was she to know that this American girlfriend would break her son's heart by landing herself in a coma after a horrible accident with a van, for godsake? All she'd known then was that Jean had danced across the stage and spoken in verse both witty and reflective, and that she had been mesmerizing.

Marion had been fifty-eight when she'd written her first play, thinking, *If they can do it, so can I.* She was sixty when it had debuted at the Adelaide Fringe Festival. Sixty-one at the Fringe in Edinburgh. She'd thought herself too old to get carried away with grand dreams of success and fame, yet there they were, coming at her as fast as the ideas for each of her plays. She was sixty-two when one of her plays showed at the Festival Centre. Sixty-four when it made it to the Opera House. Year after year she steamrolled along, wondering what had taken her so long to start writing in the first place. Her office at home housed framed playbills; a photograph of her seated next to David Williamson, both dressed in black at a long white table littered with wine glasses; a poster with "starring Goldie Hawn" in black and red chunky letters; a scrapbook of review clippings, the good and the bad, though they were mostly good. With eight plays under her belt, she was doing all right, better than all right, but what did it mean to her when now it came in the form of an obtuse check and her daughter-in-law possibly never waking up, rendering her grandson motherless and her own son lost?

Their relationship had always been complicated from Marion's side. True, they shared a love of the arts and they supported one another's passions in a way Stan could not, he being a mere admirer and nothing like a practitioner, but Marion had resented Jean for reasons she'd never been able to pinpoint. It wasn't overt resentment—they were friends and she loved Jean—but it niggled.

A strong memory, tasting bitter now, had Marion feeling guilty. Stan and Jean announcing their engagement. The riesling in her hand becoming heavy. There was no fear of the glass falling, only fear of Marion bringing it down to the table before she'd clinked it with Stan's and her soon-to-be daughter-in-law's. "Oh! That's. . . ." Rather than finish her sentence, she clinked glasses.

But she'd known it was going to happen. Stan and Jean had a remarkable story to tell if anyone asked how they'd met, and they'd been together for years. He'd taken her to Kangaroo Island, where they picnicked at his grandparents' graves. He'd flown her to Bali, and though Marion had gracefully nipped at him for buying Jean's ticket, he'd said they were a buy-one-get-one-free deal and why would he want to go alone? Who else would he want to take?

"Well, I'd like to go to Bali."

That hadn't gone too far. In fact, it had bounced off Stan's smile and landed right smack in Marion's eye, so even she winced as soon as the words had left her mouth. *What kind of mother am I?* she'd wondered, badly wanting Stan's loyalty. He'd always been her number one man.

Of course they were going to get married and one day move in with Marion, having spent all of "their" money traveling, traveling, always traveling every school holiday Stan got off work (Jean, the perennial student, could always leave at the drop of a hat), but what could Marion say? Hadn't her parents taken her in when she'd had no money?

Marion feared too much that one day they'd want to move closer to Jean's family, leaving Marion behind, aging and alone. America was just so far away and, now that she was examining this, maybe that's why Jean's American-ness had always bothered her. Her *confidence*, her *naivety*, her *optimism*. Marion closed her eyes and lay down the check, realizing it was exactly those qualities Jean needed—they *all* needed—right now.

Of course there was respect and admiration, and there was real love too. Who but Jean cared most for her when the cancer beat her down? Who but Jean? There had been midday check-ins, when Jean would bring Orion, who was only three, and both bore presents: crayon drawings and plastic containers of homemade soup. Jean drove her to hospital for chemo and radiation and follow-ups and check-ups. Jean helped her buy bras after the operation. Jean called at night just to say goodnight. No doubt it was time to give back.

Being there for Stan and Orion was the least she could do. Cleaning up the place was just that little something more. But as she held the check on day two of this mess—thinking if it hadn't been for Jean and her dance of the fallen egg, she might not have the money at all, so in fact the check should do something to honor Jean—she came up with an idea for a new project.

Day five at the house: now she was truly over-extended. A woman her age wasn't meant to care for a little boy not yet in school, all day, all night, with only a few hours' reprieve from her own son, who in these hours needed special care too. It was an emotional time and Marion couldn't find her own space where she could properly *feel*. It was all go, go, go in the day and do, do, do at night, because when the house was quiet and Digger sat with her on the couch—the familiarity of the new nightly ritual a welcomed warmth in a dire situation—Marion was putting that check to use, answering emails from the Australian Society of Authors. She'd told them she wanted to set up a grant for an unpublished female playwright over the age of fifty because surely there were budding graying playwrights, possibly nub-knuckled from arthritis, who deserved a break in a later stage of their lives, and shouldn't she help them out? The ASA asked her for the details and so she wrote that the Jean Harley Fellowship for $40,000 would support the work of an as-of-yet unproduced playwright for one year. She prayed that by the time the successful applicant got her own big check, Marion would be back at home in her office writing another winning play, and Jean would be back to caring for her family and ignoring the hassle of cleaning.

It was pure exhaustion, though. Today's checklist had included getting breakfast for herself and Orion, helping him choose his clothes and brush his teeth, cleaning the dishes and dusting the blinds, walking the dog to the park where she pushed Orion on a swing until her arms gave out and her knees did too, lunch, dinner, and all the in-betweens like going to the hospital and wiping her eyes, blowing her nose, hugging able bodies and looking over the unable one, then carrying a napping Orion from car to house, getting the boy ready for bed and into bed and somehow finding time to send the email. Jean's body wasn't responding the way anyone had hoped and the doctors were less than optimistic, you could see it in their hesitant eyes. Marion's own eyes were tired, the words on the screen blurring and shifting.

She crawled into the guest bed and her aching body sunk so far into the mattress she didn't think she could possibly turn and was sure she'd wake in this exact position when the sun came up in the morning. But there was Orion, moving in his sleep. The sound encouraged Marion to give turning her own body a go. Just *thinking it* somehow proved to be enough, because this was OK, lying in the guest bed, staring at the ceiling, letting the day lift from her old bones. Unlike Stan, at least she was lying in a bed. Unlike Jean, at least she could make the choice to lie still.

Not Dead, Just Sleeping

The red plane rose into the sky, heading for America, maybe even further than the moon. He'd built it from the little LEGO he'd been given on his fourth birthday because before four he'd only had big ones. Before four he might have stuck little LEGO in his mouth for no other reason than a mouth is a hole and holes carry all kinds of possibilities. He was clever at building with the tiny LEGO and so the plane flew far. It flew far from the city street rug he sat upon, where some days Matchbox cars drove in circles but today were packed away in an old tin because today he needed to fly. He was the pilot and he wanted to go higher, so he pointed the plane up to the ceiling and he rose to his feet so the plane could go higher, so he could go higher, and he stood on his bed and in his mind he flew his plane up above the strong rod holding his curtains and beyond the glass in the window panes and over the trees, into the sky, where he flew and he flew and he flew.

Sunlight splashed Orion's walls, brightening the green and pink racing stripes his Very Viv had painted for him. Very Viv was very nice very funny very pretty very tall and she was very good with a paintbrush. He loved the racing stripes and he loved his room, where things happened that didn't happen in other places. Like just now, he'd flown higher than the blue in the sky, then pointed the plane down, because he was the pilot and he wanted to go down. He flew along the bottom racing stripe because if he didn't follow it around the room three times, the world would blow up. It was hard work.

He looked at the map of the city street rug when he tired, deciding the world would not explode. He thought about going to Very Viv's house by the beach, where he could play a bowling game or a dancing game on her big TV that hung on the wall. Very Viv's was the very funnest house.

He could go to Juni's house, but then he'd have to fly over the city, and he didn't like to "feel crowded." It's what his mum always said after a day of running errands in the city. "Let's get out of the city now so we're not so crowded." He loved playing with Juni, but he'd never been to her house without his mum and he wasn't so sure she'd let him go by himself. She wouldn't even let him cross the street by himself. Luckily she wasn't here to see him in his airplane by himself.

He could turn around and fly to his nan's, where they would bake and read a lot of books, but Nan wasn't there because she was at his house, and if he decided to come back home, she'd be there waiting for him with a hug that would turn into hair-petting, which is how Orion told his dog Digger that he loved him. But even with Nan and Digger and his room, Orion didn't want to fly back home. He looked on the map again and decided the hospital was in the corner. He went there because it was where his mum was.

"Should we get ready to go, love?"

Orion felt himself falling. The engine stopped working. "Help! Help! I'm crashing!" The red plane tumbled in circles until it hit the hospital where his mum was sleeping (*how can people sleep so much?*). The plane and the hospital both burst into flames. Those who could use their legs were running out of the building, but most of them, like his mum, were burning in their beds. There seemed to be nothing he could do.

"Oh dear," said his nan. "I hope the pilot survived that crash!"

"No," said Orion. "He fell from too high. He's dead."

Orion's mum was sleeping too much and it was a little bit scary. She had tubes in her and it looked like they hurt, but not enough to wake her up. The tubes gave her "food and water and helped her breathe." Orion thought it odd that a person could sleep while eating and drinking. Sometimes doctors opened her eyes and shone tiny lights in them and she still wouldn't wake up. His dad told him that someone washed her. Why didn't she wake up when the water splashed her skin?

The doctors said to be "optimistic." Orion didn't know what "optimistic" meant. He noticed there was a change in the people around him, so he thought maybe they were being optimistic. His dad sure looked different. His face seemed longer. Either his hair was darker or his skin was lighter. And his eyes were different, too. Orion wondered if his mum's eyes might look different when she woke up. Her face sure looked different. And her skin. And his dad's body was longer, too. Or skinnier. His mum's body looked smaller because he couldn't see it under the covers. It was like she had no body, just lots of covers. Orion wanted to get in bed with her. He wanted his dad to get in bed with them both, but his dad looked so different and so did his mum. Orion thought they were being optimistic.

He heard his nan talking quietly to people about "dying" and "cancer" and the "coma." His nan had cancer not so long ago, but she was OK now because she had "fought it." His nan didn't seem like the fighting type because she was old and wore skirts and dresses, but she was strong in lots of ways, this he knew, even at four (almost five). When his mum and dad first told him about his nan's cancer, they'd told him that she would have to get sick before she got better, but that she could definitely get better. And she did get better, but boy did she get sick. Maybe when her hair fell out she was being optimistic and that's what made her get better.

At hospital, where his mum was sleeping, his nan asked a lot of questions about dying to the other grown-ups. She seemed to be like Orion: not so sure what it really meant. Usually she knew things that Orion didn't and she told him how bees grew flowers and what the color red might say if it had a voice, but she didn't know about dying and she looked sad when she talked quietly about it.

His Very Viv wasn't very fun at the moment. She was still the most fun of all the grown-ups because she still picked him up and tickled him when she asked what was in his belly and she ran with him down the corridors when they went to the cafeteria and she always shared a cup of Jell-O or a piece of cake, and she held his hand when they walked back to his mum's room, but now Very Viv seemed very serious, so Orion thought she was being optimistic too.

And Juni's mum—she cried a lot. She always acted like she wasn't crying, or maybe that's just how she cried. Juni had told him her mum was worried. "Why's she worried?" he'd asked. "I don't know how to say it," she'd said. But Juni didn't seem worried or even optimistic. She just seemed like Juni. Like him. So they played.

It was like no one wanted to wake his mum up, which didn't make sense to Orion. Shouldn't they talk really loudly? One day he screamed, "Wake up!" but she didn't. Very Viv picked him up and rocked him side to side and told him she was hungry. They got a chocolate bar from the machine by the elevators so at least there was that.

Today Juni was there, sitting on her knees on the blue chair, looking out the window. She was six, older than Orion, but not by much because his birthday was soon and then he'd be five. He was so glad she was in his mum's room. He went straight past his mum and tapped on Juni's shoulder. "Remember at your birthday when your dad was roaring and we were yelling so loud and running away?"

Juni turned her head and smiled at Orion. They stared at each other. Smiling.

"He's always roaring, isn't he?" Juni's mum scooped him up for a hello cuddle. "How you going, Ry?"

"Hi, Neddy." Orion felt a little embarrassed and squirmed down to the ground. He sat next to Juni and looked out the window with her. He pointed to a delivery truck and followed it with his finger. It was going to drive until it reached the ocean. Then it was going to keep driving till it reached America, where Grandma Pearl lived. They say he met her once but Orion couldn't remember. He talked to her on the phone almost every week. His finger followed the truck until he couldn't see it anymore, then he said, "Ahhh, I'm gone now. I'm gone into the ocean. I tried to drive to America but I fell in the ocean. Ahhh, I'm drowning. Help, I'm dying."

"My mum says your mum might die."

"Juniper!" Neddy squatted down and grabbed her daughter's hand. "Jean might wake up at any time, love. Anytime." She looked from her daughter to Orion, then she grabbed onto the boy's hand. "We just have to be patient."

Orion wondered if "patient" meant "optimistic" and if they were both "worried" and what did Juni know about dying because she looked a little bit confused and maybe even scared, as if she'd heard thunder and was waiting for the lightning but it was nowhere to be seen in his mum's hospital room. Orion looked at his mum, as if the answers to all of his questions were right there with her, beneath the covers, in the tubes, behind her closed eyes. He looked hard but she kept sleeping.

At first Orion liked going to hospital because of the vending machine and the cafeteria and the elevators and all of the corridors. He liked how the doctors looked like they were wearing pajamas and the patients looked like they were wearing bathrobes. But he was used to it all now; it was nothing new, nothing exciting, and so he became angry when his dad or nan said they were going to the hospital. "It's boring," he'd say; "I hate it there," he'd say; "I don't want to go," he'd say. As soon as his foot came down, someone would lift him up and cuddle him into his car seat so there was not much he could do. He'd be angry as the car left the garage, knowing that he held the truth inside him: going to hospital was not as much fun as having his mum at home. He'd be angry driving past the houses he knew, the park he knew, the Woolworths he knew. He'd be angry until he didn't know where he was anymore and then he'd forget that he was angry.

At the playground near the hospital, Orion was having fun. There was a strong breeze blowing through the park and ducks were everywhere. There was a plastic bridge and into the plastic fort with the round window he went, followed by Juni. And they'd made another friend: a boy with a patch over his eye. Together the three of them took turns being a monster. Orion imagined he was big and green. "Help, he's going to get me!" they squealed until they'd trip over their own feet and maybe cry, just a bit, then get up and have a go at being the monster. Orion felt like Juni's dad, roaring and trying to get the children so he could eat them or steal them or kill them. Yes, he was supposed to kill them because that's what monsters did. When the boy with the patch over his eye caught Orion, Orion fell and pretended the monster had killed him. He pretended he was dead. Juni and the boy kept running until they realized Orion wasn't getting up, then walked over to him and said, "Get up!" When they became bored with Orion's still body and started to walk away, Orion got up and said, "I'm not dead. I was just sleeping!" and started chasing them again, roaring like Juni's dad, big and green.

When he saw that his dad had shown up and was talking to his nan, he was happy to see him, but he didn't want to stop the game to say hello. Still, when his dad waved him over, Orion stopped. But surely stopping and looking were enough and he didn't really have to *go* to him, did he? And then Orion realized he was really out of breath. He felt his face burning red and his hair sticking to his forehead. He could go to his dad.

"Let's go back and see Mum together before we go home."

"See ya," he told Juni. "See ya," he told the boy with the eye patch. Then he took his dad's hand and together they left the playground. They crossed the road with all the other people and went through the big glass doors. They turned this corner and they turned that corner, got into the lift where his dad said, "Do you want to press the button?" and Orion said, "No." When they got out of the elevator, they turned this way and that way until they reached his mum's room where she was still sleeping, lost under all those covers, and his dad lifted him on top of his mum's bed and his dad had one hand on Orion's back while the other held onto his mum's hand and they did not try to wake her up.

On the way home neither father nor son could stop yawning.

"Dad! You're making me yawn!" Orion knew that yawns were "contagious." His mother had told him once and he'd never forgotten. Orion didn't want to yawn because he didn't want to be tired. It was still daytime and there was so much more to do. But he couldn't help it. And when he yawned, his dad yawned back.

"Sorry, mate. I didn't even know I was yawning."

Orion watched the buildings go by, looked at the signs and tried to say the letters in his head, but they passed too fast. "What's that say?"

"What's what say?"

"That."

"What?"

But it disappeared before Orion could work out how to explain the flashing pink sign with the lady's legs. It was never any use. The car always went too fast for him to move from one letter to the next; so, rather than answering his dad, he imagined they were on a conveyor belt, like at the airport or the grocery store, or even like the escalator at the shopping center. He felt the rumble of the belt in his tummy, and even his toes vibrated. He imagined people walking on the footpaths looking at him in his dad's car because wasn't he special to be on the only car-conveyor belt in all of Adelaide—goodness, he must have done something right. He waved at everyone, feeling quite chuffed with himself, but then he had a horrible thought: What would happen to him if he was too busy waving at the people and his dad was too busy yawning, maybe even sleeping, to notice that they'd got to the end of the conveyor belt and forgotten to hop off? Orion heard the sounds of the belt getting louder. "Jump," he said, barely audible over the car radio. "If you don't jump, you'll get caught in the crack and get smashed underground and you'll die."

"What'd you say back there?"

Orion straightened up. "Can we get fish and chips for dinner tonight?"

"You betcha."

Orion looked at the signs and said, "Can we get pizza?" when they passed a pizza shop and, "Can we get Hungry Jack's?" when they passed that and, getting lost in the pictures of the passing signs, he'd forgotten about the fish and chips his dad had promised him and he'd forgotten that he'd almost died. Then there was the Woolworths he knew and the park he knew and all the houses he knew, and then there was his house. It looked the same but it wasn't.

They ate fish and chips in front of the television, watching a DVD Orion had seen almost a dozen times. No matter how many times he watched it, he still laughed when the dog danced. Nothing funnier than a dancing dog.

His own dog was sleeping on the kiddie-couch his mum had bought just before she'd gone to hospital. It was meant to be Orion's couch. It had spaceships on it and Orion thought it was really cool because it was just his size. He'd given his mum a great big hug to say thank you and she'd hugged him tightly, as she always did, but Digger had made it clear that the little couch was his new napping spot. He began napping there in the daytime and at night, but not all night because Orion always woke up with Digger on his bed in the morning. Orion went over to the kiddie-couch and patted his dog to let him know he loved him. When he looked up at his dad to share a smile about how cute Digger was sleeping on the kiddie-couch and being petted by Orion, he noticed his dad had fallen asleep too. He hadn't been able to stay awake to watch the whole DVD; he hadn't even finished his glass of beer, which sat next to the greasy paper where their dinner had been. There were crumpled napkins on the lounge room table and an empty glass of milk next to a half-full carton of milk. His mum was at hospital, probably still sleeping, and wouldn't be coming home to clean up their mess. "Wake up!" Orion yelled. Digger jumped, and his father woke up to put him to bed.

Once Orion was in his bed—which wasn't as high as his mum's new bed but was much wider—he felt the all-over ache of his body. He was tired. He was sad. He was scared. He knew what all of those words meant. He knew because he felt them.

He hated the dark. He thought daytime was all right because pictures needed drawing, anthills needed flattening, swings needed swinging, clothes needed dirtying, juice needed drinking, LEGO planes needed crashing, cartoons needed watching, scooters needed riding and playhouses needed climbing. In the daytime his energy was as wide as his imagination was far, and though he "died" many times a day in his mind, he was really too busy to think about what it actually meant. But at night, when darkness covered the cluttered order of his room so that primary colors turned to gray and shapes no longer had perfect edges and there was something so strange about Very Viv's racing stripes that he tried not to let his eyes follow them around his room, Orion's energy would leave his body and he'd beg his imagination to take over so he wouldn't have to think about what "dying" really meant. If his mum died, what would they do with her? What would her eyes look like if the doctors opened them then? Would she even have eyes anymore? He begged his imagination, begged it to take over until he forced himself to see aliens drowning in soupy rivers, children turning into cookies, screaming not to get eaten. He saw trees falling on people, monsters catching him, and he wondered if the hospital really did catch fire, would his mum finally wake up? He squinted his eyes to wipe away the image of his mum burning, but he couldn't. These were awful things to imagine, awful thoughts to have, so he went back to thinking about "dying" and, because he did not know what it meant, he thought about what it might feel like, and he decided it might feel something like the dark.

Memory Is Inside Us

What defines us? Is it our history? Where we come from? What we do for money? Who we love and how we love them? Charley was sure, no matter what it was, he was shit out of luck. Abuse, crime, prison, abandonment—what did he amount to? What had he to offer?

Bricklaying wasn't such bad work and reading gave him reason to be proud, but who could love a man like him? Still, he kept trying. Dark bars with desperate smokers at slot machines usually drew him in when he was feeling lonely, but this was the city's own Crown & Sceptre Hotel. People like him didn't sit on these stools and drink these whiskeys and there sure as hell wasn't a slot machine in sight. No way was he going to find a female companion here, but he would find Mike—a young guy he worked with in the daytime who bartended at night, gave Charley a few on the house, joked with him and listened. He held a special place in Charley's life because he was such a bartender, second on a short list of two.

The first was Jimbo, up in Elizabeth, the worst time of Charley's life. Most would think his time in prison would top the list, but at least he'd been deep into self-improvement then. In Elizabeth he'd just been a thug.

He used to frequent the pub where Jimbo worked every couple of weeks when he wanted a break from the boys. The biker life was intense and Charley wondered more than twice why the hell he was living it. Jimbo never told him it wasn't any good. Jimbo listened and asked him questions—not the kind that had incriminating answers, but the kind that kept Charley talking. And Charley had never been a talker, so if someone made him want to talk that someone became a regular. Jimbo and his dingy pub were Charley's first "regulars."

"Check it out." Mike grabbed the remote and turned up the volume of the Channel Seven News. There was the scene. The gnarled bicycle. The cops and their narrowed eyes and the rain dripping from the rims of their hats. "You're clear, mate. They're not charging you." Big smile from Mike.

Was there no way to keep distance from this ruin? After the stress of the interrogation and investigation, all Charley wanted was to settle into a quiet, however somber, celebratory drink. He'd planned on telling Mike in his own good time but fucking TV got in the way. Ruined the taste of the whiskey too. Charley nodded. Mike topped up his glass.

"There's a reason I don't own a television, mate."

"Yeah, because you like to read all those books."

"It's because of all this bullshit hype, eh. People get off on tragedy. Used to be in the olden days, they'd go watch some Shakespeare. Now they just turn on the bloody news."

"You saying you're Romeo?"

"Romeo wasn't tragic, mate. He was a fool."

"So who are you then?"

"Charley."

He was a tragic, all right. Once he composed a three-line poem that read:

Memory does not walk behind us
or next to us or in front of us.
It is inside us.

But he never wrote it down. This is the memory he was referring to:

Two weeks after Runt's funeral, he was at Jimbo's pub in Elizabeth, all hard on the outside in his leather and rings, all goo on the inside, hoping tonight was the night he'd fall in love and it would change his life forever. Sometimes he wanted out. Sometimes he wanted a woman who could heal him, not just suck his cock. He was, at heart, a romantic.

A scrawny guy in an old gray suit that was way too big came into the pub with a canvas bag slung over one arm and a little kid under the other. He held the kid like a football. The kid wasn't making any noise, not laughing like they were mucking about or crying like he wanted down. The guy scanned the room like he was looking for someone or something. He wasn't right. The kid must've been only four or five and not a day'd gone by that Charley hadn't wondered what the guy was thinking in the middle of that dingy pub.

Eventually the guy put the kid down and touched the top of his four- or five-year-old head and didn't even look at him or say anything to him. Just left.

Charley yelled to Jimbo to get the kid a lemonade and said he'd be right back. Had some business to take care of.

The guy was sitting in a blue Holden, yelling at himself, when Charley knocked on the window. He jumped. His eyes were bulging and he licked his finger like he was doing lines. How sweaty he looked. How pathetic he was. Charley hated him straightaway.

He opened the door and asked the guy what he was doing dumping a little boy at a pub and the guy said, "He's not mine, he's not working out." The guy went to close the door, but Charley caught it and held it open. "You right, mate?" He hated him. He felt the hate rushing through him in a way he never had before. It was that easy to hate a man. That easy.

The guy reached for the car door and said he had to go. Too right the fucker had to go, but Charley said, "And leave that kid in a pub?" He asked him where the kid belonged and the guy said, "With you, he's all yours. Have fun with him." *Have fun with him?*

Again the guy tried to close the door, but Charley held it open, asking him if he'd hurt the kid, but he knew the answer already.

The guy shook his head no but said yes. Charley will never forget how wimpy he was. How small and insignificant. He pulled the guy out of his car and held him by his shoulders; it was just so simple. He punched him. A lot. He punched him over and over and the guy's face swelled up and turned all sorts of colors and his eyes rolled up into his head and his head rolled about because Charley was smashing the life out of him, so of course he pleaded guilty at the courthouse and didn't want to fight the rap; Charley had been completely in control.

(Once he'd composed a letter to Lisa in his head that read: *This is what I find hard to understand—I committed a crime that I was in control of and I'm not ashamed. But when someone committed a crime against me which was out of my control, I was ashamed. I am ashamed. How is this fair?* But he never translated it to paper.)

"Yeah, well, this one's on me." Mike put a shot glass of whiskey before Charley—the top-shelf stuff, the kind Charley would never spend his money on—and poured one for himself. "To fools."

Charley looked at him straight-faced with the glass in his hand, wondering what cheersing to such a thing might mean. A corner of his mouth turned up and he knew he couldn't hide his smile. He shook his head and raised his glass because, yes, it was good to be cleared of any charges and, yes, it was good to have a mate who wanted to help him celebrate and, yes, it was better to be a fool than a tragic.

Apricots

Gentle clanging in the kitchen stretched Neddy's sleep toward wakefulness. A few major clangs pointed to Juniper, her six-year-old daughter. It was a noise only a small yet independent child can make, unlike the alternatives of the dog letting itself out through a low swinging door or an unwanted stranger being far too conspicuous.

Last night's news had predicted that the unseasonable rain would last another day, then summer would resume. She knew she should be joyous for the grass and the plants and the trees but, with the duvet pulled up to her nose, she could feel herself mourning the loss of the sun. Rodd slept beside her, his closed eyes an annoyance. That he could sleep through the clamor of another morning was beyond her. He woke up when the alarm woke him, at six-thirty in the morning Monday through Friday. For Neddy, at 5:54 a.m., or thereabouts, a maternal alarm called My Child Is Roaming the House jolted her awake. And now the baby's cry. Neddy stared at the closed blinds in front of the bed, willed the light to make its slow way through the nighttime's shadows and the low morning clouds, and have mercy on their household.

With Willow on her hip, Neddy found Juniper scaling the kitchen bench. "You need a bowl, darling?"

Juniper moved quickly off the bench, singing, "I've got my cereal and milk already!" and climbed into her chair. She was a morning person.

Neddy placed the bowl in front of her eldest daughter, then sat her youngest in the highchair. Youngest daughter kicked her feet in anticipation. Eldest daughter waited for her mother to pour the cereal. Rodd said good morning to the girls on his way to the toilet, maybe forgetting his wife would have liked some acknowledgment too. They'd fought last night. Sex again. Or better put: no sex again. Neddy shrugged it off and turned on the kettle. The scent of the rain that had yet to begin was already pushing through the cracks of the doors.

She hated these days, when they were trapped inside. To leave the house in this weather seemed dreary, so Neddy clung to domestic jobs and arts and crafts like life support, praying she would not buckle under the weight of the four walls.

"After breakfast we'll go outside," she told Juniper. "Before it starts to rain." She touched Juni's head as she made her way to the fruit bowl. The last banana was deeply speckled with black spots; she was glad she wasn't the one about to eat it.

She placed half the banana into a bowl and squeezed some breast milk over it: a small puddle of bodily goodness mixed with that which came from the land. She stirred these two basics together until the combination was smooth. Willow kicked her feet some more, this time reaching out her arms, her fingers splayed. Neddy placed the food in front of her baby and fastened on a plastic bib. "Here's your spoon, little one," she said, then turned back to the fruit bowl. It was empty but for one orange, and Willow wasn't ready for oranges. Neddy needed to go to the fruit and veg shop. Did she *have* to go to the fruit and veg shop?

How was she going to manage shopping today—in this rain—with these children? After what had happened to Jean, she didn't want to be driving in this weather with them in the car, and she didn't know if she was being paranoid or safe.

"You just get on with it," she heard her mother-in-law saying. That's what country women always said. Neddy was an urban girl. And though she felt herself skilled enough at just getting on with things, she would forever think of Jean when driving in the rain.

Outside there was a drowsy heaviness in the air as the rain waited to fall; birds were everywhere. Their dog sniffed at his old poo, then moved on to whatever else smelled in the grass. Willow sat in a large plastic swing under the gum tree, chatting with life all around her. Juniper ran to the apricot tree, near-bursting with its early yield. So early, in fact, it was always a surprise when the fruit ripened.

"Mummy, look! Let's eat it!"

Neddy got down to Juniper's level to see what the apricot might look like to a small child. Indeed, it was plump and orange and ready for eating, as was so much of the tree's yield.

For weeks every morning as the parrots screeched away, trying to define their territory before someone, or something, shooed them away, Juniper had been examining the tree. Usually it was Smiley, their dog, who scared off the birds. He was in charge of all other animals in their backyard. But sometimes it was Juniper being ultra-protective of the fruit. Neddy would marvel daily at her daughter as she stood on her toes to touch the apricots. She adored Juni's love of nature, and especially trees, as it reminded her of herself as a child. She adored how already her daughter would hang and swing from the lowest branch of the gum, forming a personal relationship with the old tree. How Juni wanted to be the official waterer of the peach tree in the pot because it was just like her: small. And how the girl noticed the evolution of the apricot tree, from spring blooms abuzz with bees to nut-like balls of green expanding with juicy possibilities.

"It looks ready to me," Juniper said with serious eyes. "And I'm hungry."

Juniper was always hungry in the morning. She generally had three breakfasts before Neddy managed to have her own. But Neddy knew this wasn't about hunger. Neddy knew it was about watching something grow and now reaping the magic. "Why don't you pick it?"

Juniper pulled firmly on the fruit and when it fell from its twig, she was surprised and giddy. She held it up to her mum.

"You have the first bite, love."

Neddy watched Juniper's eyes change from concentration as she waited to find out what summer might taste like, to thrill as she tasted it.

"It's yummy, Mummy. Taste it!"

Neddy bit into the fruit. Once again life had persisted and triumphed, and it tasted good.

"I might give Smiley a quick walk before I leave," Rodd said, kissing Neddy good morning. "Before it starts to rain."

Good. She deserved that kiss. They were starting fresh today.

Neddy looked at Smiley, all languid in his soft labrador fur. He hadn't had a walk for four days because of the rain, which had caused some disagreement between Rodd and Neddy the night before. It had been foreplay to the no-sex fight. Rodd didn't see what the big deal was: you put the baby in the stroller with the plastic covering and the dog on the leash and attach it to the stroller and you go for a walk with the six-year-old striding proudly next to you in her duckbilled raincoat and gumboots. Neddy'd accused him of not having a clue what it was like to have to make decisions for the sake of two small children and to have the insight to think of your own self as well. "Sometimes you just have to realize that a dog is just a dog." She'd regretted saying it as soon as it had come out of her mouth. Her argument fared better when she'd said, "It would take us forty minutes to walk around the block; Juniper would start complaining less than half-way through and I'd be soaking because I couldn't hold an umbrella and push a stroller at the same time, probably crying like some hormone-engorged pig, just praying Willow doesn't start in too. It'd be the highlight of my day."

The argument had ended with Rodd repeating, "Hormone-engorged pig," and laughing.

"Fuck you." Neddy was angry, but not so angry that she couldn't let Rodd's laughter ease the tension and remind her that they were in this together. For the long haul.

"You wish."

"You wish I wished." And then they were both smiling.

So off Rodd and Smiley went on this dark summer morning, Rodd calling out over his shoulder, "You going to hospital today?"

"Not with the kids; maybe later tonight." Neddy gathered up the children. "Let's go inside, girls," she said, lifting Willow out of the swing. "It's started sprinkling."

Light flashed in jagged lines in the upper left-hand corner of her periphery. She was nauseous. She called to her daughter to bring her the popcorn bowl. Pain pushed hard on her skull and behind her eyes. Juniper looked up and asked if she was getting another headache. "Yes, darling," she said. "Can you please go get me the popcorn bowl?" Juniper did. It was plastic and thick and blue. It caught all of Neddy's vomit.

Migraines were nothing new to her. When life became hectic, Neddy suffered. When she was at uni and there were essays all due at the same time, she got migraines. During the months it took her to plan the trip to South America, she got migraines. In fact when planning anything—the wedding, Juniper's school fair, Rodd's fortieth—she got migraines. It was no surprise she was getting another one now. Willow was seven months and still Neddy was feeding her at night, so exhaustion added to the regular stress of daily parenting duties. But it was Jean Harley lying in that hospital that was the main cause of this one.

As she lay on the couch, thankful this migraine coincided with Willow's morning nap, Neddy wondered how she could simplify her life; migraines always told her she needed to slow down. But it was not as if she could ask Jean to please not die because it was making her sick. She couldn't ask her daughters to grow up and take care of themselves just for the short time it would take for her best friend to come out of a coma. No, there was no way to simplify life because there was no way to simplify catastrophe.

It was Jean who usually cared for Neddy when she went through a bad migraine. Once, during a steady rain, and it was a cold rain because it was a winter rain, Jean had come home to the house the two rented together, soaking, armed with two bags of vegetables.

"You got caught, you poor thing," Neddy had said from the kitchen table, lifting her head from her arms, defeated by not having had enough energy to cut a slice of bread.

"We needed vegetables. You need soup."

In fact, Jean showed up, house after house, migraine after migraine, with soup after soup, throughout all of their twenty-two years of friendship. Soup was something Jean believed in as a way to show love and offer comfort to an ailing soul. Neddy believed in doing people's dishes, sweeping their floors—those necessary things that go undone when a body is in strife. She briefly wondered if she should try to get to Jean's house and clean the kitchen for Stan.

When Jean had gone through a bad patch years earlier because she and Stan were not getting pregnant, Neddy felt the futility of her household efforts. She'd asked herself what Jean really needed. She'd considered a massage. Some bath salts. A bottle of Bailey's. In the end, she decided Jean probably needed soup.

It was nearly midnight when she had decided to soak the beans for Jean's fingers-crossed-for-fertility soup. She'd been heavily pregnant with Juniper, feeling nervous about the birth and guilty, for Jean's sake. The due date had been less than a week away. She'd gotten a migraine that night too.

Now she was laughing to herself, however feebly, at the ridic-ulousness of *why* this one came on. It was her own fault for letting the small things get so big. But the seventh day of rain in the sum-mertime *was* big. And in a house like theirs, covered in tin, it became so loud. And at ten in the morning, while Rodd was firmly seated at his big desk in his city office, sketching away at someone else's luxury, eco-friendly home that probably kept the thundering sound of rain on roofs to a bare minimum, Neddy was struggling for ways to stop worrying about the worsening day and forget the oppression. So, yes, it was exhaustion and, yes, it was Jean and, yes, it was the rain and being stuck indoors, but it was also that one small thing—the missing puzzle piece.

Willow had been rocking herself back and forth in the crawl-ing position, ready, but not quite, to take off, and her body had just given up. She was on her stomach, beginning to grizzle, ready, but not quite, to cry. Juniper and Neddy were doing a puz-zle, and Neddy desperately wanted to finish it before Willow dragged her away for the late-morning feed and nap. She felt the letdown in her breasts, which were wet and fetid with perspira-tion and the scent of milk.

"Wait, where'd it go?" They had done this puzzle many times and Neddy knew it hadn't been missing a piece. She looked under the bed. She picked up toys and smoothed out the rug around Willow in case it was hiding under there. She turned her head in every direction but up. The puzzle was missing a piece.

Juniper had dumped another puzzle onto the floor, having become bored with the unfinished one. In her world, everything was all right because something better was always waiting. She knew how to "just get on with things" without having to analyze and find a solution. Missing pieces carried no burden. Death was still an unknown.

"But it was here before we started; I know it," Neddy had said, panicked. "All the pieces were here."

Juniper didn't look up—she was happily putting together the Goldilocks puzzle—while on the floor Gretel was missing the hand that held onto Hansel's. Willow had begun to cry, but the missing piece, in Neddy's mind, somehow outweighed her daughter's frustration, hunger and fatigue. She kept looking, her breasts beginning to leak, her forehead soaking and now she could hear the drip from the ceiling in their hallway where the rain had managed to work its way in.

"Fine!" she yelled at Willow. "Fine!"

Twenty minutes later she'd felt the migraine.

Neddy had met Jean and Viv at university. At a party, actually, where they'd sat on someone's outdoor couch drinking rum and Coke until three in the morning. Twenty-two years later none of them could remember the name of the host, though Viv was pretty sure she had slept with him once before the fated party, but what they all could remember was waking up the next morning with that sickly sweet taste in their mouths, hungry to continue the previous night's conversation.

Food had been fairly unstomachable that afternoon, which was why at the outdoor café they ordered only a bowl of wedges to eat amid sips of the house white. It was then that they brainstormed what would become their first Adelaide Fringe show.

Neddy had outlined it for them, as she was clearly the organized one of the trio. She would write the poetry Jean would perform and dance to, and Viv would build the set. They had visions of a discarded ovum, at first comfortable, then journeying down a lonely and confusing vaginal path, until finally bursting toward freedom in a deluge of blood. They would call it *A Celebration of Menstruation*, half avant-garde, half taking the mickey, largely a coping mechanism for Jean as she'd only just received the news from her doctor that she had dysfunctional uterine bleeding.

Reviews weren't favorable (though some pointed out that the obvious talent was not yet matured and asked of readers "to watch out for these artists in the future"), but the experience had cemented their lifelong friendship. That first lunchtime meeting would evolve into semi-regular Thursday night drinks that Neddy, always Neddy, made sure happen. Overseas trips would follow, an abortion would be had, bridesmaid dresses would be fitted and worn, babies would be born, Neddy would stop writing and Viv would become intensely successful while they both, unknowingly, geared up for Jean's accident.

Neddy wondered what would happen if Jean died. How do two friends, so accustomed to being a part of a trio, make a happy duo when seeing one another might only remind them that something is missing? Neddy loved Viv and always thought of Viv and Jean as being equal—they were *both* her best friends—but since Jean had gone into a coma a week earlier, Neddy saw Jean as fatally perfect while Viv was becoming immortally flawed. Jean was the good one, so much like Neddy, a devoted mother and partner. Jean was the caring one, the one who knew how to comfort Neddy with soup when she suffered from what Viv referred to as "a headache." Jean was a dog-lover, like herself, while Viv had a snobby cat. Jean was the one who might die, and Viv had always been so selfishly alive.

When they'd met at the hospital when they'd first learned of the accident, Viv had been dressed in heels and a trendy short skirt and she'd brought along the man from the night before. Neddy was wearing a T-shirt stained with spit-up. Yes, they had hugged and of course they had cried, but when Viv said she needed to get to work after less than an hour at the hospital, Neddy had felt her anger surge.

Neddy hadn't reached out to Viv over the painful days of waiting. In fact, she had been ignoring Viv's texts and calls. She knew it couldn't go on like this forever. She knew Jean couldn't go on like this forever. What if there was a funeral, a wake, and all of those Thursdays to follow? If Jean was going to die, Viv would still be alive.

Nearly six, later than usual for the girls to have dinner and later than usual for Rodd to get home. Rodd entered quietly, as if he didn't want to disturb the usual noise of the household. Neddy didn't turn to look, instead felt a twinge of anger. *Typical gendered household*, she thought, slicing the fish with more precision as she said hello. She was tired. Her head, the rain, the everyday of these long days.

"I stopped by the hospital on my way home."

This time Neddy lifted her head. Her eyes met Rodd's, where she looked for clues. They were red—bloodshot—and he was biting his bottom lip.

"What?" A tightening in her gut.

"You need to go. They tried to take her out of the induced coma. She didn't come out."

What already felt like slow-motion slowed all the way down to pause: Rodd's face, Juni's song, the drone of the heroic refrigerator and the monotone of the rain. "Did you see her?"

"Ned, you should go."

Neddy's chest tensed and everything on pause gave an enormous shiver. She scanned her mind quickly and flashes of steaming vegetables and frying fish, the avocado, the breast milk, *maybe I can pick up some fruit on the way*, sped things back up to their regular hectic pace and, as if fated, the sound of her baby's cry. But with her cry came focus. "I need Willow."

In the lounge room, next to Juniper and her Duplo tower, with her seven-month-old forehead pressed to the floor, lay Willow. Such a teeny face, and Neddy knew it was filled with so much frustration. Her heart momentarily broke before she picked up her daughter and held her cheek to the baby's head, where hair became the gentlest of drugs in which Neddy could lose herself.

"Let me just breastfeed her first," she told Rodd with her eyes closed. "Can you take care of dinner tonight?"

"Course."

Neddy felt Rodd's eyes on her, watching his wife with the complete understanding that life was full of pain, and life was full of joy.

"Stan asked me to tell you to call Viv."

Neddy shut her eyes tighter. Rocked her daughter with a stronger sense of purpose.

"Come on, Juni. Let's go make us some dinner."

The tiny suck of Willow on her breast drained it all away—the empty fruit bowl, the lingering pain of the migraine, the claustrophobic feeling of the house surrounded by raindrops, and the impending call to Viv—everything but Jean. The tiny suck of Willow on her breast filled her with calm, and she did not need to cry. Jean would die, maybe not tonight, but she would die. She saw it in Rodd's face. She would die and then she'd be gone. The tiny suck of Willow on her breast was slow and it was practiced and both mother and child were absorbed in the act. Neddy marveled at the size of Willow and thought, *I did that, I've grown her, I'm still growing her*, and pondered the life-giving production and receiving of milk. Before long, Willow would turn her head from her mother's breast in search of bread and meat and, like her sister Juniper, apricots from the tree.

Neddy opened the door. Jean had been in a coma for over 150 hours. No one knew if she could hear anything so, to be safe, they talked about their fears in hushed tones.

"She's not in any pain at least." Marion, Jean's mother-in-law, frowned.

Neddy guessed that Marion, in her late seventies and a recent survivor of cancer, didn't have it in her to watch her son go through this. No matter how he seemed to hold his pain, it was sure to be severe, and it was probably more than Marion could handle.

"What can they do for her now?" Neddy stared, realizing that a body is medically just a body, and she wondered if the doctors were considering Jean's organs.

The sheets on the bed were starched near horizontal over the top of Jean's sagging form. The whiteness and the fine edges made a person forget that underneath was warm flesh, a body still raging with blood and cells, lungs still taking in and discarding breath, a heart still keeping rhythm to life's ticking away. Jean was probably going to die, but now she was alive. Neddy couldn't decide if one was more important than the other, or if they were both equally depressing.

Marion touched Neddy's arm. "Stan's in the cafeteria now. You just missed Vivian. She took Orion back home."

"Viv was here?" Neddy's heart jumped, conflicted with feeling guilty for not having called and jealous that Viv had been the one to take care of Orion. "How is Orion?"

Marion shrugged her shoulders. "I don't know if he fully understands, but he knows something's wrong with his mother. I'm going to him soon. Stan's going to stay here with Jean again. I'm getting too comfortable at the house, though. Don't like what that means."

"He's lucky to have you."

"It's hard to believe there's any luck in that little boy's life right now."

Neddy thought of Juniper. She and Orion were nearly the same age.

A single light over the stove lit the kitchen in a dull and warm nighttime way, the silence a perfect companion to the soft shadows, and in every bedroom people slept. Neddy put her bag on the table and sat down, resting her head in her hands, pulling the hair taut from her scalp, staring at the gnarled but polished wood of the kitchen table that her husband had made for them when they bought the house. Rodd must have cleaned up after dinner, usually not his thing. She looked toward the counter. Wiped down, dishes stacked in the drying rack. How could she ever thank him for this simple chore?

She imagined his long body stretched out to feel the relief of sleep. Maybe she would wake him, touch him under the covers with her own body. Maybe they would make love in the silence of the house now that the rain had stopped. Maybe the rain would start up again and muffle the sounds they might make.

She imagined Juni's breathing, listened for it. Listened for Willow's breath in the stillness of the night. She couldn't hear them, but the thought of their bodies functioning perfectly made up for it.

She was hungry. She wondered if Rodd had left her some dinner, but rather than getting up to look in the fridge, Neddy swivelled her head and searched for the last orange in the fruit bowl. On the shelf, where the sea-green paint was peeling and the ants made straight paths up and across and down again, sat the large wooden bowl, now filled with apricots. Neddy broke down and cried for the simple way they were piled to almost-overflowing. There must have been thirty, maybe forty apricots. She imagined Rodd and Juniper picking them while the rain lessened to a fine mist, the sun setting lazily in the cloudy sky, and she cried for the simple fact that life went on.

She rose and made her way to the fruit bowl. She searched for the perfect apricot. She chose one and twisted it to reveal the stone, which she plucked out before placing the fruit in her mouth. It was summer. It tasted like summer. She chose three more and sat back down, pulling her phone from her bag. She rang Viv. She wanted to tell her about how sad she was that Jean could not wake up. How sad she was that Jean would probably not live to see Orion become a young man. She wanted to ask Viv if she thought Stan would remarry if Jean ended up dying and give Orion a second mum. She wanted to ask Viv if she'd be able to accept another woman in Jean's house. She wanted to ask her if she ever thought about the applause on the opening night of their Fringe show and share with her that sometimes she was afraid she would never feel that sense of creative accomplishment again. That sometimes she was afraid she would never feel that way about friendship again. She wanted to tell her about how she missed walking Smiley without a stroller, about Willow almost crawling, about her anxiety over Juniper growing up too fast, about her love for Rodd and how even during the most mundane evenings her body ached with that love. She wanted to tell Viv that she missed her, that she needed her. She wanted to tell her about the apricots.

PART
3

This Was Their Family Now

Never, *never* should a man be so afraid to let go of his wife's hand that was his that was hers that was his that was hers, afraid to let go because she would let go and it would all be lost: the morning songs, the hair in the dinners, the hair on the pillows, the small gap between her two front teeth and the way she stuck her tongue there when she smiled, each freckle, each foot rub, their past, their dreams and the potential for more more more because that's what love is, that's what love is. And before the accident, when Stan's hand held Jean's held Stan's held Jean's, there'd been a tight presage of love then, and of their son and of the years and of each other and of their love, such an endless love, all within their two hands, but now her hand was limp and he couldn't let go, her hand now limp *inside* his, not right, never, *never*, this saying good-bye, no, one, could, understand, how so unlike Jean it felt, maybe like who she was before she was born, but *I knew you then*, he cried and he did know her then, a fetus looking up at the stars. It was Jean and it had always been Jean, his hand never fitting a thing until it held hers, and then he understood love, their love, Stan's and Jean's, Stan and Jean, and now, and now, *don't let go*, he was saying, *don't let go* to himself because Jean was letting go. Jean had already let go.

★

It felt as though it wasn't his house, or as though he hadn't been in it for years. It was familiar, eerily familiar—how long had the red teapot been on the stove and when had it ever not been there? His mum had clearly cleaned the house and Stan felt he wanted to live in it just to mess it up so it would remind him more of Jean. There needed to be some dirty dishes, just a few, piled by the sink, and a stack of them in the drying rack, one precariously atop the other, all working together to hold the last one up. Maybe a random Band-Aid or rubber band on the counter, something that had been there for months, too small for anyone to bother moving. Toys needed to spot the floors just here and there, just here and there. Had his mum straightened the magnets on the fridge? He wanted to ask Orion if this felt weird, but the boy had just said goodbye to his mum so everything in his little life must have felt weird. Stan bent down and held Orion at arm's length. "What do you want to do, mate?"

"I want to lay down with you."

Father and son, holding hands, walked to the door of the son's room.

"Your room," said the son.

"OK," said the father.

There was too much light pouring through the window of the master bedroom and the bed was tight, having been perfectly made and then untouched. How long had it been since he'd slept in his bed? Almost two weeks, of course. The last time had been with Jean, and after they'd risen and dressed for the day, they made the bed in their own way: the duvet rumpled, the sheets showing, his clothes (now washed and folded and put away) hanging over the post at the bottom of the bed. *Bed*. The word was almost too much to take in. Stan just stared, unaware of how long he'd been staring at the bed and in no way digesting how long would be seen as too long to his little boy.

Orion took off his shoes and crawled in first. Turning to the wall and closing his eyes, "Come on, Dad," he said.

Stan undressed down to his jocks and crawled in next to Orion. He held the boy, hoped it would warm him up because he was so incredibly cold. He tried to still his own body as he cried, unsure of why he was doing such a thing because he was sure he wanted Orion to know it was OK to cry. But perhaps he didn't want Orion to follow his lead and cry again because he just wanted the boy to sleep. He stopped himself from crying. He felt cold. So ridiculously cold.

Sleep came heavy and when they woke it was dark outside. Orion was the first to move. He touched his dad's face and Stan wondered if it was something he'd learned from Jean and would he please hold onto it for the rest of his life?

"Dad," he whispered.

Stan tried to smile.

"Are you going to hospital?"

"No, Ry. I'm staying here with you." Stan closed his eyes again, just wanting sleep, sleep until the new morning when they would start their new life in their old, clean house, but Orion whispered, "Dad" again, so Stan opened his eyes. "I'm hungry." And though he'd thought of it so many times in the past two weeks, what it might be like to parent this precious child alone, he now understood. Orion first. He'd always be first.

His mother had said the same to him when they set off from Adelaide to Kangaroo Island, leaving his father to the opal mines up north. He was confused, didn't understand how life could change so quickly, but his mum tried to reassure him. "Don't worry, bug. We'll be OK. And with me by your side, you'll always be first."

He'd been twelve then and he never saw his dad again. Orion was only five and one day.

Eggs and bacon sounded the easiest but Orion said no, that eggs and bacon should be for breakfast, so Stan then ruled out oatmeal too, which also sounded easy.

"Can we have a barbecue?"

"It's too late, mate. It's dark outside."

"Can we have fish fingers?"

Stan opened the freezer and saw a dozen plastic containers he'd never seen before piled neatly, with the largest on the bottom and the smallest on the top. Most of them had names on them: chicken curry, beef stew, pasta sauce, bolognaise, vegetable soup, potato bake. Who had done this for them? Who did he need to thank?

Fish fingers were on the bottom shelf, where the frozen peas and corn were. "Got it," he said, taking out all three, then winking at Orion who sat swinging his legs, one hand holding up his head and the other scratching at the clean table. Poor lad. His birthday would forever be cast in the shadow of his own mother's death. Christmas too.

"Dad?"

"Yeah, mate."

"Are you going to cook for us every night or is Nan going to come over?"

"I'm going to." Stan opened the oven door to make sure it was lit. "Blimey," he said to the cleanliness.

"Dad?"

"What is it, Ry?"

"Do you miss Mom already?"

And this is the way life would be for them. Everything they'd say to each other, everything they wouldn't say, would begin with the traces of this question.

"I do. Very much."

"Are you sad she's gone?"

"I'm very sad."

"Do you think she misses us?"

"I do think she misses us."

There was a great sense of weariness not only in Stan's body, but also settling over the entire kitchen. Digger was still in the bedroom. Stan thought about calling to him to bring a bit of life to the room, but Digger was sad too. When Stan had come home from hospital during Jean's coma and went into his room to change clothes or get some small thing for Jean, who would never wake to know what it was, Digger would follow and sniff Jean's side of the bed, his eyes classic puppy-dog-eyes, like the black reverse of two full moons spilling out the night. "Digger!"

"Digger!" Orion yelled back, sitting up and perking up, and the dog came trotting down the hall, his claws clip, clip, clipping on the hardwood floor. He nudged Orion's hand, wagging his tail. Orion got down from his seat and onto the floor. He placed his head on top of Digger's back, smiling into his wealth of fur. "Good dog, Digger." And this was it. This was their family now.

There was so much to do, so many photos to look through, music to choose, the eulogy, the phone calls, and tomorrow the choosing of the urn, discussions of proceedings, timing, cost, but tonight Stan just wanted to sleep. He deserved it too. If ever there was a time for sleep, it was when you could not be with your lover while you were awake.

They'd only been up long enough to have dinner, Stan leaving the dishes for tomorrow when the world would not stop for them.

Let them pile. A rinse was good enough. Jean would've done the same. Jean would approve.

Though he desperately wanted to crawl back into bed and cry and cry and cry and cry, Stan didn't want to leave Orion alone, or maybe he didn't want to be left alone. He couldn't decide which it was when he tried to analyze this need for Orion, but either way it came down to the question, "Do you want to sleep with me tonight?" Orion reached his arms up to his dad and Stan understood that this is what it meant to want something so badly there weren't any words, so he picked up his son and carried him to his own bedroom, feeling the warmth of the boy's head resting on his neck and resting his own head on the boy's, knowing that this, now, was his place of love. No longer Jean's hand.

It hurt again. Would walking into their room ever not hurt? Would they eventually have to move? And was he going to have to get rid of her things? Her jewelry on the dresser, her books on the bedside table? If he got rid of her clothes, what would he put in the empty closet? What would he put in the drawers that held her knickers and bras and socks? What would he *do* with those things?

He set his son gently down on Jean's side of the bed. "Do you want me to read to you?"

"Yes, please."

"Which book?"

"*You Are My I Love You.*"

"I like that book."

"That was Mom's favorite book."

It was. That and so many others. But it was that book she sometimes quoted when she played with Orion—"I am your quiet place; you are my wild"—like when he squirmed and giggled while she tried to dry him off after a bath. Stan wondered if every book he read to his son from this day forth would hold for him a memory of Jean. Would it do the same for Orion?

Stan walked back to Orion's room and found the book among all the others he'd never really realized were there. Had she read *all* these books to him? Stan had always read to his son, but not as much as Jean. He realized he would now be reading all of these books to him, over and over.

Back on the bed, Orion was wide-eyed, staring at the ceiling. "Dad?"

"Yeah, mate."

"I like your room better."

"You do?" Stan got down to his jocks again, freezing in the summer night, glad Orion had picked a short book because he was tired, had never been so tired in his life, and even though he was especially tired, still he wondered if he'd be able to fall asleep, and did he even want to fall asleep? He wanted to think of Jean and think of Jean and he wanted to cry and cry and cry and cry, but now there was Orion. Just him and Orion and their dog Digger at the side of the bed that used to be Jean's, so he'd force sleep to come, tomorrow being a new day, a huge day, a hard day, a sad day, the first day of their new life. "But your room's got all the toys. And you've got those cool racing stripes going round it."

"I like my room in the day . . ." he drew the last word out like it explained so much, ". . . but I like yours at night," and the emphasis on "yours" explained even more.

"You think you want to sleep with me for a few nights, then?"

"Yeah. Maybe four nights."

"OK. You can sleep with me for four nights."

They fell asleep with the bedside table light on, Stan only waking up at two in the morning to turn it off. And when he woke to the confusion of a light being on and the confusion of not being in a chair at the hospital beside his wife and the confusion of her being dead, of it all being real, and the familiar but foreign bedroom of his and Jean's and now only his, he also woke to the sound of Digger's deep sigh, for Digger had woken and shifted too, and he woke to the soft, pale eyelids of his sleeping son, and he saw the boy for what he was—so very, very small, so fragile, so tiny, so needing of Stan—and he cried and he cried and he cried and he cried. And then he couldn't sleep. And then he slept.

Thank You, Jean Harley

"Truth is, Stompy, she was always tryin to leave. She came too quickly out of the womb. Near tore me to pieces and put me in such a state I didn't know if anything were real or not. Nothin like childbirth. Pain you can't even imagine, but it's a good pain. A right beautiful one. Otherwise we wouldn't keep doin it." Pearl strained her eyes, trying hard to see into the past. "I swear when Jean was born she weren't even cryin. And when they brought her over to me that first time, she still hadn't a cried. Just looked up at me with those big blue eyes of hers and stared into my own. I know they say babies don't see nothin but fuzz when they're born but I'm no dummy, Stompy. A mother knows. She was lookin straight into my eyes. She *saw* me. Just wished I coulda looked into her eyes and seen her when she was dyin."

The old woman smoothed out the pink and cream woolen blanket, all of its history told in the many holes and stains. The fabric was more scratchy than soft but she liked the feel of it under her hands. It was as much home as the house they'd built in the Ozarks with their own hands, as much as the rich soil on which the picnic blanket lay, surrounding her husband's grave. She looked up to the clouds, which seemed to spin the earth faster this afternoon. "Guess there ain't a thing I can do about it now. I just hope she forgives me for not bein there."

The woman was sixty-one years old, with a birthday coming up later in the month. She looked and felt ten years older because her life of raising two children with very little money had been a hard one. Worrying about food and clothing can put deep furrows on a woman's face. That and smoking more than the chimney of the pot belly stove in the kitchen ever did. And though she wasn't quite sure how she would manage getting up from the blanket she was sitting on, what with her knees so riddled with an arthritis she'd gotten at only forty-three, she liked being nearer to the earth where her husband rested. She'd gotten the idea for the picnic from Jean. It's how Jean had met Stan's grandparents when he first took her to his childhood home. It's how Pearl knew the boy was the right one for her daughter, even if he did live on the other side of the world.

"What about that time she went missin? Only seven years old. Wanted to get to the state line. She been studyin that geography in school and thought the line between Missoura and Kentucky was a real line. Like someone took one a them permanent markers and drew one right there next to Hickman." The clouds had now completely covered the sun and the woman shivered, feeling the chill bore into her shoulders, her fingers and especially her knees. "I always did blame myself for that. Member how I told her if she could get there she could stand with one foot in Missoura and the other in Kentucky? She liked that. You liked that too, Stompy. I member you sayin you'd like to go one more. You'd like to stand with one foot in America and the other in Mexico. You member that? Good thing she didn't take up your idea that night." The woman looked up, as if the continental border lay in the clouds. "I also member the moon was big and low that night. We was settin out on the front porch, sharin a bottle a beer, wonderin if we'd ever get to Mexico one day, or any other country. Didn't even know she done snuck out. Course we didn't ever get to Mexico, did we, Stompy? Even when our girl went and found herself in Australia, got herself that scholarship—she always was smart, both her and the boy—but we never left to visit her. Missed the wedding too. I don't think she was mad at us, though. She knew we was simple folk. But her leavin us like that, livin so far away . . . didn't think I'd ever forgive her for that. Too painful watchin her get on that plane, but wasn't she a sight? So much spunk, and she was little too. Short, like you. She was a beauty, wasn't she?"

Pearl clasped her hands together, sniffing the water the clouds contained. It wasn't much different from the morning after Jean had slipped out of the house to find that black line between Missouri and Kentucky. The thick chill had not been ideal for a missing little girl in a flannelette nightgown and wearing no slippers. Pearl and Stompy and a neighborhood of worried souls wore jackets and strong boots while they joined the police in their search for Jean. Now Pearl wore an old green cardigan and her shoes were white and orthopedic and her daughter was dead.

She sniffed the air some more, sure she could smell Jean if she only focused hard enough. "I thought she was gone then. I never did think anyone had stolen her—I knew better than that in my heart and I knew that Curtis fellow was a fine man, even if his skin was as black as the inside of a broom closet. Didn't ever bother me none. Did you, though. But I thought she was gone for sure in a different way. She was old then. Even at seven she was old. Curious too. A wild seed likes to blow in the wind and that's what that girl was. But we got her back. Dolly Fife's son found her sleepin in that hollow tree, member? She musta been so cold, Stompy. Such a cold ground in those early hours that time a year." She looked off in the direction of the forested patch of land where her daughter had lost her way long ago. "But we got her back, didn't we? And she wasn't even scared." Pearl remembered the love-making that night too. The shared desperation so strong that it was both physically and emotionally painful, and that the pain was a thing of great beauty.

From a basket with a woven rose near the latch, Pearl retrieved a thermos and a plastic container of three peanut butter cookies. A Ziploc bag of a ham and cheese sandwich cut in two escaped un-smooshed. She felt relieved, old enough to know it was sometimes the tiny things that could ruin a day. Big things, like finding out your only daughter had died in a hospital bed while you slept soundly in your own thousands of miles away, too afraid to fly over the ocean to be with her in the end, did not ruin a day. They shaped it. This was the saddest day of Pearl's life and in some strange way she felt it a perfect day in its tragic proportions. There was something beautiful to be had in an encompassing sorrow, and that beauty could be shattered by any number of tiny things.

"I member when I found out Jean was doin the dirty with that boy from school. I member him, all right. He played the football, but he wasn't very big. Wasn't very good neither, if I member correctly. I reckon she left us then too. She had that womanly way about her. She was prouder. Wore her shoulders back like this." The old woman's back cracked twice below her shoulder blades, then quickly spasmed above her coccyx. She flinched, though no one would've guessed had anyone seen, such was her way with just getting on. "I never did tell you. No need to make you angry at your own blood. And you woulda been angry, Stompy. You woulda let that girl have it, through silence anyway. You never did touch her, did you? Just had to look at her the wrong way and she knew she was in trouble. She'd be sorry straightaway. Besides, you woulda just said that boy was only sweet talkin so's he could get our Jean pregnant, cause we got pregnant, didn't we? Not everyone is as unlucky as us, Stompy. Or as blessed."

After Pearl poured her tea from the thermos into a plastic cup, she looked to the trees to find the lone redstart singing *see, see, see,* wondering if it had a partner who might sing back *me, me, me.* Courting is courting, whether it is done by bird or man. Stompy had put on airs to win her over. Wore that checkered hat as if he was something too big for their small town. Of course he was tethered to the land by his own blue veins and that was what had won Pearl over in the end. That and the fact he was a real man, ten years older than her seventeen. Each time she thought she saw one of those redstarts in a faraway branch, a flutter in another tree would distract her. It seemed the birds were everywhere and nowhere.

"That boy didn't have to do no sweet talkin to Jean because she didn't need no winnin over. If Jean wanted to be havin relations, it'd be her doin the winnin over. She was a whipper, that one." There was the bird, its orange underbelly pushing through the limbs of an elm. Pearl rested with ease then, slumping further into her bones. "I member that boy too. He died a long time ago. Only young. Felt so bad for his mama. That's when I forgave our girl for bein so silly as to risk havin a baby. I member thinkin that I was happy he got to know Jean in that way. Young boy like him didn't need to die no virgin. Glad he got the chance to know what it was to lie down with a girl and have your whole life change. She was a good girl, that Jean. No matter how old she was when she lost her innocence, she was good then and she's good now. Don't know why all the good people have to go and die on me." She wiped away a tear before it had a chance to fall, as if it tested her and she wanted to win. "Lordy Lordy, let our Johnny outlive me. Let him get on that plane with our grand-daughter safe and sound and fly across that big old ocean and say goodbye good and proper, then get on back to *this* country, where he *belongs*, and let him live a *long* time, till he's old and crippled and lost his sense."

The hot tea felt soothing against the cool breeze at her throat. She knew where the sun had gone, wrapped up in that steady flowing river of white, but still, she looked for it. She closed her eyes, imagining the darkness before her was nighttime in Australia, and thought about her grandson sleeping. They were separated by distance, and neither could get over the fact that they could talk on the telephone when it was both today and tomorrow, both yesterday and today. They were separated by age too, and joined by their love of Jean.

"Ah, Stompy, how'd it ever get to this?" The woman cried and didn't let it bother her now. Outliving a child was the hardest thing a person could take. Even the redstart had quietened his song out of a curious respect. Animals know death. They know the sound of a mother grieving for her offspring. "She didn't have no time to tell that little boy goodbye. She didn't have no time to kiss him goodbye or leave him no note or nothin. Member when she left us for real that first time? Went to Colorado for the summer? Full of dreams and big ideas. Thought she could dance her way around the country but it turned out to be the world, didn't it? She left a list for us. She was always makin those lists. I member two things on that list. One was real practical. She said: *Put a nail in the wall by the back door so you can hang your keys on them and they'll never go missing again.*" Pearl giggled, thinking back to Stompy's old ways. He'd have lost his britches if he hadn't belted them to his waist. In the end he'd lost his mind, and nothing could've kept it in its place.

"The other was a real sweet one. She said: *When Clover has her pups, kiss each one for me.* Member that? Those pups lived under Jean's bed when they was born. When she came home, what was left of them were sleepin *on* her bed." The woman smiled. "And there was another thing she said but it wasn't on that list. It was in a note she left for me. She said: *Find love with Dad again. Let it in. Hold onto it.*" Pearl closed her eyes and breathed in thickly through her nose. Her nostrils flared and her lungs filled and a wave of vertigo came, then left. "Them were hard times, Stompy. I never thought I was the type to overlook adultery but there I was, and you better thank your dead daughter for that one." She opened her eyes and looked for a break in the clouds where blue might have a chance. Where sun might have a chance. She wanted to see the arcs of clouds against shafts of light, not the single white plane that presented itself to her like a blanket of snow in early February or a soft shawl around her cold shoulders. There was no blue. Not even through the thinning clouds where it might seep in if stretched far enough. It was a tiny thing, and it was OK. If winter wanted to settle in for the long haul, it was OK. She wasn't going to run to someplace warmer, someplace better. This was her home. This was her life, painful as it was, but here on this picnic blanket, talking with Stompy and remembering Jean, she knew it to be a beautiful thing.

"Let's both thank her, Stompy." Pearl closed her eyes but kept her chin raised to the sky, in case her daughter was there, looking down upon her on the woolen blanket. "Thank you, Jean Harley. Thank you."

Baumgartner's Jump

He'd been sitting in the dark for fourteen minutes. The sun had gone down and the room was a large beige shadow. Years ago, back in the minimalist days at his shack in Katherine, Philip would have closed his eyes and meditated, letting the nerves of his body go somewhere beyond the hairs of his skin and emptying his mind. Such was the impact of Jean Harley's death that he'd actually considered giving it a go, but the deeper he went into remembering that time, all the damage and the urgency, the more he did not *want* to empty his mind, and his first beer was going down so well.

Jean Harley. It'd been more than twenty years since he'd heard her name out loud. His old friend Jim Sanford had left the message on his answering machine. "I thought you might want to know." This was the girl he'd left his partner and job for, even though he was nothing but a transient love affair to her. A reckless experience. An older man. Hell yes, he'd want to know.

He would call Jim back when he finished his beer. He would forgo the marking, just for the night, and suffer his students' complaints that they'd turned in their essays a week ago and how long does it take to assess them, anyway? He would search the Internet instead. Type in a few keywords and obsess over Jean's accident. A van and a bicycle on Diagonal Road, a road he knew well. She'd been on her way to Flinders University, where she'd been a casual tutor in dance; Flinders, where they had met so many years ago when she was the girl he'd lost his marbles for. They'd spilled all over the place: one rolling this way, another that way, one falling down the sewer, another being kicked by a passer-by, and by the time they were completely gone, so was she. That's when he had packed some belongings into a ute and driven off into the bush, leaving his partner and his job behind. The last thing Philip had said to Jim was: "I'll ring you once I've settled. But you've got to promise me you'll never mention her name again." And Jim hadn't, not until today when he had left the message on the answering machine.

Rebecca was a child psychologist who worked in linguistics. From Monday to Friday she would listen to small children learning to speak and, through their speech, she diagnosed and offered therapy, theorized and applauded. After five years of cohabitation with Philip and at the age of thirty-six, it had been time to have a child of her own. Not so with Philip, though. He hadn't wanted a baby, but when she'd said they didn't have to try, she could just go off the pill and "see if anything happened," he thought it reasonable. He certainly didn't want to lose Rebecca and if a baby would make her happy, he could give it a go. He'd warm to the idea, surely. He himself was thirty-six and had a permanent position at a university. He *felt* like an adult.

But nothing had happened. Rebecca kept getting her period and Philip kept hiding his enormous relief.

After a year of the same, the sex had become more frequent and, in due course, mechanical: this hand goes here, this tongue there, just a little faster, just a little deeper, slow down, babe, you're going too fast, are you done? Each orgasm made him feel less of a man and more of a prop held up by the V of Rebecca's legs. It was at this point in his great confusion that Philip had met Jean Harley.

She was barely out of high school. Her stomach was flat from what Philip assumed was proper metabolism and the right of youth, but later learned was from regular exercise. Jean was a dancer. And she had an amazing aura.

He was a new-age hippie who believed in material pleasure and was willing to pay top dollar for it. They had a good life. A beautiful home. He and Rebecca were both vegetarians, he meditated every Saturday morning, was active in campaigning for Indigenous rights and environmental issues, smoked weed from a small bong and wrote bad poetry afterwards. He saw the connectedness between the earth and his body and other people and other living creatures. He saw auras. Looking back now, he thought it was a load of rubbish.

Jean's aura was the brightest mix of red and yellow—but it wasn't anything close to orange. It incorporated citrus fruit and blood, distracting him the moment she walked in the room. What he knew about her was that she was young, she was from America, and her studies proved her to be diligent, zealous and confident. One day after class she'd told him she was planning to cycle around Tasmania for three weeks and would therefore miss the first lecture back from holidays. "I love Tasmania," he'd said, though Philip had never been.

"Really?" The corners of her lips rose to her soft, brown-freckled cheekbones, her eyebrows and her interest rising too. "I've just begun planning my route, but I don't know anyone who's actually been, so I don't have any local knowledge. Just maps and travel brochures."

"I've got some time now if you want to grab a coffee."

Jean looked like she'd been caught off guard, but only momentarily. As if she didn't understand his accent or the common tongue of their shared English language. Philip thought, *This girl is the purest thing I have ever seen.*

"Come on. I'll shout you a coffee." He opened the door for her and turned off the light, leaving the lecture room empty.

She was majoring in dance and psychology, wondering how to stay in Australia once her student visa was up. Philip imagined Jean teaching dance to troubled children as therapy, then realized it was quite close to Rebecca's field of work, and then felt a pang of guilt.

"Maybe I'll marry an Aussie," Jean'd said.

Was she flirting? Was she flirting? Philip felt his insides brighten as he briefly imagined she was thinking of him. Then his insides slouched into his bones, as he realized she could never marry him; he was already committed.

"Maybe I'll marry you," he'd said. Had he? Really? Said that? He'd then felt the need to shit. Something toxic in his body wanting out.

Their next cup of coffee had led to merlot. Philip kept his cool, though Jean Harley had him on a gossamer thread snagged on a hangnail she hadn't even known existed. All she had to do was talk about something, anything—the black swans in the River Torrens, for instance, and how they compared with the white swans of her America—and there was that accent, the freckled flesh of her breasts as she leaned forward in a defining movement of keenness. He wanted to touch her and show her what passion was, what an older man could do for her, do *to* her, but he kept his cool. He played the sophisticated philosopher, the laid-back academic, the new-age hippie older man, and sensed that it was working.

That evening, when they'd said goodbye amid the just-getting-started folks of Rundle Street who were dressed in black and walking in small groups to dinner and drinks, they shared that moment where no one existed around them. They both returned to their teenage days (which wasn't much of a stretch for young Jean) and felt nervous and anxious and compelled to kiss, or at least say something awkward.

"So don't study too hard this weekend," Philip had said. But then Jean had kissed him. An unstoppable kiss. He knew then he would fuck her. Even when she pulled away and said goodbye, he knew that he would fuck her.

When he got home, Rebecca was still dressed in her work clothes, busying herself with a few groceries. She'd been prepped earlier during the week that he would be attending a debate at the university between a philosopher and a theologist on the prevalence of God.

"It was fascinating. Really impassioned. I felt I was on the edge of my seat for at least three-quarters of it."

"What did they say?"

What *did* they say? "Nothing new, really, it was how they said it, I suppose. Inspiring, if not enlightening. I reckon I can get a poem out of it. In fact, that's what I'll do after we're done here. That's exactly what I'll do. I'll write a poem." *Just shut up*, he'd told himself.

"How's Jim?"

Philip went to help Rebecca put the groceries away but got flustered because there was only one bag and he was getting in her way so he started going on and on about sin and redemption and free will and natural instinct—where he got it from he did not know because it certainly wasn't the debate. Except, of course, he did know—it was from his rendezvous with Jean.

"Have you eaten?" he asked.

"I'm late," she said, her smile almost devious. She moved to put the kettle on. "Only by two days, I mean it should have come Tuesday, so technically two and a half days."

Philip walked to the freezer to get himself the chilled vodka for the martini he suddenly wanted. He moved past Rebecca, sucking in his stomach, not touching her. "Let's not get too carried away, Bec. Don't want to get disappointed over two and a half days." He knew his words were cruel. Could he still fuck Jean if Rebecca was pregnant? He hated himself.

"Don't shit all over my hope, Philip."

He watched her kick off her heels and walk toward the toilet, all tailored and business-like for her appointment with a urine stick. No, he did not want to be a father. He did not want to be a father to Rebecca's baby. He did not want to—suddenly this had stopped being about a baby; Philip realized that his relationship was hanging in the balance.

She came out of the toilet crying. "Bloody negative."

Philip breathed out, walked over to Rebecca's defeated body and put his arms around her waist. She put her head on his chest. He held her and kissed her forehead. He told her he was sorry. And he was. For everything.

Over dumplings, he knew he would fuck Jean Harley. Later it was "Dance with me!" and Jean pulling him toward the other bodies that jumped and fist-pumped and jerked their hips at some club Philip hadn't known existed. The first thing he thought of was what if any of his students were there? Then he became conscious of his age. Was mid-thirties hip? But then they'd started dancing, rocking, mocking, laughing, holding each other closely, then letting themselves get loose; sweat beaded and dripped.

After the tequila they'd found a new rhythm. They were practically fucking now. He said, "I don't want to leave," and she said, "Don't," and he said, "I have to," and she said, "Is there someone waiting for you?" and he said, "No."

Then, in the tiny bedroom at the share house where she lived with four other students he'd managed to avoid in the sneakiest, most immature way, Philip dressed slowly, wondering what he had done with this naked girl, leaning on her elbow, her breasts full and her hips barely there.

"So maybe we'll see each other when I get back?"

Who knew? While she was in Tasmania, Philip just might find his way back to Rebecca and forget all about the girl. Remorse setting in, he began to realize he couldn't see her again. "I'm already hard just thinking about it." And as much as he'd wanted it to be, it wasn't a lie.

Jean Harley filled his thoughts. He became agitated and absent-minded. Each essay he marked reminded him of the fact that *she* was his student, such a young woman, that he had marked *her* essay, *her* essay! And he thought about her hot tequila breath. And he thought about the noises she'd made when he went down on her. In the evening, as he fluffed the couscous and stirred the chickpeas so they'd be waiting pretty for Rebecca's arrival home from work, he dreamed of a time he might cook for Jean and teach her what an older, cultured man knows: that cumin loves ginger, that sex is always better if fueled by chili. At night, as the switched-off light cued Rebecca's ovulating body to fold into Philip's deceptive one, Jean Harley was in bed with them. In the morning, there was sun and Jean Harley.

A typical afternoon might have even gone like this: Philip checking his emails, anxious for one from Jean; the computer not working fast enough (it was still the twentieth century); Rebecca coming home in a couple of hours and no new messages in his inbox. Jean had not emailed him—how could she email him?—the point being maybe she hadn't thought of him at all, was maybe meeting a boy her own age, perhaps another adventurer like her who would drink with her until they were both drunk enough, cheeky enough and confident enough to take the risk and kiss and touch one another, go further and deeper, and Rebecca wouldn't be home for hours, how good it felt to jerk off!

But the fantasies were short-lived. Eventually the sound of the garage door and the subsequent slam of a car door had Philip's chest high, his shoulders up. He tried to grumble at the televised face of John Howard so that Rebecca would think he was his normal self when she walked through the door, but the minute she touched his shoulder, kissed his lips, pushed her tongue inside his mouth, Philip pulled away, said, "No," and she said, "What's wrong?" and he said, "This," and she said, "What?" and he said, "Everything." "Everything?" and he said, "I'm in love with one of my students."

Philip phoned Jim. No answer. There was no chance of hearing Jim mention Jean's name tonight. Philip felt like he should be annoyed at this, but instead he walked to the refrigerator for another beer. In the crisper he found half a sweet potato that needed eating. He grated the tuber, rustic skin and all, and mixed in an egg. His food became a dirty orange concoction, so pleasing to turn, to smoosh and release with his own hands. He had never made this dish before, but he understood it intrinsically: when the oil started to sizzle he threw in some diced onions and garlic, then the dirty orange mixture, which he moved quickly and regularly with a spatula as salt and pepper and more than a pinch of tarragon were quickly added, quickly dispersed. He moved the patty to the side of the pan and set a fat gourmet sausage smack in the middle of it. Vegetarianism went out of style with the daily yoga. He'd reunited with meat when he moved to Newcastle and began teaching again, a welcomed downgrade from university to TAFE. A new city. A new job. A new man.

As he ate he thought about Felix Baumgartner, the man he'd recently watched on YouTube suspend his toes over a void of twenty-four miles, below him solid ground. Philip's own stomach had caught in his throat as he anticipated the more than four minutes of freefall awaiting Baumgartner. When he had exhaled, his lungs still felt inflated. Now he was poised in full knowledge that there was poetry in the moment before the moment: in the moment before Felix jumped; in the moment before he'd told Rebecca he was through with their relationship; in the moment before he'd turned in his resignation; in the moment before Jean Harley had walked through the door of his Intro to Ethics tutorial after her cycling trip to Tasmania. Philip knew, too, that he was not so different from Felix Baumgartner, who'd stepped off his small capsule and become nothing more than a lonely body plummeting through the void.

He'd been trying to busy himself as students began filling the room, and he continued to busy himself when he felt Jean enter. He was tight, nervous, completely wound. When he did look up, there she was. She was darker. She appeared to have more freckles. Her aura was different.

When Philip caught her eye, Jean smiled quickly and looked away. What was that? But maybe she didn't want anyone to catch on that they were having an affair. He began talking about Kurt Baier's essay on egoism. Watched Jean while she wrote.

After class Jean waited for the others to leave before she approached Philip. *Ah*, he thought, *she comes to me!* He smiled at her as if to say, *I knew you'd come.*

"That's interesting, the consistent egoist not being able to make a moral decision." Was she nervous? She sounded nervous. Was she making a comment about his ego and lack of morality? He quickly freaked out and thought, *Was Baier?* But how good it was to hear her voice. He could smell her when she was this close to him. He kept his cool. He was a grown man, after all.

"How was Tasmania?"

"Amazing." Her smile grew; she relaxed. He could see she wanted to talk about it and he wanted to do everything he could to keep her talking.

"Do you want to grab a coffee?"

"I can't. I've got to get to the library. I want to get started early on an essay due next week."

This was more than awkward for Philip. No, this was wrong. Jean started to move away.

"Are you OK, Jean?"

"Yes," she said. "No," she said. And *No*, he thought, *no no no no*. "We can't do what we did ever again."

"What's happened, Jean?" Philip got out of his seat, moved dangerously close to her, thinking she would change her mind if only he could touch her.

"I met someone in Tassie. Well, I already knew him. From America. It's a long story, but an incredible story. He's an Aussie, but I met him in America and then I met him again in Tasmania. Anyway, he's . . . I just know I can't be with you after seeing him again. It's not right. It's not fair."

Philip wanted to ask how old he was, did she sleep with him, was she in love with him, did she despise Philip for being so old? But he just looked at her, crestfallen, and then she said she was sorry. And then she was gone.

Seven years of new mornings and lotus positions in the bush had passed before Philip realized what he was doing was more insane than what he had done to get to this point. Cutting himself off from the world was literally getting him nowhere. When he gave it all up it had been surprisingly easy. Not the sex, though. Not really. Seven years of celibacy is a long time and maybe that was the problem: it had been too long. Over the next fourteen years, during his time in Newcastle, he'd had only a handful of flings and they'd made him feel awful: the two tourists from America had become his first threesome (and it did bother him, this penchant for American accents and unbridled energy); a widow from town had drunk herself into his bed; he'd felt sorry for a lonely friend with severe chronic pain. There were a few more, but Philip couldn't even remember the details they were that insignificant. Jean had been his last truly significant fuck and it was decades ago. Of course it had been different with Rebecca. He rarely thought of them as *fucking* when he remembered sex with her. Sometimes they got dirty, and that might've been fucking, but Philip had loved her body *and* her soul when they'd been intimate. During the best years of his life, he'd felt such a strong spirituality with Bec he now wondered if he'd ever feel anything close to it again.

After dinner and five beers down, Philip knew this to be his burden: to spend the rest of his life thinking about how easy it was to mess things up. "Rebecca." He began a mantra, laughing at himself but curious as to where it might go. "Rebecca." He tried to focus on what she'd looked like. "Rebecca." But he couldn't find her. Jean Harley filled his mind instead.

The phone rang once. "Jim," he answered.

"Philip." An old friend's laugh on the end of the line. "How you going? Long time."

"It's been a bloody long time."

"Too long. When you coming back to Adelaide? We need to catch up."

"Well, when's the funeral?"

"Yeah . . ." An old friend's silence followed by the two words he'd promised he'd never say: "Jean Harley."

Call Me Charley

The train engine settled in the noise of its own long sigh, deserving rest after traveling through the South Australian desert. At the platform, Charley fidgeted. He had no pockets and didn't know what to do with his hands. Finally, he settled on an old habit of picking at the skin surrounding his nails. He had a twitch in his left eye that attracted a determined fly. He wanted a shot of whiskey—another old habit—but it was only ten and he wanted to be at his best for Lisa.

When he'd found out Jean Harley had died, Charley wrote to Lisa. Just as he'd written to her the day he'd worked up the courage to go to the hospital to find out if his victim was OK. Just as he'd written to her after his first (ill-fated) relationship began when he'd left prison and tried to lead a quiet life. Just as when he'd left prison and grappled with what "a quiet life" might entail. As with all of these and so many more letters to Lisa, he needed to write in order to think clearly. He needed to ask himself if he had the right to go to the funeral, so he asked her. Charley had always seen Lisa as much a teacher as she was a friend. She'd opened up reading and writing to him, so how could he not put her on a pedestal of Biggest Influence and Supreme Mentor?

He wrote to her that he was an outsider in the worst way, asked her what he should say if someone asked him how he knew Jean, said he wanted to avoid her family at all costs because he didn't want to tell any of them his name. Lisa's reply was: "I'm coming to Adelaide. We'll go to the funeral together."

Now, on the platform, watching the passengers disembark and hug their loved ones, Charley wondered if he'd ever been so nervous. It had been thirteen years since he'd seen Lisa and in that time they'd shared so much. Too much? It had never seemed too much when there were so many miles between them and only pen that translated thoughts and paper that reflected feelings. Charley had never been good with speaking. He stumbled over big words and hid the most complex ones far from his tongue. It was through writing letters to Lisa that he got beyond his fear and really looked at life and language. Now, with Lisa nearing the space he guarded, with Charley over-burdened by his own bulk, how was he supposed to communicate?

There she was, carrying more weight than he remembered, carrying more age, a roughness in her skin from the heat of the Alice sun, more lines from what he assumed to be frequent smiling and laughter—she had a husband and four children to thank, triplets for fuck's sake. There she was raising her hand to her mouth when she saw him. Charley, who'd not gained more weight but lost a lot of muscle so that he'd grown a fatter gut. Charley, who'd taken on a darker color from his work outdoors yet still carried that ashen skin reserved for someone so much older, a smoker with his big toe in the grave. She raised her hand to her mouth and he lifted his in an uneasy wave. She didn't bother wiping away her tears as he approached, allowing familiarity to lightly drown him. Still, what to say at a time like this? What to do with one's body?

"Look at you, you big old bear," she said and hugged him.

Charley patted her back at first, self-conscious of their closeness. Then he stilled his hands, let them rest on her warm back.
Then he let them hold her just that little bit tighter.

"I was always a blubberer," she told him, laughing. "You had
to expect this."

"I didn't know what to expect," he said, looking at the train.
"Never do."

At first he'd had to get his cellmate to read him the letters.

My dear son Charley,
I won't ask you how you are because it would probably break my
heart. The only advice I can give you is to take each day one at a
time. That's what I do. Each day that I get out of bed and take my
shaky legs to the bakery, I survive another day. The doctor said the
tumor is the size of an orange! I'm surprised my brain can hold
something so big. It's bad more than it's not, but I won't let it get me
down just yet. As long as I'm up I'm winning. That's what I tell
myself. It surprises me that on days when there's pain and I feel like
there's no hope I'm actually glad because those are the days I have to
look hard to find strength and those are the days I end up being the
most thankful. I hope you're seeing your time in prison as a way to
search for strength. I hope you can forgive yourself. I also hope you
can be thankful for the life you still have ahead you. You're a good
man, Charley. I know this even if you don't. And I love you, my
beautiful son.
Mum

It was OK for a while, but after he'd begun feeling the weight of
his mum's devotion and the ache of her tumor, he hadn't wanted
anyone else to read them.

"I want to learn to read," he'd told Doc.

"But that's wonderful, Rascal!" Doc clapped his hands together. "And how do you think you might go about learning to read?"

Charley shifted in his chair. Having never outgrown the boy he was in school when the teachers called on him for an answer, he didn't know what he was supposed to say. "There's that lady who teaches here—"

"Ah yes, Lisa. A lovely woman. But how do *you* plan to go about learning to read?" Doc's smile brought rows of wrinkles to his face.

This was a trick, right? Like some kind of riddle? So he sat for a long time, staring at the turquoise diamond shapes on the dirty red carpet under his feet. If he put his hand out he could make the diamonds disappear. Just like that. Then he got it. "You mean I have to really want it."

"Yes, Rascal. You have to change." Doc's eyes looked tired from staring so deeply at Charley in his regulation uniform, as if he was worn out just thinking about all the pain that lay below, beneath Charley's skin, under his muscles, packed into his bones. "Learning to read could quite possibly be the first step to really helping yourself."

Sometimes, the man referred to as "Rascal" thought of the man referred to as "Doc" as the sort of man he might've liked for a father. Then he wondered what it would've been like growing up with a father. Any father. Even old Charles Cromwell.

Rascal wasn't his real name. When he was harmless and punching the foreign air with those angry fists in the first seconds of his life, beet red and already screaming of injustice, he was Charles Cromwell II, named after the no-good father he would never really remember.

The elder Charley spent the first two years of his son's life in prison for poking a water pistol through the pocket of his jacket and demanding money from a shop clerk, who then died of a heart attack. After he was released from prison (with "Born Bad" tattooed on the inside of his forearm and a halfway-vacant look in his eyes), he gave his son a water pistol. Eight months later he died outside the Star Hotel, a broken pint glass by his head.

The boy had his father's sense of misadventure sure as he had his rotten luck. It was enough to secure his fate as a Chip off the Old Fucking Block. Of course he'd land himself in jail, but for Charley it had been a time of healing, where he'd learned to find strength, to forgive and be thankful. It was also where he'd learned to read.

If it had been a dark night rather than a Wednesday morning on the first day he began his studies and if he and the teacher had been on an empty street rather than in a prison and if he'd been walking behind her rather than sitting in front of her, Lisa would've been bloody scared. Charley knew the effect he had on people. At more than six feet tall and carrying a grand bulk of equal fat and muscle, while sporting a beard that was long and gnarly and matching it with the inverse of a shaved head, Charley understood the power of intimidation. Being bald, though, wasn't his plan. When he'd started losing his hair at twenty-four—only two years older than his father had been when he was killed at the Star Hotel—he felt there wasn't any choice but to shave it all off.

Sitting in the room where the other inmates had moments ago either leaned back in disinterest or hunched forwards while honing their penmanship, Charley stared at his teacher, not sure how to ask her to help him. He studied her as she packed up her books and journal into a shoulder bag and placed her pen into a plastic pencil case—a present he would later find out was supposed to be for her two-year-old son. She wore her hair loose. It was thick. He thought about how nice it would be to feel it, to crush it in his fingers and watch it spring back when he let it go.

"Is there something you want to talk about, Rascal?"

He fumbled in his front shirt pocket for his mum's letter. "I get these," he told her. "I want to read them."

Lisa stood tall as she approached her student. "You want me to read it to you?" she asked.

He looked away from her, ashamed of who he was, of his history. Ashamed he'd never learned to read. "I want to learn how to read me mum's letters."

He'd expected a sigh. Instead her face softened. "If you hang in there and have patience with the class, I think you'll find you'll be reading the letters on your own quite soon."

"No time. Mum's dying."

Lisa sat down in the chair next to him. "I'm really sorry about your mum, Rascal, but I just don't know how we can manage to get any one-on-one time."

Charley looked at her, wondered if she loved her own mum, if she was someone else's mum, if there'd be a man sleeping next to her at night. "We're getting one-on-one time now."

Just then a guard came through the door, took away their one-on-one.

Three days later Lisa had asked if he'd happened to bring his mum's letter. As slow was his usual pace, Charley was still seated, gathering himself while the other prisoners were leaving. He stopped and watched them, unwilling to answer his teacher until everyone had gone, then pulled out his mum's letter from his front pocket. He'd brought it to class not because he was going to ask Lisa to help him read it again, but because he carried it everywhere, always trying to work out the words. He could make out some—*the, and, want, day, hello, love, Mum*—and some he could have a go at. Sentences formed. Sentences fell away.

"You've got me for half an hour twice a week." Lisa moved into the seat next to him. "Let's see how far we can get today."

Charley felt a jolt in his chest—relief? excitement?—but he didn't indulge in it, didn't want to give too much of himself away. He was quiet when he spoke. "I know what the first line is. It's pretty much the same every time."

"Well, when you're saying it to me make sure you're really looking at the words. Make sure you're *reading* them." Lisa nodded her head and tightened her lips, encouraging him.

"My dear son Charley." He looked up at Lisa straightaway. "That's what she writes every time. Sometimes with my name, sometimes without it."

"Your name is Charley?" She said it as if she had just discovered he cared for injured animals.

He shifted in his seat and looked back at the letter. "It's Rascal." He felt the back of his neck beginning to itch and went to scratch it, first digging into the scar under his ear.

"I'd love to call you Charley. Can I call you Charley?"

He stared at his fingernails, expecting to find flakes of skin, dirt, blood. "Mum's the only one who calls me that."

"What can I call you?" Lisa sat with her back straight. She was patient with him. "You have to give me a better name than Rascal. I don't want to call you by your biker name. I don't think you're a biker anymore."

Charley raised one eyebrow, crinkling the other.

"I think you're a sensitive man who hides behind a particular image."

He thought about a new name. Thought about how easy it had been to discard "Charley" and accept "Rascal" all those years ago. Thought about how expendable names were. How expendable people were.

"I'll come up with something. But call me Rascal for now."

My dear son Charley,
I hope this letter finds you growing stronger and wiser. I think of you
so much and I imagine the loneliness you must feel in that prison.
Then I think it can't be any worse than the loneliness you were
feeling before they put you away. I'm sorry for that. I wish I
could've been a better mum. I wish you'd agree to a visit, although I
probably couldn't handle the travel anyway. I've been doing a lot of
soul-searching since I've been having more pain. I find it hard to
leave my bed before noon on the days I don't work and more and
more I'm taking days off. Soon I'll have to leave the bakery for
good. Sometimes I feel like it's all I have so leaving makes me
very sad. But then I think about other things I have, like the
crochet club and Mavis and June and the wilderness of our own
backyard. It used to be your playground. I think of you the most.
I'm so sorry your life has turned out the way it has but I will never
think that it is over, Charley. I have to believe your life is about
to begin.
I love you so much.
Mum

It was true what his mum had said. In prison he was lonely, but that was nothing new. His pain had always been his. No one could touch it. But as he'd come to depend on the letters from his mum, he was working through it. Her letters were like scripture to him which he poured over daily, though struggled, became frustrated, short-tempered and angry.

Lisa had used the term "dyslexia" and came up with exercises for him. Repetitions of vowel sounds like *boy* and *toy* and *soil* and *toil*. He studied three pages of short words every week and at night he returned to his mother's letters. Now vowel combinations were taking shape on the page and manifesting as sounds in his mind and on his tongue. They were bonding together, helping to form words, and words upon words upon words made thoughts. He believed his mother's letters were going to change the direction of his life.

Twice a week he went to class with a letter in his pocket. Sometimes two. It took them half an hour to get through half a letter and, when their time was up, Charley could see that Lisa's heart seemed to fall and thud in her gut as he folded the paper and put it in his shirt pocket.

"Do you want me to read the rest to you?" she'd always ask.

"I need to," he'd say, looking hard at the deep creases in his hands. At only forty-two he felt he was getting old. Look at his skin. His bald head. His gut. He couldn't imagine how old his mum must've looked.

Lisa would nod and look at his hands as well. They were big hands, weather-worn. The right one had a cigarette burn on it. Indeed they were hands with stories to tell; Charley would say there were too many stories.

One day Lisa had asked if she could take a letter home with her and make note cards for the difficult words. "If you see a word you don't know, you can just flip the card over, and I can spell the word out like it sounds so you can work out what the word is." Once Lisa had discovered Charley's dyslexia, he could see confidence in her teaching. "I'll bring it to you tomorrow and you can have the letter and the note cards to work on by yourself."

Charley's eyebrows were two thick, bushy wrinkles. He stared hard at Lisa, and it was as if a conversation was continuing in their eyes. This small freedom seemed too good to trust, and he so rarely trusted in anything good.

Charley had been surprised to see Lisa the next day in the visitors' room. He'd thought she'd just leave the letter and the note cards for him. Perhaps Lisa thought he was an OK bloke.

"I just wanted to give you them in person." She took a deep breath, gaining new momentum. "Rascal, I wanted to see you. I wanted to tell you I think your mother is the most amazing woman."

Charley nodded, looking hard at the hairs on his fingers. Five long black hairs on each stout finger. He made a fist, stretched his fingers, made a fist again. Scratched the back of his neck.

"My mother died when I was fifteen," she told him, and the space between them fell away. Charley put his hands in his lap. He thought about himself at fifteen, stealing radios from cars, smoking half a pack of cigarettes a day, roaming the dark streets at night and suspicious of his world. He thought about how different Lisa's life at fifteen must have been. He thought about how soon they'd have the death of a mother in common.

She gave him the letter and note cards. "You have a long list of sight words now."

Charley knew this. He also knew that difficult words like *tumor* and *remember* rested on his eyes and settled in his mind easily. It wasn't that the letters in those words made sense to him, because in fact they were always jumbled, no matter how many times he'd seen them; it was that they'd been written over and over again so many times he just knew what they were without having to look too closely.

"So between that and sounding-out, there were really only thirteen words I was worried about."

Charley looked at the cards. *Infinite* was rewritten as *in-fin-it*. *Acceptance* became *ex-sept-ans*.

"I have to say I did struggle with the science of what I was doing: taking away the heart of the word to get to the body." She rummaged through the cards and held up *journey*. "I'm sorry," she said, smearing the wetness into her cheeks, "but her love for you . . . her love for you. . . ." She shook her head and laughed at herself. "I don't even know the words to finish the sentence. How ironic is that?"

Charley had never known this kind of openness with a woman before. Tears went with anger or alcohol or drugs. Maybe he was more than a student. Maybe he was a friend. And it was that thought that gave him the courage he needed. "How'd you do it?"

"Do what?"

"How'd you say goodbye?"

She looked off in the distance, maybe recalling an image of her mother that lasted for only a flash of a moment, maybe recalling a memory of her that went on longer. "I never said goodbye while she was alive. I'm not even sure I did after she died." Her eyes returned to his, staring. "I haven't."

"Were you with her when it happened?"

"It was the middle of the night. I knew when the phone rang. I knew instantly."

"Ain't no call in the middle of the night's gonna be a good one, eh? Don't reckon I'll get a phone call, middle of the night or afternoon."

They sat in silence for what seemed like minutes. Charley felt Lisa's hand in his own, even though they weren't touching.

His first big book was *Of Mice and Men* and it took him months to get through it. Sometimes he read the newspaper and, by the time he finished, it was old news. Reading certainly took a lot of time, but time was something Charley had.

My dear son Charley,
I think about you most on these cold nights. Now that it's winter I'm settling in. Maybe too much. My bones shiver and my muscles don't want to stretch. I read a lot. I remember when you were a baby. I was so tired from feeding you and loving you that I couldn't get past three pages of a book. I dreamed that when I was old I would lie in bed for

days reading all the books I spent a lifetime saying, "One day I will read this." Well, I'm doing it now. Sometimes I read all day and night, but I know I'll never read them all before I die.

When the first week passed without a letter, he thought his mum must be feeling really bad or maybe she'd died and nobody'd told him. He worried. But at night, when he pulled out an old letter, he didn't *feel* his mother's death, as Lisa had her own mum's. But then the second week without a letter passed and he was sure she was dead and no one had told him. And then he had a dream, one that moved him so much that when he woke up, he didn't know where he was, had forgotten he was in prison.

"Did you ever have nightmares bout your mum's funeral?" They'd just finished discussing a children's book, *Danny, the Champion of the World*, just finished discussing fathers. The thirty minutes were almost up and Charley wanted to talk about mothers.

"I'm not sure if I did while she was sick. I can't remember. But I did after she was gone."

"I dreamed she was in a coffin. Her face was white."

"Did she look like you remember her?"

"Been so long since I seen me mum I'm not sure if I remember her right, eh."

"I always dream about mine being young and healthy. Not at all like she was near the end."

Charley picked at a callus. Hard on the outside, soft on the inside.

"Don't you want to see her, Rascal? Before she dies?"

When she said his name, he shook his head no. Rascal didn't want to see her. Charley did.

His mum died in hospital. Three of her friends from the crochet club had been with her, crocheting small floppy flowers in all colors. It had been his mother's request to have them decorating the church at her funeral, then to let people take one with them as they left. She herself had been crocheting them for months, before the pain became too much. Charley got one of hers. A woman named Shirl gave it to him. She'd cried and told him he would've been proud of his mother in those final days, that she'd never known a braver woman. The flower was purple and green with a yellow center. "It's the smallest one we made," she said. "We weren't sure how well a bigger one would go over here."

Charley put it under his pillow, fell asleep at night holding it in his hand. He did so for the rest of his days in lock-up.

He'd meant to show it to Lisa after the next class but class was canceled. Lisa wasn't there. The next week someone else began teaching.

Dear Rascal,

I'm sorry I've missed our classes and our one-on-ones. I've been sick. But the good news is that I'm actually not sick. I'm pregnant. In fact, I'm having triplets! This has been quite a shock as I was convinced we'd already done the kid thing with Clayton and once was enough. Apparently once is not enough. We've decided to move back to Alice Springs, where we're both from. We've decided to be closer to our families. We're going to need them. This all seems to be happening so quickly. I'm sure you've noticed that there is already someone else taking over the class. I'm so sorry about our one-on-ones. I promise I'll visit before we move, and it's not an empty promise. I want us to remain friends, Rascal. You do know that the only way to do that is through letters, and I love that you can now read them and write your own. There are so many more books to discuss, so much pain and joy still to work through. I look forward to our continuing journey.
Your friend,
Lisa

When Lisa came in for the visit, he told her about his mother's death, about how the warden had told him there was a phone call. It was the middle of the fucking night. He hadn't been able to bring himself to ask for a pass to the funeral. Lisa cried. She held his hand. By then the leaves that had greened and the flowers that had blossomed in the outside world, only to dry up and fall away in the summer's unforgiving heat, had completely disappeared, winter returning for another long slog. Lisa's belly was big.

"It's Chuck," he'd told her. "I've told the guys in here to call me Chuck."

"A derivative of Charley."

"I reckon that's what I am. *A derivative of Charley.* Me mum wouldn't have minded it."

"Aw, I don't know. I reckon she'd still call you Charley."

"You can," he'd told her, picking at what wasn't peeling from his hands, creating new broken skin.

"I can what?"

"Call me Charley."

And Lisa had smiled. "OK, Charley."

Charley was well aware of his less-than-average economic status and he knew he reflected a much sadder social one, but it didn't usually bother him. Because of the shit life he'd led up to this point, he was OK with getting by. But if made to show a woman his home—his small and lonely ex-con home with his two-seater couch and a stained-to-buggery coffee table and all those books on the shelves he'd built, with the single bed in the room with nothing but a reading lamp and a single three-drawer dresser and piles of books, with the moldy shower, the dank outdoor toilet, the wonky-springed recliner under the awning in the backyard— if made to show a woman his home, Charley stiffened till it hurt.

"You should be proud of yourself," his parole officer had said, hands on her hips, surveying his lounge room. "You're doing really well." Charley had felt small then, just as he'd felt the master of losers when a mate's wife looked around nervously, with pity, as if to say, *How do you live like this, you sad and awkward man?* A woman he'd been wooing at the local pub in a very self-conscious way came over one night drunk and horny and said his house was depressing, "needs some bloody curtains," and she would be the one to make them. He felt hopeful and hopeless all at once and she, of course, never came back. Now, here was Lisa. Here she was in Charley's new cell, a space within the vast open prison that was his world, and it said, *This is me; what do you think?* And he hated himself.

"Look at all of these books. Camus. Robert Dessaix. Cormac McCarthy. You're certainly diverse."

"Not really," he said, his shoulders loosening. "Takes me ages to get through one, eh."

"You like poetry?"

"Sometimes."

"I do too." Lisa looked back at Charley. The room felt warm. "Funny we never brought it up in our letters."

"Mmm," he said, not sure what to say.

"I love the Romantics. Shakespeare's sonnets. When my mum died I went into an Emily Dickinson phase."

"I like Dickinson."

Lisa laughed quickly through her nose, said, "I wonder if it's because you've lost your mum too," and returned to his books.

"I didn't read poetry when she died. Only been reading it the last few years."

"What made you start?"

And here they were, having a conversation about poetry and life in his somehow ample home. They talked about Alice Springs, how much she liked it, how much he'd like to go, though she didn't invite him to visit. They talked about her family, about how he was sure he'd never be a father. They talked on the car ride to her hotel about how driving was for him, since the accident. Later, at the hotel's restaurant, Lisa asked Charley how he was feeling about the funeral. He took his time answering, at first trying to escape it by swirling his whiskey in his glass and letting the words *golden amber, bronze urine* roll around his mind. Though he read poetry, he never wrote it. Sometimes, though, he silently composed it.

"I guess it's pretty hard naming your emotions right now."

Charley took a swig. *Fire ants' piss and splendidness.*

"I feel nervous for you. I'm sorry, but I do." Lisa picked at the calamari in the basket in front of them but didn't take a bite. "You know, I can't believe you can write these confident letters, so insightful too, but you can't speak out loud without second-guessing yourself. I mean, in your letters you ramble on, and it seems like you've got it all worked out because you really have no idea. Does that make sense? Like *not* understanding gives you clarity and comfort." Lisa looked up from the food to see Charley once again swirling his whiskey. "They're amazing letters."

"Clarity? No. Comfort? Don't know. Maybe."

They arrived at the funeral late, as Charley had wanted. It meant he wouldn't have to shake hands with the family if the funeral was to be traditional. His plan was to get in and out without having to talk to anyone other than Lisa. True, he wanted to apologize to Jean Harley's son, but there was no way to do it without imploding. Lisa agreed. Talking to the boy would be hard.

Although late he had plenty of time to look for the people he'd seen in the ICU waiting room. He couldn't help wondering how each of them might handle their anguish now that she was gone.

There was Stan. There was the boy he now knew to be Orion. There was the woman with her two children. She was holding her baby close to her chest, as if she might grieve too loudly if she and the baby were to separate. Her older daughter seemed to be singing.

It was a large flock of mourners. He guessed two hundred. There were blown-up pictures of a smiling Jean on her bike, a smiling Jean with Stan, with Orion, with her friends, as a child with her brother, as a baby with her parents. There was an open casket, the body in it soon to be ash. Charley and Lisa found two seats near the back.

The preacher wasn't like Charley would've imagined, having seen only males, for starters. She didn't wear the right clothes. No black pants and shirt or robes. No collar. Charley then realized she wasn't a preacher, this wasn't a church and God hadn't been invited.

She spoke about the meaning of life, the meaning we make of our own lives. Charley's gut was heavy with regret, almost touching the ground with shame. Here was a man who'd made so many wrong turns the only thing he knew to do now was go straight, and even that wasn't working for him. His mother must have been cursed to have a child like him, and yet she'd loved him and he hadn't even been there to bury her. Now there was Jean, who'd done good in this life, whose death was giving the people in this room reason to cry. Charley suddenly became aware of his arms and legs touching Lisa's. He couldn't give her any more room; his body wouldn't allow it.

Who would speak at his funeral? One woman said that Jean's life was an adventure and she'd known how to be a damn good hero. Her brother spoke as if she'd been a star, shooting through two hemispheres. Her husband said it was love. "With Jean, it had always been about love." Charley's insides were tight and twisted.

He felt the only way to loosen them was to let out a howl. What had he done to this poor woman's life? To her son? *At least he has a dad*, he thought. *At least he has a dad*. And then he missed his mum. And then the pain made its way to the back of his throat and he made a sound like hissing gas inside a moan, the inverse of a howl.

"For those who are able, Stan has provided envelopes in each of the memorial cards so that you may write to Orion about his mother. It is no minor tragedy when a young child loses his mother and this is a way to ensure we keep her alive in his memory."

Lisa took hold of Charley's hand and whispered, "You can write him a letter." And without having thought about it first, Charley squeezed Lisa's hand in reply.

There was a space between the funeral home and the parking lot that Charlie thought of as a holding pen, and if the decor of the holding pen could talk, the green vase in the center by the ficus tree might complain of its color, bemoaning that it wasn't black or white, something less vibrant in such a solemn place. The ficus tree itself might scream that it wasn't fair being in here, away from the other trees that had roots in the earth. The eyes that skimmed past his own might say, *Who the fuck are you?* Charley stood next to the ficus, looking down into the vase, wondering why there was nothing in it, all the time avoiding as many eyes as he could. But he could feel them on him, staring at his stiff shoulders boxed in his navy shirt, the sorrowful slant of his eyebrows, the dead weight of his belly. His hand flew up to shield his guilt, so sure he'd been giving something away: *I do not belong here; I wasn't her friend; I caused her death.* In each corner of the room stood the guards of the holding pen, waiting for their moment to tell the people it was time to leave.

There were too many whispers and he couldn't make out any particular phrases or words. A series of esses, some chopped consonants, a few ohs. Outside the sound of cars moving forward as a light turned green, someone yelling abuse. Charley wished Lisa would hurry the fuck up. It was getting noisy and he was cramped. He thought he might need to shit. She was talking to the woman from the hospital, the one with the two children, the one who'd held the baby tight during the funeral. They smiled and hugged and chatted like two long-lost friends, which Charley would later learn is exactly what they were. He wondered how Lisa might explain to the woman what she was doing at Jean Harley's funeral.

A girl with black hair to match all the swarming black in the holding pen bumped into him. He prayed she'd keep to herself.

"Lot of people here." Small talk much like "nice weather we're having," but more suited to a funeral.

Charley nodded.

"My aunt must've had a lot of friends."

Charley nodded again.

The girl looked absently at all the others in the room. "How did you know Aunt Jean?"

The whispering seemed to have risen to a roar and he hoped she wouldn't hear him when he said, "I knew *of* her, eh."

"Oh. How was that?"

"It wasn't too good," he said, beginning to move away, but then the girl picked up the little boy Charley hadn't seen standing there—the boy called Orion, Jean Harley's son—and stopped Charley in his tracks.

Orion looked like Jean in the photos much more than the Jean he remembered lying on Diagonal Road. He had curly hair and a look that suggested he, too, would like tire swings, as Jean's brother had said in his eulogy, and he, too, was a deep thinker with a high-pitched laugh, as Jean's friend had said, and he, too, had a very big heart, as Jean's husband had said. The little boy rested his head on the girl's shoulder and said, "Who are you?" pointing to Charley. Both Orion and the girl stared at him, waiting for an answer.

"I'm Charley." Then he made himself small and forged a path through the holding pen, past Lisa and the woman with the two children, all the way to his car where he was able to breathe. Then he howled.

Fifteen

Coraleen scanned the room and wondered who would die next. The woman who'd read the poem at the service while holding her baby the whole time? Her dad? She began playing a game with herself, making up stories for how each person would die. Lightning might strike dead one of the little kids running around the garden. The man with the large cheeks who seemed to be laughing too much for a wake would choke on his own vomit after the annual Big Night Out with the old gang. The baby sleeping in the carriage under the tree would grow another year then get stung by a bee. The boy at the food table, who looked as if he were having a telepathic conversation with each individual platter, his heart would stop the first time he took drugs.

Coraleen approached the food table with trepidation. "My dad picked those out. They're Oreos. We brought them from America." She could tell she'd startled him. He'd been checking out the food with such intensity, yet hadn't put a thing on his plate.

"I think you can get them here." His voice was deep. He wasn't a boy. Coraleen guessed sixteen, though he could've been older. Eighteen. "I mean, you can . . ." he continued, "get them here."

"My dad wanted to make sure we had Oreos. Jean loved them growing up." It surprised her how easily she'd said her aunt's name. She found it harder to say "Jean" when talking to her dad. As if she might upset him more than he could handle.

"Are they brother and sister?"

"*Were* they? Yeah. She was my aunt."

The boy looked uncomfortable but he held Coraleen's eyes. "She lived next door to me."

Something in the way he said it made Coral think that he knew Jean well enough to feel sad about her death. She wanted to know how well he knew her. She wondered if he had any stories to tell. Any story. How she used to honk her horn when she backed out of the driveway so no one would get hurt. Or maybe how she'd once had a garage sale and he got some cool relic, and then he could describe it to her so she could see it in her mind's eye. Any small story. Anything.

"I play with Orion sometimes on Saturday mornings." He looked at his feet, perhaps fumbling with the present tense. "I guess I *used* to. They liked going for bike rides to the hills once a month. I don't know if Stan will be wanting me to do that anymore."

That was the story. That's what Coraleen needed to hear so she could make the connection. Now she wouldn't feel like such an outsider.

"I'd like to, though. Keep doing it."

"Take one," she said, pointing to the Oreos. "For Jean."

The boy seemed to endure a short-lived panic attack, looking at the biscuit. "I haven't made it to the end of the table yet," he told her with pleading in his eyes.

Coral picked up the Oreo and put it on his plate. "It's just a cookie."

They followed each other to the bench along the fence, neither sure who was leading. When they sat down Coral said, "There are three types of people at this wake. First, there are the little kids. They're pretty much untouched by it all. They don't *get* death. They get *now*."

"Do you? Get death?"

Coral looked at him as if she could talk for hours. She was a Goth, didn't he see that? A *do-I-get-death!* look sufficed. "Then there's the grown-ups," she continued while eating some nuts. "This is heavy for them, but they don't want to let other people know how heavy. So they keep telling jokes."

The boy pointed to a couple near the back screen door. "My mum and dad have lived next door to Jean and Stan for twelve years. Mum and Jean used to water their plants at the same time in the summer so they could catch up. Now look. Mum and Dad are laughing. It's sort of quiet, though." He looked down at his plate, still untouched. "So what's the third type?"

Coraleen turned her eyes to him, again as if the answer was obvious. "Us."

The girl dove headfirst into the death of her aunt, whom she'd only met three times—four if you count when Coral could only crawl. She clung to the powerful mixture of sadness and confusion that accompanies an end and seemed to float with it easily, as if a ghost herself. She somehow blossomed in her grief, however dark the color of her rose. No one was surprised or concerned about it; she was fifteen and dressed herself daily in black clothing and wore thick black eyeliner, a black-red lipstick. She'd been this way ever since her mum and dad's first lengthy silence. Coraleen hadn't known the fight lasted for five days; she'd only caught onto it after three. Given her outward appearance and the fact that her parents were going through a separation, it didn't seem extreme that she took on her aunt's death with such passionate gloom.

It was Jean, the exotic aunt from Australia, who'd walked her to school every day for what seemed like ages when her mum had gone through her first big bout of depression. Coraleen had been only eight and didn't much understand the emotion in the house, but she did know that Jean was the best. They played dress-up and dance school while her mother rested and cried.

Two years later Jean had come with Stan and their new baby. Coral had adored Orion, carrying him everywhere. She remembered Jean breastfeeding on the living room couch, as if her breast hadn't been hanging out for all of the family to see, for her father to see, as if she hadn't heard her mum say, "Would you like to go somewhere more private?" She remembered Jean just smiling at Orion and saying, "We're happy here," as if they were the only people who mattered.

Three years later it had been at Grandma Pearl's home in Missouri. There had been talk of selling the old house when Grandpa Stompy passed on, but Grandma Pearl held strong, saying, "If I move from here, where will we have Christmas?" It was Christmas then, and little had they known that two Christmases later Jean would be dead.

That last time, Jean and Stan had taken off with Coraleen and her dad on a two-day drive west to Colorado. Coral's mum, being waist-deep into avoidance with her dad, had stayed behind with Grandma Pearl and Orion. Jean had wanted to see the mountains again, wanted to return to the place where she'd first met Stan and take them all snow-shoeing and skiing, things Coraleen had never done before. And Coraleen was hopeless, but oh how she laughed with almost every gawky foot placement and disastrously slow fall. There was an unsullied elation about Coral during that trip, but then it ended. It had to end.

"So were you close to Jean?" the boy asked. They'd put their plastic plates beside them on the green bench: hers a mess of near emptiness, his neat with a single Oreo, untouched. They settled into watching the younger kids running in and out of small groups of grown-ups who laughed in place of crying. Coral thought his discomfort interesting and cute. "I got a question for you: why are you so afraid of the food here?"

"I like to make plans first. It's just something weird about me."

Coral thought about him considering the platters of meat and antipasto, the deviled eggs, cold chicken, the chocolate and coconut sponges piled in a pyramid. She wondered if he'd been freaked out by the bowls of nuts sitting so near the bowls of chocolates. Did he ever consider mixing them or would he have spontaneously combusted? And weren't dips something you needed to try before putting some on your plate? How did that work?

"I'd made a mental note to take an Oreo before you came up to me."

"Then you're OK to me. So was I close to Aunt Jean? Yeah. Totally."

★

Though they shared a heinous loss that would eventually bring them closer, the rolling sound of the suitcase over the hardwood floor set the men apart: John was a stranger, Stan at home. And so he felt uncomfortable, claiming part of Stan's space for the next few days. He felt uncomfortable without Jean in the room. He felt uncomfortable wanting to unpack his suitcase right after his sister's wake. He'd planned on getting settled at the house days before the funeral, but things don't always go to plan and death doesn't afford a body time to wait.

He'd gotten the call five nights earlier as the rest of his small town slept. Wide awake with a focused urgency pushing his grief aside, John booked a flight immediately. It was high-priced and lengthy, but his sister was dead.

By morning he and his daughter were more or less packed and ready to go—"We'll buy whatever we forgot"—and they were off. Problem was there'd been so much snow. In this flat land of all-horizon, John Harley couldn't have separated the white earth from the white sky if he tried. Ventilated heating worked to warm him inside the cubicle of his car and morning radio worked to cheer him, but that feeling in his gut of being caught between two places and not having a single step of solid ground on which to stand was bearing down on him; nothing had felt right. With his sister gone, with his marriage ending, John wondered if anything would ever feel right again.

Coraleen had curled herself into an unshapely S on the passenger seat, exhaling the softness of a fifteen-year-old's breath. John wasn't in any way *glad* he was traveling across the world to collect a handful of his sister's ashes, but he couldn't help think the opportunity perfect for him and his daughter. Soon he'd be moving out of the house. He'd have to get used to weekend visitations, shared holidays and school breaks. He'd have to watch Coraleen flower into womanhood on prescribed days. Jean's dying in a foreign country at least gave John and Coral this: the chance to share a specific time and place with one another; the chance to embrace family; the chance to grieve over its loss.

And at the airport, no, nothing was right. The ground flight attendant had told him that snowstorms generally didn't last for more than a couple of days, but he knew this to be false. He'd lived in the Wheat Belt for eighteen years and he knew how snow could build. How it could fall horizontally from such a strong wind that you didn't dare push against it. How schools and workplaces and highways and airports closed down. "I have to get to my sister's funeral." Could he have made it sound any more dire? He'd already missed saying goodbye to her while she'd been alive and that made him feel a complete failure as a brother. He had to go now.

The storm lasted three days. They spent two nights sleeping among strangers on chairs and on the floor against the walls of Chicago's O'Hare Airport. The quality of food in cardboard boxes and wrinkly bags ridiculous, the bar and grill airport lounges' and restaurants' food dull and lonely. And they'd had to buy new books. They took long walks to stretch their legs and shrug off boredom, went into shops that hadn't interested them.

"You think Mom's OK at home?" Coraleen squished a U-shaped pillow three times then moved onto another. It was Christmastime. Not the best time to be left alone with your own sad thoughts. "I bet she's lonely. It's a huge house. I wouldn't want to stay there alone."

They'd been avoiding it, the separation, and John knew this was his daughter's way of bringing it up. He tried to sound a little cheery and nonchalant. "She'd be missing you, that's for sure." And he'd known it to be true. John had felt his need for his daughter growing stronger as his marriage had begun its steep slope downwards. It had been on a gentle decline for years but at some point—and neither his wife nor he could determine when, exactly—the grade had changed dramatically. He saw it happening between his wife and his daughter as well: this *need*. He saw how they lay upon each other watching TV and how sometimes Lynn would take Coraleen's hand when Coraleen was asking her a simple question, as if Coral was a small child again and everything she said was a wonder. John expressed his love for his daughter differently. It was more distanced and hesitant, but it was no less deep.

"She'd be missing you too. It's not like she's ever lived without you." And here the conversation stopped, Coraleen's eyes challenging him with adolescent insight. John had wondered when she'd gotten so old.

Things were changing rapidly, too fast for John to feel safe, and now, after Jean's funeral, after digesting the fact that a portion of her body would soon fit into a small urn he'd bring back home, after the eulogy he gave on behalf of the family back in America, after the wake and all of those condolences from absolute strangers, he was exhausted, wanting a shower and a bed.

"You can have this front room. It's sort of a study and a guest room."

John set the suitcase near the tall table where two African figurines were mated for life. He picked up the male. "Did you get these on your trip to Sudan?"

"We did." Stan looked as if he wanted to say something, and John was waiting for him to continue, but he didn't. John had been in love once too and, though he'd fallen out of it with Lynn, he understood that there was too much to say about the people and the streets where Stan and Jean had traveled together. She'd told him about the trip—about all of their trips—in letters, on the phone, during visits home, and John knew there was no way Stan could sum up that Jean had fallen in love with the mothers who carried babies on their backs, that their journey to Sudan was the first time the two of them had ever talked about having children, that she and Stan both agreed they had never felt so foreign before as in Khartoum, though in years to come they would always consider the city "theirs." How could Stan have said any of that?

"You guys love your travel." John set the figurine back on the table, inwardly wincing for not using the past tense when referring to Stan's life with Jean and knowing that, really, it was still too soon after her death to worry about using the present tense unapologetically.

"I guess this is our travel room too," said Stan.

John looked around the room at all the other objects that told a million stories. It was a purple room with refurbished second-hand furniture and, yes, relics from all over the world. Instruments, posters and prints, forget-me-nots of carved wood. A black-and-white photo of three sets of footprints in the sand hung above the couch.

"That folds out to a bed," Stan said. "I'll get you some bedding."

Stan's footprint was three times larger than Orion's, who must have been a toddler when the photo was taken; not surprisingly, Jean's was the most deeply indented.

"Great room." Coraleen leaned against the doorway. "Did Aunt Jean paint all these rooms herself?"

"Most of them. But not Orion's." Coraleen would be sleeping in Orion's room.

"That's a wild room. I love the stripes going all the way around."

"Our friend Viv did that. Did you meet her? Viv?"

There had been so many people at the funeral and the wake, and they were so tired from the long days at the airport and the equally long flight, that neither Coraleen nor her father answered.

"You probably can't remember anyone's name," Stan said, looking rather hopeless. "Viv was her best friend. Along with Neddy. Neddy's the woman who held the wake." He moved his eyes around the room, back and forth and up and down, then seemed to return to this particular moment in time. "Anyway. John . . ." He pointed at his brother-in-law. "Beer?"

"That'd be great. I'll just jump in the shower first?"

"Go for it, mate. I'll keep the beer cold. Coraleen? You want some water or juice or anything?"

"No thanks." Coraleen looked at her dad when her uncle left the room. "Isn't this weird?" she asked. "Being here?"

John continued looking around the room. "She's everywhere," he said. "She's in all these pictures and knickknacks. She's in each book on the shelf."

Coral walked over to the bookshelf and picked up something bright green: a novel she'd probably never heard of by an author she most likely didn't know. "I wish I could ask her what her favorite book was. Then I could read it."

John scanned the large bookcase, wondered which book his sister had read last. When the thought began to take on a shape he wasn't prepared to follow through, he changed gears. "You want to shower first?"

"Sure," she said, turning back toward her dad. "I'm tired."

"Me too."

When Coraleen walked down the hall, the sound of her shoes seemed to rebound off the hardwood floors and echo from the high ceiling. It was a lonely sound, and John immediately missed her. He had a longing to ask her to sleep in the purple room with him, to share the bed with him as she would have done if she were a small child, but there was something wrong about that now since she was fifteen, and what it was, he wasn't sure. He felt like yelling down the hallway, "Hey, Coral! What's your favorite book?" but he had closed the door to the purple room before the feeling stood too tall, and across the hall from the bathroom, in Stan and Jean's king-sized bed, was a five-year-old boy he didn't want to wake.

★

When her dad had asked Stan if he was sure he wanted them to stay at their house, Coral hadn't wanted to know of any other alternative. She wanted to stay with her cousin.

"It'll be good for Orion. He remembers Coral. He's really excited." Perfect.

Soon they'd fly to Uluru, that big rock she'd grown up with in their coffee-table book at home, and get there for New Year's. Then to Queensland to see the Great Barrier Reef, another thing in the book. Then down to Sydney for more "touristing" (as her Aunt Jean used to call it). They'd worked out a plan on the long flight over and John made himself busy in the day booking flights and accommodation. Coral guessed it was as good a reason as any for her dad to stay out of Stan's way.

She couldn't believe they'd be leaving in two days, couldn't believe that in less than two weeks' time they'd be back in the arms of a cold and heartless American Midwest winter. She was torn between being ready to leave Adelaide and wanting to stay. She felt tongue-tied around Stan, wanting to tell him how sad she was for Orion, how awful it must've been for him to have a birthday cake in the hospital room where his mum died, how she wished they all lived closer so she could look after him, just a little. She wanted to tell Stan that it would be good for both her and Orion, talking about their absent parents, only her dad would just be living somewhere else, not dead. She really, really wanted to tell Stan that she was sorry for him too, but words seemed unoriginal and meaningless.

Death lay thick in the air of Stan and Orion's house, like fumigation, but it lifted for Coraleen when she was with Orion. She liked doing little-kid things with him, and he had the best room in the house. Just now she was helping him to cut and glue paper to make a card for his Aunty Lynn.

"She loves you so much, you know. And she *loved* your mom."

"Then why didn't she come with you?"

The rays of a sun were particularly finicky to cut out with a pair of children's scissors. Coraleen concentrated on her art while answering the boy. "My mom and dad are splitting up. They make each other sad."

"What do you mean *splitting up*?"

"We're not going to all live in the same house anymore. My dad's moving out. Can I use that glue?"

Orion handed her the glue. "You mean you're not going to have a dad anymore?"

Coraleen knew he'd understand.

After the craft session they played dress-up and dance school, Coral's way of winking at her Aunt Jean in heaven. She had previously thought there wasn't a heaven, like there wasn't an Easter Bunny, but now she wasn't so sure. Fifteen is a fine age to contemplate such things.

"Nice moves," Stan said from the doorway, smiling with every deep crease in his face.

Coral stopped dancing and started laughing, like she'd been sprung for enjoying her childhood while heavily into her adolescence. Then she wondered if some moments made her Uncle Stan feel lucky for his life, and if this was one of those moments.

Her dad had popped his head in the room too. "What's going on in here?"

"We're dancing!" Orion yelled, running on the spot with his arms straight out in front of him.

"Well, come on then, dance into the bathroom. It's time to brush your teeth."

Orion kept his arms straight in front of him and ran into the bathroom yelling, "Goodnight, Coco!" His pet name for Coraleen.

"He's going to miss you when we go," her dad said, sounding somewhat lost between cheerful, bemused and concerned.

"I'm going to miss him too," she said, feeling just about the same.

But Orion wasn't the only person she was going to miss. He was a big reason for wanting to stay on in Adelaide, but not the biggest. *Kyle* was the biggest. *Kyle*, the strange boy with the food fetish who'd taken Coraleen to the city the day after the funeral. Down Rundle Mall they'd gone, stopping in front of every busker. Coraleen had been drawn to them, thinking them exotic and utterly "Australian" because there weren't any entertainers like that in Galena, Illinois. Through Rundle Street, where they'd looked in windows at the brightly colored dresses draped on mannequins. Where *Kyle* had asked her why she wore so much black. It had been a black-singlet-with-a-pair-of-black-men's-cut-off-pants-bunched-at-her-waist-with-a-thick-black-belt-and-black-army-boots-to-match kind of day for Coraleen. "Don't I look tough?" she'd asked, nudging him.

"Not really," he'd said.

"You must see right through me, Kyle."

They'd gotten gyros and eaten them at a park, absentmindedly swinging on two swings.

"You seem kind of uptight sometimes," she'd told him, licking garlic sauce from the corner of her mouth.

"I am," he'd said. "But I don't feel uptight now."

They'd walked along the Torrens River, paid for a paddleboat and made their way to the fountain springing from the middle. Water had rained over their bodies, relieving their adolescent pores, and they'd laughed and felt very young and simultaneously quite old. At least ten. At least twenty.

While they sat among the seagulls and swans that claimed the river and all of its food scraps, Coral wanted Kyle to kiss her. His lips were large and soft as he licked the Jaffa ice-cream cone, and she stared at him staring at her, as if she'd known what he was thinking, as if it was what she'd been thinking too.

"Your ice-cream's dripping," she'd said, and she thought he was sweet when he licked his cone and his fingers. "What do you think it's going to be like for him when he's our age? Orion."

"I don't know. I can't picture him as a teenager."

"I can see him being sad." Coraleen had imagined the boy heartbreakingly cute, crying quietly on his bed.

"Maybe he'll just get used to it. Maybe he won't think of her much because he was so young when she died."

"Maybe." Coraleen took a bite from the bottom of her cone, sucking the melted ice-cream out of it. "I wonder if I'd be better off if my parents split when I was five. Then I'd be used to it now and I wouldn't be sad."

"Maybe every teenager is sad about something. Maybe it's what teenagers are supposed to be. Just sad."

"Are you sad?"

Kyle had nodded his head then, kneaded his knuckles into the grass, dropped his head to his chest, and Coraleen had leaned into him and hovered over his shoulder until he turned to look at her. She'd kissed him with her lips, then with her tongue. It was sweeter than the waffle cone and as big as overseas travel. "Are you sad now?" she'd asked when they had finished.

"No."

Now, waiting for her dad to close the door to Orion's room and leave her to dreamy thoughts and the single bed, the memory of that kiss made Coral want to stay in Adelaide. Made her want to drop out of school and move to Adelaide so she could kiss *Kyle* anytime she wanted to. She imagined them falling in love, getting married, having babies who would play with Orion. Was there anything as good as that waiting for her back home?

But she was leaving for the Red Centre the day after tomorrow and soon she'd be back in America, 13,000 miles away, where her house would look different with all of her dad's stuff gone.

"Well, don't stay up too late, OK?" John hesitated, and Coraleen wondered if that was really all he wanted to say to her.

"OK, Dad." She thought maybe she should say, "I love you," but she thought about it for too long and then there was no time.

★

John cooked meals for the four of them that they ate at the kitchen table. Orion poured his own cereal and Coral's too, and together they ate at the kitchen table. Stan poured coffee, tea, milk, water, juice and wine, and they drank them at the kitchen table. Jean was there with them too. In every story, thought and breath.

"Eighteen years, huh?"

"Yep. Makes it difficult to separate 'mine' from 'yours,' that's for sure." John didn't envy Lynn the task of boxing up his things during the time he and Coral were in Australia, but it was the plan. He knew when they returned to the house on South High Street, dead-eyed from the flight and craving only sleep, he wouldn't go up the stairs to his bedroom where he could undress and climb into the bed with the feather duvet bought especially for their winters; he'd say, "OK, see you soon," and turn into the freezing night, leaving his daughter behind.

"Jean hated that you and Lynn were going through this. She'd cry whenever she hung up the phone with you."

John and Lynn had gone through the Anger stage, first a simmer then a constant boil, occasionally completely out of control, and Anger butted heads with Numb, which was the stage that had lasted the longest. John counted two years, though Lynn once told him four. When they first began talking about separating, they moved into the Amicable for the Sake of the Child stage. It was the most unnatural of them all and John, therefore, knew it'd tipped Coraleen off. Now, with Jean's sudden death and the hotel he'd booked for a week in his own hometown and the real estate agent waiting to call him to give him news on properties, John and Lynn were at the stage of Downright Sad.

"If my sister were alive, *I'd* hate this for her."

"They really got on, didn't they?"

An image of Lynn and Jean with brown paper bags full of antiques and craft crowding every space on the kitchen table. "How am I going to pack all this?" A bottle of wine between them, dinner cooking on the stove, the women laughing at the kitchen table. Yes, they really got on, and John suddenly missed his wife. "She really wanted to be here. It's my fault. I told her she could come, but she knew I didn't want her to. I tried to do the right thing. I get that she's still a part of your family, Coraleen's mom and all, but I was glad she said no."

"Oh yeah, Orion will always know her as Aunty Lynn. No doubt about that."

John wondered, with Jean now gone, if Orion would ever see his Aunty Lynn again. Ever talk to her on the phone. Galena's as far from Adelaide as a place can get—how often would John see them now or talk to them on the phone?

"You know, I was a few years younger than Coraleen when my mum left my dad."

"Did you see him much after that?"

"I never saw him again."

The men finished the dregs of their beer.

"Maybe Lynn knew it would be better if you had the time alone with Coral."

"She's always been intuitive."

"Is it a female thing, like they say? A mother thing? Jean had it too. Intuitiveness. Intuition."

A photograph John took of Jean with Stan and Orion in front of the Christmas tree: Jean has her finger in Orion's mouth and the baby is dead set on chewing it. "He's teething," she'd said before he took the shot. Orion's cheeks are a fiery red; Jean's looking at her son, laughing.

"Want another?"

"Most definitely."

John went to the fridge this time. Brought two beers back to the kitchen table.

★

Morning brought chocolate chip pancakes a la Coco and Orion. They messed that kitchen up good with goops of yoke and flour castings, somehow putting a smile on Stan's face and getting John busy with a washcloth like Coral had never seen before. After the dishwashing and during the full-bellied ten o'clock rest, the doorbell rang.

Coraleen could almost see the knot in Kyle's throat as she stood peering over Stan's shoulder.

"Kyle. How you going, mate?"

She thought he looked as if he was bravely willing the knot to go away.

"I was hoping I could see Coraleen."

Coral smiled, knowing he could see her right then. "Hi!" She stuck out her neck a little bit further.

"Oh, hi." He acted surprised, and Coraleen liked him all the more for his embarrassment.

"Come on in," Stan said.

"Hi."

"Hi."

"I was just reading." Coral held up a bright green book. She tried to act like she was bored, but her heart was skipping rope double time. She felt the energy jump up and reach her eyes, which became large with a teenage-lust she had never known before. *What is he doing here?* she thought, and, *We're going to kiss again today!*

"Do you want to go to the beach?"

Seriously? "Give me a minute. I'll come over when I'm ready."

She told her dad she was going to the beach with Kyle, knowing he'd say it was OK because she was, after all, fifteen, and he said, "Sounds like fun. You'll be home for dinner, though. Gotta pack tonight too."

"Yep." Dinner was seven or eight hours away. Plenty of time for kissing.

She ran into Orion's room, feeling giddy, like she was back in eighth grade again when Scott O'Boyle had asked her "to go with him," before her parents had gone silent on each other. She felt young and innocent, like she was thirteen years old. She looked at herself in the mirror once she was in her swimsuit and the feeling went away because she didn't look thirteen at all. She looked and felt older: maybe a dangerous and thrillingly sixteen.

She threw clothes on over her bikini, stuffed a towel into her day bag and grabbed her wallet, then looked at herself in the mirror one last time. She thought about her mum back home. She wanted to tell her about how Kyle was making her feel. She wondered if her mum had ever felt this way about her dad.

As she stood in front of Kyle's house waiting for him to answer the door, Coraleen's lungs sat uncomfortably in her throat, making her wonder if this was what had been happening to Kyle's throat when he'd stood in front of Stan's door.

"Hey."

"Hey."

They walked down the hallway, which was long like Stan's and Orion's, but there were runners on the floor, muffling the movement of feet.

"Are your folks here?"

"They're both at work. Mum's a doctor and Dad runs an outdoor clothing shop. They don't get time off at Christmas."

Coral breathed quietly but deeply through her nose. She hadn't wanted to meet Kyle's parents again. The wake was one thing, but now they'd kissed. How self-conscious would she have felt? How aware would she have been that she didn't look like the other people at the funeral with her red-black lipstick and her dyed black hair? That she didn't look like someone their son should hang out with?

"Is that your room?" she asked. It was the first room on the left. Impossible to ignore.

"Yeah. It's nothing great."

Under the loft-style bed was a large desk that had a jigsaw puzzle on it, three-quarters completed. Books too. Scattered pieces of paper of all sizes. Dirty clothes were on his floor, but not many. Coraleen spied his jocks. They were blue briefs. When she looked up she saw the red in his cheeks. An old green futon sat under the window. More books on it. More paper. A poster of Einstein decorated his wall. That and a map of the world. Coraleen walked over to it. "That's my home." She pointed to a nameless space slightly above and to the left of the red dot labelled "Chicago."

Kyle leaned in close to look.

"You should visit someday."

He smelled of sunblock and shampoo. Her small breasts were touching his bare arm: only just, but just enough. Coral thought she could feel that his breathing had become irregular, but then maybe it was hers. She didn't want his arm to move. Suddenly, her breast touching it was all she knew. His arm, her breast, the closeness of their bodies, the desire to swallow his tongue again, and this time to not stop.

Coral made the first move, and after three minutes of kissing on the green futon, Kyle made the next. They alternated moves.

It seemed an easy way to communicate to each other that *this was OK*, that *we can keep going*, and though she'd thought about it in a very hypothetical way the night before as she lay in Orion's small bed, unable to sleep, staring at the ceiling and the pink and green racing stripes, she somehow seemed surprised and amazed when Kyle entered her. It was like she had suddenly become a woman as soon as his penis had broken through. Like she was at least twenty-one.

So this is it? she thought, moving through the discomfort of the bones between her legs. It was awful and she tried not to wince, but the pain was intense. It wasn't until after Kyle had come in a clumsy spill on top of her belly that Coraleen would think of the encounter as terribly romantic. And when the saltwater of a foreign ocean cleaned the dried blood from the inside of her swimsuit, she felt young again. They splashed one another. She squealed. He yelled, "I love being here with you!" and she thought he was perfect. He was perfect, the day was perfect, the beach, the sun, and none of it could last. Nothing. Ever. Lasted.

*

When they finally left O'Hare Airport they'd had more than thirty hours of travel ahead of them. John had wondered if they were even going to make it to the funeral—it'd be tight. Two hours in, over the desert fields of the American Southwest on the morning after Christmas, it hit John that he felt empty. The earlier feeling in his gut that nothing was right had calmed to such an extreme that he now knew hollowness. Maybe it was all that space seen from such a height mixing with his burden. Maybe it was all that dirt. He remembered Jean telling him about the desert in Australia and how it compared to the desert in America, how Aboriginal Australians compared to Native Americans. She'd seen so much, had such insight into the worlds of others, and this, at the age of forty, was his first time flying overseas.

Maybe that was it—he'd just turned forty. Wasn't forty a time when most people evaluated their lives and decided whether they were going in the right direction or not? Nothing was right, and now he was hollow and old.

On the first leg of their journey to Australia he'd leaned over Coraleen; she'd been napping in that same S position as earlier in the car, which had seemed like ages ago, ages ago, and he watched the crumpled mountains of the desert below him, knowing at that moment he was saying goodbye to something, and it was more than his history and bond with Jean, it was more than the hope he'd built his marriage upon. He couldn't put his finger on it, but it had been very real.

In another airplane, heading for another new place, the earth below them was red and flat, riverless, lakeless, waterless once again. It was almost like flying over America's Southwest, only a different shade of loneliness. Who lived down there? John couldn't picture a white face if he tried because the book at home made it seem like only the Indigenous people lived where they were going. He let the "otherness" of Australia take hold of him while Coral sat next to him, the complimentary earphones sounding off an American sitcom even he could hear.

John jabbed her leg with his finger until she took out her earphones. "Look out the window. Look at the color. It makes me feel like we're finally in a foreign country."

"You didn't feel like Adelaide was foreign?"

John didn't know about the buskers on Rundle Mall or the black swans in the River Torrens like his daughter did; he only knew that Adelaide was Jean and Stan and Orion, but mainly Jean. "Maybe Adelaide felt more like another home." *Home*, he thought. What did it even mean to him now? It might as well be the airplane since the only family left to love was sitting there beside him. Not fair to his mother, though, and he knew this, but what had she to do with his melancholic mood? No, Coral was his home.

Coraleen turned back to the screen but didn't put her earphones in. John turned back to look out the window, continued talking to his daughter. "I wish I'd seen Jean with Orion a lot more than I did. I know she was a great mother, but I wish I could've seen how she did it. Just to watch someone hold this tiny baby and then through the years mold it into a little person. It's really special, being a parent. I just wish I could have seen that part of her more."

"Do you think Mom's done a good job?"

"I think she's done a fantastic job."

"Do you think you've done a good job?"

"I think I've done an OK job. I think I can do better." *Tell her you love her. Tell her you love her every day of her short life and tell her right now. Tell her not to grow up too fast, to keep playing dress-up and dance school as long as she can because simple things like that bring joy.*

They locked eyes, and what John saw in those seven seconds was a young woman who had fretted over a stain on a boy's futon as the boy had tried to wipe it away with a discarded sock. He saw a mixture of the shame and curiosity she felt when she looked at the boy's drooping, wet penis before he'd gotten dressed. The assuredness of a girl who'd loved her breasts more than she ever had as she exposed them to the boy the moment before she reached for her own swimsuit. He saw the guilt, the pride, the adrenaline of having such a big secret and all he could make of it was that he was looking into the eyes of his fifteen-year-old daughter, who he wasn't ready to give up on. John touched her knee. "You're not a little girl anymore, I know that, but I'll be damned if I'm going to watch you grow up from afar. Just because I'm moving out, I won't lose you, Coral. There's still some molding left in me."

Coraleen popped her earphones back in and returned to the sitcom. John returned to the cracked earth below them, and it seemed as if it was trying to tell him that life goes on, no matter how much the dust tries to choke you. No matter what foreign country you're in. No matter, even, if you're home.

Sometimes

Some days he woke up in the morning forgetting she wasn't there. He'd open his eyes and straightaway think he'd see her getting dressed or hear her singing, or when he'd walk into the kitchen he'd find her doing something with food, her back to him, just shaking a little because she'd be putting peanut butter on toast or wiping down the bench or washing the dishes. Once he asked his nan when his mum would be home. His nan had sighed and said, "Come here," and told him a story about when her mum had died. Once he told his dad he wanted his mum to read the book. His dad had ruffled his hair and begun reading.

Sometimes he thought his dad didn't know how to do things because he did them differently than his mum had. Like never have his glass of milk on the table *before* he sat down. His dad always seemed to forget. And he wanted him to put sunblock on him *slowly*, and rub it all in so you couldn't see any white streaks. Sometimes he said, "You're not doing it right!" and his dad would say, "Well, I'm doing it."

Sometimes he didn't want his dad. Sometimes, he thought, only his mother would do. Sometimes he had to sit quietly in his room and remind himself that she was gone. Sometimes he thought she might come back. Sometimes he thought everyone was wrong. Sometimes his dad would come in and talk to him and sometimes he'd cry, his dad. But not always. But when he did, then Orion would cry too because it felt like the right thing to do and it felt like the only thing he could do. Sometimes, when he was thinking about his mum, his dad would peek in his room and leave him alone.

His mum was gone, Uncle John and Coco gone. Orion was in the bath and it was his second bath since his mum had gone, his first since his rellies had gone. His dad wasn't super keen on baths, so Orion had been the one to suggest it. His dad had suggested it two nights earlier but Orion had said no, he wanted to keep watching the movie with Coco, and his dad had told him, "Fair enough," then must have forgotten the next night. His mum would have said, "Come on now," and still made him have a bath the next night too. The only reason he suggested a bath all on his own was because earlier that morning they'd gone to the beach. "Digger needs a run." His dad probably would have suggested the bath in the end but Orion had beaten him to it.

They'd gone at Dog Time, when all dogs were off their leashes and they ran to each other and sniffed bottoms and chased each other into and out of the shallow water. Orion splashed while his dad kept an eye on both of them, which must've been hard with one over here and one over there, but he seemed fine just sitting in his spot being very serious with his sunglasses on. Sometimes Orion would go underwater and all he could hear was a loud noise that was empty of everything except the water and when he came back up there was a lot of noise: the waves, a seagull, a dog, other people. He'd look at his dad and wave to him and his dad would wave back.

When Orion got cold he sat by his dad and buried his feet in the sand, which warmed his feet up quite a bit while the sun warmed up his body. Digger sat down next to them, panting and panting, all sandy and wet, and Orion began to bury his legs and then rub the warm sand all over his body. "Look, Dad. I'm making myself into ashes." His mum was made into ashes. It's what people had to do sometimes when they died. Some people were buried underground. Orion wanted to be buried underwater.

So with ashes all over his body and then the saltwater washing him off (and don't forget the sunblock his dad had rubbed on fast and not all the way in), even he knew he needed a bath.

Along with the bubbles up to his chest, the bathtub was filled with toys. He had dinosaurs, all sorts of colors, and pipes he could play only if he filled them up with water, and he had boats he always ignored but still put all five of them in the bath. He could stay in there for an hour if his dad let him.

"You OK in there?"

He was usually OK in the bathtub because he knew how to wash his body and, though it was a little trickier, he knew how to wash his hair too, but sometimes he wanted his dad to do it because he used to like when his mum did it and she wasn't here but he was. She did it softly. His dad scrubbed fast. Like with the sunblock. Orion said, "Yeah," thinking about how his dad did it wrong so he'd just have to do it himself.

There was a lot of shampoo and it felt so nice so he rubbed it in for a long time until his dad came in and asked again, "You OK in here?"

He said, "Yeah," but he wasn't OK because there was too much shampoo and he didn't know how he was ever going to get it out.

"Here, lie down, Ry."

His dad helped him down slowly so his head was in the water but his eyes were still above, and he rubbed his hair gently, like his mum might have done if she had been there, and it felt so good he closed his eyes and hadn't known his dad was talking until he opened his eyes and saw his lips moving. Orion didn't ask him what he was saying and didn't try to come up to listen, either. He liked this underwater world with his dad rubbing his head like that and he felt very safe and very, very clean. There was a loud silence under there. Like he could hear the blood in his ears.

His dad dried him fast too, with a grown-up towel.

"Mom always uses the frog towel with the hood."

"Well, she's not here so we'll just use this one."

Orion didn't like when his dad said that: "She's not here." Juni's mum had told him that his mum would always be with him so really she was here, wasn't she? Orion looked around the bathroom. Somewhere, his mum was watching his dad let him use the wrong towel, so he said, "Dad, use the frog towel the frog towel," and threw a fit. He knew he was throwing a fit, but he really couldn't help it and once it started it felt really good, yelling and crying and demanding to be heard, until finally his dad said, "OK" and finished drying him with the grown-up towel, then gave him the frog towel and pulled on the hood and said, "All right, let's get you in your PJs." Everything was OK then.

"Can I sleep in this?"

"In the frog towel?"

"Yeah."

"Do you think you'd be comfortable sleeping in a towel?"

"Yes."

Sometimes his dad smiled at him and it made Orion think that he was glad he had his dad with him and not his mum. He missed having them both with him at the same time and he missed having his mum all to himself but sometimes, if he had to choose only one, he was happy his dad was the one with him because his dad said, "OK, mate," and his mum would never have let him sleep in a towel. But sometimes Orion knew it was wrong—wearing a towel to bed *and* being glad it was his dad and not his mum who was still alive—and then he thought that maybe he was bad and she'd know he was thinking bad thoughts because she was always with him, right? So when he crawled into bed he began to cry.

"What's wrong, Orion?"

"I miss Mom."

"I know you do. I miss her too." His dad looked sad but still he smiled. How did he do that? All Orion could do was cry and cry and cry and cry because this was their family now: him and his dad and Digger the dog at Orion's side of the bed.

His dad kept rubbing his back and it felt good, even good enough that he could stop crying, but he still couldn't stop sniffling.

"Dad?"

"Yeah, mate."

"When are you coming to bed?"

"Not too long. I'll be in soon." He kissed Orion on the forehead and Orion reached his arms around his dad's strong neck, and it felt good, even good enough that he could now stop sniffling. "I love you, Ry."

"I love you."

And his dad turned out the light, leaving the door cracked because Orion hated the dark.

In the dim room he could see the dresser his parents shared. His mum's jewelry still sat in little bowls. The books she'd been reading before she got run over were still by the bedside lamp. He looked around the room, taking note of everything he knew to be hers, then gave up and looked at the ceiling.

Some nights Orion would lie awake for a very long time staring at the ceiling and imagining his mum's face. She'd be looking down on him and smiling and her lips would be moving but he couldn't hear what she was saying, like when he was in that underwater world in the ocean or the bath, only he was lying in the bed that used to be hers and now was his. Some nights he would tell her, "Goodnight," and wonder if she heard him. If she was always with him, then wouldn't she hear him? Or was death like an underwater world too? But she was ash, like the sand on his skin. But she was looking at him from the ceiling too; sometimes it seemed so real. But she was also in heaven, like Coco had said to him and like Grandma Pearl had told him on the phone. But she never woke up, she *never* woke up, so was she still sleeping?

"Goodnight, Dad!" he yelled to the dim room, and through the crack at the door that let in the light he heard, "Goodnight, Orion!" and then he could close his eyes, and then he could fall asleep.

PART
4

The List

If ritual makes the horrible seem normal, then here was Stan, pulling nails out of pallets of wood with a horrendous hangover. Morning breath still coated his tongue at two in the afternoon and a dry tongue it was. A six-pack-of-beer-and-half-a-bottle-of-wine kind of dry. The beer was Sierra Nevada because it was an American beer, and Stan found himself drinking only American beer these days in memory of Jean. She used to say it was worth paying the extra money every now and again for good craft-brewed hops, and no place crafted them better than her home country. She loved them, and now he did too. The wine was a Langhorne Creek cab sav because Jean never drank anything but South Australian wines. Though he'd never been a big wine drinker before Jean died, he drank plenty of South Australian wines now. Luckily for Stan, Jean hadn't had a strong affinity with spirits.

Firewood tended to be Stan's go-to hangover job, no matter what time of year it was. It was now March, as good a time as any to be sorting out the winter wood. And the wood pile was, indeed, plentiful, as hangovers had been a regularity the last two months. The pain of Jean's death seemed to be worsening, not lessening, over time.

"Got another pile for you, Ry."

Orion looked up from the sandpit under the passion fruit vine and said, "More nails, Dad?"

"More nails."

The boy ran to where his dad stood, hammer in hand, sweat that smelled of alcohol sticking fast to his forehead, and Stan smiled at him, despite the thudding in his skull, because he realized that, for a five-year-old, placing a dozen nails at a time into a plastic bowl must be an exciting job. "We make a good team, hey?"

Orion beamed at his dad, said, "Yep," then moved his loose tooth back and forth with his tongue. "Still wobbly!" he announced, then ran back to the sandpit. The nails, the tooth, the sandpit—it was all very exciting.

Having dug it up and filled it herself, Jean had loved the sandpit. She'd specifically placed it under the passion fruit vine, where she'd buried Orion's placenta to give the soil richness and the word "passion" new meaning. She called the corner "Orion's Spot" and painted a sign to welcome him in.

A cloud layer moved west, opening the warmth of the sun. Stan bathed in it then remembered he didn't have a hat. *The ozone layer*, he thought, remembering Jean's list of things she'd lost. Then, with each nail pried from the wood, Stan added his own entry to the list. *Things that hold other things together.* And just how was he holding things together? Grief was tearing at him like the hammer the nail and the nail the wood but somehow he was managing, wasn't he? Somehow they were getting by.

Jean had been a true list-maker if ever there was one, leaving Post-it notes all over the fridge. Lists of what to get done over their breaks, even though she knew they'd only tackle a third of them. Lists of people she wanted to catch up with, even though she always chose the same two friends when the opportunity to go out arose. Lists of things she wanted done to the house once they'd saved a little money and lists of places she wanted to go once they'd saved a lot of money. When Orion was inside her belly there were lists of boys' names and lists of girls' names, separate lists for first names and for middle names. Stan could not help but puff up in pride when he had seen those lists, and he'd always made an effort to look at them for the six months they were there. When Stan's mum was going through chemo there were lists of soups Jean would make for her, then recipes for those soups posted on the fridge, even though Jean never followed recipes. Those lists had made Stan's gut feel empty, and it wasn't that "mung bean and turkey" reminded him that there was an absence of food in his belly; it was the possible absence of his mother from his life.

Jean had kept an ongoing list of things that had gone missing: a single green earring, the thick woolen sock, the cap to the toothpaste, Digger's tugging rope, the spare key to her bike lock, her bookmark, her emergency safety pin. Initially Stan thought Jean might have a touch of the obsessive-compulsive in her, but Jean rationalized that it was only a silly game she played with herself because losing small things drove her mad and crossing them off once found made her happy.

"What if you made a list of the things you've lost that you'll never get back?"

Jean had taken up that challenge and made a new list for the fridge. A flowery list. Sometimes funny, sometimes sad. A little work of art. *Snow, mountains, my youth, my faith, my virginity, the northern night sky, sleeping in, my father, the ozone layer.*

Stan bent over to pick up the dismantled pallet pieces and begin the task of carrying them over to the woodpile. How *big* was the blood vessel in his brain? How *hot* was the sun? Maybe he needed a hair of the dog.

"Dad! Look at the airplane." A jet stream split the sky.

"Where do you think it's going, mate?"

"America!"

Stan watched the silver point disappear, the white line lose its precision, thought about the last time he'd been in a plane, wondered when it might be again, envied the passengers their flight and their freedom. He looked back to his son in the sandpit. He picked up an armload of wood. *Freedom to fly.*

Just then the backyard gate scraped loudly on the concrete path. Stan's mum tried to close it so Digger wouldn't run off, but the gate was stuck, and Marion looked very frail.

"Let me get that, Mum." Stan put the wood aside while Digger ran past him to be first to greet Marion properly. She smiled and bent down to pat the happy dog, who shuffled in tight circles at her feet until finally he sat, staring up at her and thumping his tail. Digger wasn't running through the opened gate. He seemed to have everything he needed.

Stan shut the gate and kissed his mum. "Perfect time to knock off. Got a white in the fridge." Stan raised his eyebrows, hoping his mum would join him.

Marion's eyes took on octagonal shapes, fraught with worry and urgency. "It's back, Stan."

Stan had taken his sixth-grade class to the Adelaide Gaol and, as they sat outside eating their lunches, he heard it first, coming from the west. It was a rough bowling rumble, and when he looked up to the low layer of cloud, he thought that the sound of the train might be affected by it. Might echo more, bouncing from track to cloud and down again. Or would the clouds absorb the sound and muffle it? He wondered whether the River Torrens felt its momentum. Whether it trembled. Whether it danced. The high wall prevented him from searching for ripples.

"Hey, it's The Ghan!" Christos was one of the excitable lads who had many friends.

"Duh." Julian wasn't.

"No, it's the Indian Pacific," said a third. "It says so on it."

Stan recognized the significance of a train speeding by a jail where whipcords soaked in water once broke skin and spirit, their echo so loud that birds must've flown away, forgetting how to sing. This could be the lesson the kids would take away. What was freedom and in what ways might perception change its definition?

He could see the passengers who'd probably crossed the Nullarbor and wouldn't have minded a walk along the river. All those eyes trapped inside, marveling at the symmetry of a barbed wire loop, gawking at the immobility of brick on bloody brick. And what of him? Hungover again, stuck in time, unable—no, unwilling—to get past his longing for Jean so that days were suddenly too long when once they'd seemed so short and nights were a fucking nuisance. And what of his poor mum, confined in her dying body, mind sharper than ever and honed to a point of penning truly great works of art but the body sinking so far into itself that soon there'd be nothing left but the cancer licking its wounded lips? We are all prisoners in our own points of view.

It seemed, for a moment, that every one of his students contemplated the train, and that when the train had disappeared, so had their interest in it. Back to apples, sandwiches, juice boxes, muesli bars.

"Did anyone take notice of those passengers? Did anyone think them lucky to be traveling on a train, free to leave their homes for someplace new?"

Heads rose in mere ambivalence, though some surprise because it was lunchtime, their time, no real place for their teacher to comfortably fit in. These kids were young. All they knew about freedom was that they had it.

"Anyone?"

"Yeah, we're in jail and they're on a train."

"We're not *in* jail. We're visiting."

"Yeah, we're really at school."

"Hey, that's like jail!"

Stan smiled and shook his head. They were allowed their own points of view. "So are you free in a jail?"

"No." Varying degrees of interest mingled murmurs with answers that suggested an echo of Julian's "duh."

"What about in a train?"

"Yes." Slightly more interest in their tones. The discussion might build. Then Danni said, "No, because you can't get off."

"What about school? Are you free when you're at school?"

"No!" They almost yelled this time. Then Danni said, "Well, we are, sort of, because we're learning, and you don't get to learn in jail."

"Yes you do!" another girl countered. "Remember the library in there? Some people probably read more here than they did when they weren't in jail."

"Maybe *you* need to go to jail so *you* read more," said Jack, always sarcastic. What sort of prison did he live in?

Stan thought about Charley Cromwell, the ex-con who'd run over his wife while she was riding her bike to work. He'd found out about him through Neddy, who'd learned about him from an old friend she'd run into at the funeral. In the beginning Stan had thought about him incessantly, but eventually the obsession faded so that he'd almost forgotten his name. But when Stan and his students arrived at the Adelaide Gaol, the name appeared in neon from the deep fog of his tired depression. Charley Cromwell was a murderer. Apparently a model prisoner, learning to read on the inside. He'd gotten out early for good behavior. The cops saw no reason to punish him for Jean's death because it had been an accident. Was he free? Was Charley Cromwell a free man?

He felt like asking, *And what of the old woman who finds out she's dying of cancer and chooses to forgo treatment? Is she a prisoner because she's dying or is she free because she's decided to die on her own terms?* But that would be morose. Inappropriate. Might give him away.

As the students returned to their social circles, Stan considered how he fit in. He was a single parent now with a mother who was in need of serious attention and he was unable to get away from it all. His week-long mountain biking trips with his mates were a thing of the past. Leaving his son for a week with Jean and just getting on his bike. Just going. What he wouldn't give to go a few hours north, get on a trail and camp when the day was done. Or put his bike on a plane and travel somewhere, his jet dividing the sky as it left Australia behind. He punched himself inwardly because this was not about being dragged down by his five-year-old son and his seventy-seven-year-old mother. He was free to leave if he wanted. There were friends on hand, eager to help. Neddy called at least once a week asking if there was anything, big or small, that she could do. And just last week Viv had asked if she could have Orion over for the weekend. "It's too soon," he'd told her. Too soon for whom? Orion couldn't be the problem because Orion was most often the solution: why he got out of bed in the morning, why he laughed in the evening. And it wasn't his mum, either. She'd been such a help, so indispensable, both physically and emotionally, when Jean had been in the coma and during the planning of the funeral that Stan felt ready to give back. It wasn't something he *had* to do, but something he wanted to do.

It was Jean. Memories imprisoned a person in the past, but what would he do without them? Stan went back to first hearing the Indian Pacific rolling nearer, imagined Jean had been with him and heard it too. He imagined they'd talked about Perth, where they'd spent their last holiday together before the accident. He imagined taking hold of her hand, seeing, once again, the crinkle of her freckled nose when she smiled. He thanked god he had the memory of her crinkling and freckled nose. He looked to where the train had just been, now replaced by an overcast horizon. *Freedom.* He knew he'd added "freedom" to Jean's old list of things she'd never get back, the big things, things she missed, as he watched the airplane in the sky the day before, and it made him feel guilty then, but he couldn't erase it now. That was the problem with a mental list.

At first he'd left the list of little things Jean had lost on the fridge. He was hoping for the day when he'd find something on it and could cross it off: the reading light that was supposed to be with their camping gear, the acupuncture voucher she'd bought for his mother—Marion could certainly use it now; the cancer was in her lymph nodes. But as weeks turned into months the realization that he wouldn't find the little things, and the fact that the little things had become really big to him, was painful. He took the list off the fridge and filed it away in a folder in the office, where he'd put the list of big things Jean had lost. There, they would always be safe; there, they would always be out of sight. Obviously they weren't out of mind because, though he'd filed away the list of big things the morning after Jean had died, he was mentally adding to it now. Clearly it was an obsession.

There had been three additions already today. Hungover again, Stan had placed *morning clarity* on the list. The recycling bin mocked him every morning when he chucked in new bottles. It smelled sticky, sweet and foul and made him gag just a little bit, made his head swim momentarily. Then, when picking up bread after school and before going to his mum's, he added *books*. He'd seen a woman reading at the crossing and, when the light changed and the pedestrians began to move, the woman moved too, still reading. Jean had loved to read. Had been in a book club. Had two floor-to-ceiling shelves in the spare room packed with novels. Stan wasn't much of a reader so, now that Jean was gone, books weren't really an obvious presence in his life. And at his mum's, when he picked up Orion because it was Tuesday—Tuesday was always Marion's afternoon with her grandson and she insisted it remain that way, cancer or no cancer—he'd seen a hairbrush on the kitchen table and thought, *Mum's hair*. She wasn't losing her hair now and, with chemo and radiation out of the question, she hadn't planned on losing it ever again, but her hairbrush had made Stan remember her first bout of cancer. He'd had a memory of being at Marion's just after her hair had started to grow back, when the cancer and her breasts had been forced from her body, the malignant cells secretly lying dormant in her lymph nodes. Orion had fallen asleep on the couch, next to Stan, who'd been watching football. He remembered his team had won that day. There'd been a fire. He'd been eating something. Jean had been brushing his mum's hair. "I used to love brushing my friends' hair when I was a little girl. Guess I still do," she'd said, and Marion had said, "I love you," just like that. Stan knew that if Jean had been with him earlier this evening and had seen the hairbrush on the kitchen table, she would've remembered it too.

"She'd miss brushing your hair," he said out loud to his mum that evening.

"What?" Marion turned to her son as she pulled on oven mitts.

"Jean. I remember a time when she brushed your hair."

His mother touched his shoulder and looked up toward the ceiling. Was it memory or angels she was searching for up there?

And now there was Orion's first tooth.

~

"How's the Tooth Fairy going to get in our house?"

"She's magic."

"How do you know it's a 'she'?"

"I've seen her before."

"When?"

Stan kept it rolling, knowing if he stopped for only one second to think about his answers, he mightn't know how to continue. "When you were born. She came into the hospital and told me when you turned five you would start losing your teeth, and that she would come and take them."

"Were you scared?"

"No. I could tell she was nice."

"Was Mom there?"

"Yes."

"Was she scared?"

"No. She was holding you."

"Where's the Tooth Fairy going to put my tooth?"

"She said she turns the teeth into stars."

"But I already have stars in the sky."

"I told her that. She said she was going to add them to your constellation and make his sword even brighter."

Orion looked off to the side as a smile took over his face, and Stan could see his little imagination lifting to the skies. He ruffled his son's hair, pulled the blanket to his chin, kissed him good-night. "See you when I come to bed," he said, because Orion still slept on Jean's old side of the bed. As he ruffled his son's hair a second time for good luck, he told himself not to forget about the tooth. He told himself to go looking for some gold coins as soon as he turned off the light. Tonight he was more than a single parent; he was the Tooth Fairy, and he couldn't mess it up. He would have to slide his hand under the pillow, Jean's old pillow, now Orion's. He would have to find the tooth and take it out and put it on the bedside table, where a couple of gold coins would be. He would have to pick those up, slide his hand back under the pillow again and leave them for Orion. He would have to carry the tooth to the pillbox Jean's mother had given to her, the one Jean had said she was going to put Orion's first tooth in. Then he would have to fight the urge to cry, lamenting the minute she'd lost the beating of her heart, the minute she'd lost the use of her lungs, the minute she'd lost the chance to share in this moment with the people she loved most. He would then tell himself that there would be no more mental additions to Jean's list because he was pissed off with its abstraction, with its absurdity, with its relentlessness and its implications of "what's been lost." How vulgar. He would take out a piece of paper and write down the words "first tooth"—nothing more, not even a title, though he knew the title was understood: Things I Want to Share with You—and he would stick it on the fridge so that he could add to it at the end of every day. His own list. Not hers. And he would be freer because of it. Stan didn't want to be free from Jean, just *freer*, and it would turn out to be a far better alternative to his daily hangover.

Licking the Wound

There was a flash of two crazed dogs in an urgent moment over the fence, barks and snarls, the two dogs jumping high enough for Digger's paw to find its way into Pyro's teeth, and when they started falling back to the ground the drag of poor Digger's leg against the fence skinned him raw. Other dogs in other houses and backyards were barking frantically in response, as if they all wanted a piece of the action, but no beast would choose to be on the receiving end of this madness. No beast would choose to be Digger.

★

The dog licked the black oil of his paw. It had been a hard day and he found comfort at the feet of his man. Digger looked up at his man's clean and friendly face and wondered if his man knew how badly it throbbed. How could he know the violence of the thing—he hadn't been there. His boy hadn't been there either and his woman was still gone. Digger missed his woman's clean and caring face. He missed her neat hands and how she fed him scraps while she worked over the kitchen bench. He missed nights when she let him onto the couch where his man would not. He missed her pale skin around his animal coat and the way she burrowed her nose right into him. No, his woman hadn't come back so she hadn't been there for the trouble.

They'd been pups when they'd first met, sniffing each other through the tin fence, one smelling like the bottom of a brown river and the other like the film that might rest on top. They'd had their routines: Pyro did a series of high jumps first thing in the morning to find Digger over the fence; Digger told Pyro what he was getting for dinner and Pyro let Digger know with one gruff bark when he'd had enough of his bragging. Hadn't they been friends? What had turned them against each other so suddenly and violently?

Digger rested on his forepaws and fell asleep, so tired from the day, and the warmth of the fireplace felt so good. He woke only to lick his paw, this sleep-then-lick, this sleep-then-lick seemed to be an obsession. His man touched him on the head.

"What have you got there, Dig?" His man got down close to him on the floor. There were small drops of darker red on the lighter red carpet. "This still hurting you?" His man had seen the paw when he'd first come back from work because Digger had been limping. His man had come back. His boy had come back. His woman had not.

The neat hand touched the furred paw and his man held it as if it were a flower. His woman used to hold flowers this way. His boy would give his woman flowers from the garden and she would hold them as if they might break, as if they might go away and never come back. Then she would put them in her hair, where they always fell out and died.

"What did you get into today, mate?" His man held the paw and Digger moved to lick the neat hand, grateful for his man's touch and his words and his clean and caring face. Digger felt the love. It was a full feeling, shining inside him, round and big, like what he knew the moon to be, and he would always love his man like he would always love the moon.

Since his woman had gone, his man had been reaching for him more often and staying with him longer, and Digger knew that his man, too, was full with the love. But it was love and something more. It was a deep sadness that they shared, which came from the same place as the love, only the sadness didn't shine inside; the sadness carried stones to give itself more weight, then laid down its burden and rested.

"We'll take you to the vet in the morning." Digger liked the vet with the treats, but his woman and his boy used to take him to the vet, so he looked at his man curiously, then looked at the skinned part of his leg and licked it.

"What's this?" His man got off the couch again and moved to the floor to be with him. Digger felt like howling just a little when his man saw the leg.

"Jesus, Dig. What happened?"

It was the trouble that had happened.

"We're definitely taking you to the vet tomorrow."

He liked the vet with the treats so he laid his head back down again and swiftly fell asleep. He did not know that this time tomorrow he'd be wearing the Cone of Shame, so he dreamed of the waiting room, where other dogs were and other animals like cats in boxes, then he woke up again to lick his paw. Sleeping wasn't working. It was all too hard. He stared at his man, telling his man everything important with his eyes, and his man stared back, having heard it all. "You'll be right, mate. You're a good dog."

Digger beat his tail twice against the carpet, the thickness of the tail a thud of effort. His man was here, with him.

When his man turned off the light and went to his room, Digger raised himself, shaking a little, and stretched his body long. Slowly he walked to his boy's room where he could sleep on the bed. His man had told his boy that Digger would sleep with him if only he'd return to his own bed. His boy had said he missed his mum, then started sleeping in his bed again. Digger loved the bed and he loved his boy. His boy often got down on the floor with him to show him the love. His boy often laid his head and his chest on top of him so that they were almost the same. His boy fed him at night, now that his woman had gone. On the safety of their shared bed, warming each other in the winter's night, he thought his boy was the only person who would never go away.

What We Don't Know About Animals

Dawn stretched itself out for what seemed like an hour. Was that how long he'd been writing? Only now the sun was rising above his roof and holding the promise of heat. Charley laid down his pen and walked over to the window. A koala was breakfasting on the leaves of a tree in his backyard. Not a usual sight. Charley watched as if it were giving birth or ripping apart another animal for a feed—as if it were nature at its peak rather than an animal barely moving. Truth: two things that shocked Charley when he first left prison were colors and living things, and after all these years on the outside, both still blew him away. He wondered how long the little fella would take refuge in his backyard. In his experience, animals didn't live long around him, no matter how much he willed them to. He thought it just bad luck, but knew it could be something more.

Charley picked up his letter, lit himself a cigarette and sat back down at the table to read what he'd written. It was enough to make a grown man cry, but not him. No, he'd got all his crying out when his mum died. He'd been so riddled with guilt for the man he'd become that he refused to see her in lock-up. How could he have asked to go to her funeral to say goodbye when it'd been far too late to say anything at all? So he hadn't gone to her funeral but held a vigil in his cell. The photo, the prayers, all the letters she'd written to him laid out to read. The tears had come on heavy, then stopped. Heavy, then stopped. The problem with tears was that once you let them out, they wanted to come out and out again and again, but what good were they? Charley was a big man. He'd plenty of room to hold them in.

He was trying to write a letter to Orion and it wasn't any good. He didn't know how to talk to a kid. He didn't know what to say, especially to this one. Did he tell him what kind of man he was? What kind of son he'd been? Did he tell Orion he killed Jean Harley one rainy morning just as he was about to mail a letter and, hey, *here's a letter for you!* For some reason Charley had answered yes to all of these questions and the letter read like a bad confession. He crumpled it up, then thought that writing to Lisa wasn't such a bad idea because this was where his comfort lay: cigarettes, coffee, morning sun, writing a letter to Lisa.

He stared at the paper long and hard, then closed his eyes and breathed three times through his nose. He was ready to compose.

Dear Lisa—I'm trying to write to Orion. I wonder what his favorite thing to do is. I started out telling him I liked to read and build things like houses, pergolas and decks. Did you know I once sculpted a naked man? It's true. I've built cages for animals too.

The first cage was out of scrap metal he'd found in the bush from burnt-out cars and the springs of old chairs. He was twelve when the people round town started complaining about the mangy dingo. They said it was probably half dog/half dingo and dangerous. They wanted it dead. Charley thought he might catch it and keep it as a pet but some old farmer got to it first. *I cried when me mate Runt told me. He was my best friend and I never cried in front of him before. I never did again. But I couldn't help it because they killed that dingo and they didn't need to. I would've looked after it. I would've loved it.*

Charley began transcribing onto paper. By the time he'd finished, the sun was well and truly up, light pushing through his dirty window. He got up to look for the koala, afraid it'd be lying dead on the ground or wounded to the point of needing to be put out of its misery. But there it was, still as lazy and round and plush as you'd imagine, feeding off the biggest tree on Charley's small, wild property. "What're you doing, you silly bugger?"

He finished his coffee watching that koala. He'd have liked to stay at that window all day long but there was work to go to, bricks to be laid and he'd had it in his mind to get a good chunk of the letter to Orion written first. One to Lisa would have to do. He rambled on in his head:

Not long after, Drillbit gave me a turtle. He visited his cousin in Adelaide who took him to a pet store. Drillbit's cousin was saving for a pet turtle for months and finally he saved enough. They named it Lobster. Funny name for a turtle but it seems like names are sometimes the opposite of who or what we are.

Example: his old friend Trev was Bat even though he was part deaf and the old saying goes, "blind as a bat." He was one of the Warriors. There'd been four of them: Bat, Runt, Drillbit and Charley, who they called Rascal. Together they were a group of boys who got into fights with the Indigenous kids at their school. They weren't racist, just needed to fight. None of them liked their homes and they didn't much like themselves, but when they were together, things were different. They were different.

Kids made fun of Bat because he talked funny on account of his disability, but Bat knew how to get back at them. He worked out their weaknesses. Back then Charley thought it was crazy that Bat used words instead of fists to hurt those who'd hurt him but years later, during his time behind bars, Charley thought it was crazy that he'd turned it around. Wondered why Bat ever had to change.

Bat's mum's old boyfriend used to make fun of him and that guy was the one person Bat didn't know how to get back at. The fucker had too much power. Bat told the gang that the one thing he hated more than anything else was knowing that his mum cared more about the old man than she did about her own son. He said one night she walked right past Bat in the kitchen while the guy was pretending to be a spastic and making fun of the way Bat talked. His mum saw it all and didn't do anything about it. Eight years later the guy was arrested and went to prison for identity fraud and the Warriors celebrated by pouring beer over Bat's head and staying up all night.

Stevo was Drillbit because he liked to joyride in other people's cars. Not that stealing a car has anything to do with engine mechanics or building a car body but nicknames come in roundabout ways. Drillbit's dad wasn't around—none of their dads were—but his mum was and she was a drunk, throwing things at him and calling him "weak" and a "girl." Drillbit used to say he never understood why his mum called him a girl like it was a bad thing because it seemed to him that his mum loved his sister and hugged her for no reason at all. She stopped hugging him when he was six. That was the year his dad left and his mum was pregnant and started drinking so much she lost the baby on the kitchen floor. He said he had to clean up the mess with half a roll of paper towel.

Charley's best friend Jack was the short one so they called him Runt. He hit puberty late and didn't really grow until he was seventeen so there wasn't much mystery to his nickname. Runt made up for his shortcomings by being the toughest in the gang. In sixth grade, kids made fun of his mum because her tits were big. Runt beat them up. Later, in high school, the jokes got less funny because they called her "slut" and "whore" even though they didn't know that she had different men over all the time. No one but the Warriors knew, so the stupid kids didn't know they were hitting just the right spot. "In their sleep," he used to say, slamming a fist into his open palm like some wise guy in a gangster movie, "when they're dreaming about fucking Mum." Instead he took care of them in the schoolyard. It's like he couldn't ever punch enough kids to make the jokes stop, so he punched more kids than deserved it.

Charley was the quiet one who didn't want to do anything bad so he got the nickname Rascal since rascals always got into stuff, couldn't help themselves. Charley was the boy with his head down and textbook open and unread. Thought he was stupid because he couldn't read. He was the biggest kid in the class so Drillbit, Runt and Bat wanted him in their gang. And he was angry, just like them, so he felt like he fit in because they all had shit lives. None of them were winners, but they knew if they stuck together, no one would ever call them losers.

Charley was angry because of his old man, a thief and a drug addict found dead outside the Star Hotel. He used to hate walking past that pub, let alone teasing the bloke who delivered the beer because he had no teeth. Why would he tease a man he didn't even know in front of a building that made him sad? The Warriors were doing it and it was "all for one and one for all," but if it hadn't been for the teasing would the bloke ever have come up to Charley in the park when he was minding his own business, kicking a ball around by himself?

When Drillbit and his cousin brought Lobster back to the house, his aunty said, "No way," so Drillbit brought it home with him, hiding it from his mum the whole way back. When he finally took it out of the car like it wasn't even a secret or surprise, you can imagine what she said: "No way." So I got it.

Much transcribing to be done and it was already nearly eight in the morning. There wasn't any time to write about how Charley didn't want to risk his own mum saying no to Lobster, so he stuck a small plastic bin inside the cage he'd made for the dingo because he loved that cage and didn't want it to go to waste, but in the morning Lobster was gone. It would've taken an hour to write how he found its shell a couple days later about a hundred feet into the bush, how he'd wanted to see the death trail, where the hunter went with the soul of the turtle heavy inside its stomach. Where had that animal gone? What type of animal had it been? He'd guessed a dingo.

He'd wanted to look for something fresh inside the shell. He didn't know why; he just wanted to see something of its life still inside. It seems like we're meant to turn our heads from death and gore and the unclean nature of a body that has yet to go stiff or crust up, but Charley hadn't wanted that, so he looked inside the shell and stuck his fingers in there and smelled for something maybe yellow and spoiled, but there was nothing. The shell had been licked clean. Charley had thrown up.

If he wrote how angry he was that another animal had died under his watch, he'd be late for work, so he didn't write that he'd lifted the shell above his head and screamed like a warrior and threw it hard onto the dirt, but it didn't crack. That he jumped on it until it became many shells, screaming the whole time. That, when he finished, he'd walked into the kitchen and felt like he'd changed because this was one of those big events in life, those ones you end up talking about years afterwards, and he didn't really know that turtle just like he hadn't known that dingo, but this event and the one with the dingo had changed him.

Charley had asked what was for dinner even though he'd felt sick to his stomach. His mum walked into the kitchen to check the oven and she touched his shoulder when she went to the fridge for a beer. She asked him if he was hungry. How could he answer such a question with the memory of an empty shell so raw and vomit still coating his tongue? She told him to go wash his hands, who knew what he'd gotten into.

Charley shook his head, trying to transfer meaning from the dingo and the turtle onto Jean Harley. There was life and there was death, and in between there was more and more and more of the same. Is that all it boiled down to? And if that was the case, what the bloody hell would he ever say to Orion? *Your mum was a big event in my life, like the dingo and the turtle?* Charley felt dirty, went to shower, made sure as he passed the window that he didn't look at the koala.

★

Dear Charley,

I'm sitting on the veranda again with a lukewarm cup of tea. I let it go cold—school holidays so the triplets are home. It's never an ideal time to sit out back and read. I set them up with their daily dose of Freddy Krueger. They have a wicked plan to watch the entire Nightmare on Elm Street *series and then move onto the* Friday the 13th *series. I'm not a fan at all but you should see them. Luke, Stephy and Grace are all sitting there together on the couch, their bodies touching in some way like they're still in the womb. So comfortable with each other's skin it might as well be their own. The TV is blaring and their eyes are stuck to Freddy Krueger and his fingernails. When Grace screams, Stephy laughs and Luke gets these really big eyes. They can't be more different, yet they all agreed on the summer bloodfest, and turning back now would be admitting they aren't old enough to handle it. At thirteen, are they? I'm unconvinced. It seems a ridiculous initiation to the teenage years but they want to do it and Cam thought he'd been about their*

*age when he'd watched those flicks so I gave in. I miss the days of
G and PG family films, but fine—let them watch it. Let them
scream then laugh because it's not real. What's real can be so much
worse.*

Much worse, yes. At thirteen Charley was in the park, minding
his own business, kicking a ball around by himself. The toothless
man who delivered beer to the Star Hotel said, "What do we have
here? It's the little shit, is it? Or should I say 'big shit'?" He was
old. His hair was thick and dark, needing a good comb. His face,
too, needed a shave. He asked Charley where his mates were.
"Not so tough without them, are you?" He kept walking toward
Charley, tilting his head. "You're just a little boy, aren't you?" Yes,
he was. He was thirteen and he was scared. The toothless man got
so close to Charley he took the ball out of his hands and tossed it
up and down. He had an evil smile on his face. Charley knew he
needed to get away, but something stuck him to his place. He
couldn't move. The man asked Charley his name and Charley
told him. He hated that part of the memory most: that he told the
man who pushed him into the toilet block and raped him like a
fucking dog that his name was Charley.

Without even finishing the letter Lisa had sent him, Charley
got out his writing pad, found a pen, scribbled on the pad to make
sure it worked and took them back to the table where he lit himself a cigarette. *Dear Orion,* but he ripped it in half, then in half
again, then in half, in half, until it was too small to rip anymore
because all of it had been out of his control, just like the accident
with Jean Harley. He hadn't expected the bike to be in front of
him but then it was, and it was like it had happened in slow
motion. He could still see her falling. Each thrust of the toothless
stinking arsehole man. He could see her fingers spread like she
was trying to catch the rain and why the hell had it been raining

in December anyway? Why had he ever teased the bastard moth-
erfucker? If it hadn't been raining, would this have even happened?
If he hadn't teased the man? Would it have? He swore he could
count the seconds it took him to brake. He swore he counted each
thrust. He could feel the van drive over her body. The man's dick
when he'd come inside him. It was the second person he'd killed.
It was the first time he'd died.

The House of Noise

There is nothing sadder than an unmotivated philanthropist. A woman with her fists full of good intention—and yellow, too—intention the color of fifty-dollar bills. Watch her fists open. Watch the yellow intentions drop to the floor, swaying in slow motion like a sheet of leaves falling as the wind whips them from their branches, and the heart just breaks.

Marion's heart was breaking at ten o'clock this Sunday morning because Jean Harley was still dead. Almost eleven months had passed since they'd pulled the plug on her daughter-in-law, though it had been much gentler than it sounds. She doubted Jean had felt any pain, and the fact that she'd been in a coma led Marion to believe that Jean hadn't had the means to mourn her own passing. But the pain in the waiting room had been heavy as Marion held her grandson in her lap while he played with an old pocket Etch A Sketch, completely oblivious to any colors in his periphery, not to mention the gravity of the situation. When she imagined her son saying goodbye to his wife's sunken body, so sunken she seemed lost in the sheets, so white she blended in, the thickness of the pain had shrouded her.

While Jean had been in a coma, time, for Marion, had been too grand to be ticked off into seconds or even beeps of the wretched monitors. And then, when the beeps had ceased, time seemed to have stopped. It certainly had for Jean. And now, eleven months later, with cancer eating away at her own sunken body, time was mocking Marion. It seemed to be moving too slowly and too fast all at once. Lately the days dragged themselves as if through sand, weighty and long. Always the certainty of Marion's own death, the refusal to rest her eyes on a calendar in a news agency or gift shop, knowing she might not see the year out. She'd forgone the chemo and radiation so of course she knew time was limited. She could hear it and see it lagging behind her and racing ahead of her in the strong wind that seemed determined to blow the lake's surface to the shore of her back doorstep. Yes, she lived on a lake, but today it sounded like an ocean.

In the days before Jean's death, while she'd been planning the grant and getting things in order, it had all seemed so urgent. Then Jean died. Aside from signing official papers to tie things up, the project went into hibernation. Now, with the application deadline five weeks past and the applications from women-of-a-certain-age-wishing-to-be-playwrights sitting before her, energy was lacking and she did not know how to get it back. The house was too silent; the house was too lonely. Maybe it was time to consider Stan's suggestion of moving in with him.

Marion walked to the glass doors that opened to the violent wind and its compliant lake. She felt sorry for the borders of the artificial lake, that the wind could go on and onto far-off places but the waves of the lake stopped at the shore. And though the water tried to leave its prison and come closer to her back door, it was no use. It would never know the kind of freedom that the ocean had, being both here and there, both Adelaide and Antarctica, both Sydney and America. The ocean. The ocean.

~

In her son's front yard two birch trees bent to the ground, finding nothing there to help them stand. It had been a relentlessly windy spring, and now, four days into summer, it seemed as though it was going to stay that way.

"You don't have to do this, Mum."

"I want to, love."

"You sure you're up for it?"

"Well, I'm having a good week. I feel strong and I'm not dead yet."

Stan had aged five years in the last eleven months and, though Marion knew it was not a good thing, she had to admit, as clichéd as she knew it to be, a bit of gray never hurt a man, a bit of crease around the eye only added character; it was the sudden onslaught which had brought it on that hurt her to consider.

Orion came running out the front door with a backpack fit for a boy at least seven years older than he was. Digger the dog pulled him toward the car.

"Let him go, Orion. He'll jump in."

"Go, Digger." Orion laughed at either his dog's eagerness or his dog's ability to follow orders. Whichever it was, it made Marion smile at the pair of them. Stan's brow remained creased.

"The wind will be worse at the beach, Mum. You know that."

"We'll be fine," she said, patting Orion's car seat for him. The boy took off his backpack and handed it to his nan. Marion said, "Thank you," then grimaced and shook her head. "I can't stay in that house another second. It'll kill me and no one will know I'm dead."

"I think I might know what you mean."

Marion touched her son's face, the strong male skin with the weekend's stubble. He was close to the age she was when she'd left Donald, and he looked so much like him now. She pulled him to her, cherished his linger, felt she could safely melt because it was Stan, not Donald, and Stan had always been the biggest love of her life. "We'll all be better for it."

"I'll pick Orion up around noon. I'll bring a chicken over for lunch."

"Oh, my lucky day! My favorite grandson and my favorite dog are spending the night with me and my favorite son is going to buy me lunch." Marion bent over to buckle Orion into his car seat and felt her back momentarily lock as she tried to move within the car door's frame. It was not only the cancer that her body hated, but age too.

"Let me get that, Mum."

"I'm fine, Stan. Just old. Just riddled with tumors. Nothing new." She moved aside for Stan to say goodbye.

"Have fun, mate." He kissed his boy. "See you, Dig." He patted his dog.

From the driver's seat Marion looked worriedly at her son. "Just get some rest, Stan. Or go out and have fun tonight. Do *something* worthwhile. I'll have a bottle of riesling chilling for us when you come tomorrow."

"Ah, my favorite mum taking care of my favorite son and my favorite dog and I get wine, too?"

"Against doctor's orders. Just watch us enjoy life."

"Yeah, how dare we?" Stan looked down at his left foot, which kicked at a clump of weeds growing through the cracks of the drive. He bent over to pull it out as Marion started the car.

If Marion looked at the waves long enough she became light-headed. No one else was at West Beach—they must've all known that being in wind like this would be far less than pleasant—but who would've known by looking at Orion? The boy wrote his name in the sand with cuttlefish; he picked up piles of seaweed and threw them back into the ocean, yelling, "Live, seaweed, live!" he walked into the mutinous surf and screeched when he got wet past his swim trunks; he searched for snails in the foam, yelling, "Nan!", his smile as vast as the shoreline. And then there was Digger, who hopped and danced across the wet sand and in and out of the inevitable waves. He peed on every pile of seaweed he sniffed and kept coming back to Marion for "good dog" pats. Marion felt feeble and small holding her body against the wind but her lungs felt enormous. She would sleep well tonight. They all would.

Back at the house by the roughness of the lake and nestled within the silence of the walls, Marion washed Orion and his clothes, made them toasted ham and cheese sandwiches and heated up some pumpkin soup for tea while Digger slept on a rug in the lounge room. How good it felt to fill the house, bringing it to life. She'd lived alone in it for more than twenty years. There'd been small gatherings, dinner parties, out-of-town guests and friends down on their luck, just as there'd been lovers, but never for long. Stan and Jean had once lived in the spare room for ten months following their year abroad. They'd discovered new landscapes— mountains, rapids, cities and a jungle—then found they needed to save money when they'd returned. They used to try to muffle their lovemaking so Marion wouldn't hear, then giggle after it had clearly been impossible. Jean's exuberance made Marion cringe while the low tones of her son's pleasure never ceased to amaze her. They were sure and young and in love, and the house had been alive then, like never before. Jean had turned thirty that year. Marion and Stan had baked her a cake.

There'd been other birthdays too, and Christmases and Mother's Days and sleepovers for Orion. The first time he'd spent the night

Marion rose to his cry at two in the morning and rocked him to sleep with a warm bottle, humming a made-up tune. The house had continued humming after she'd stopped and laid her own body down that night and it had lulled her to sleep. From the time Orion was two until Jean died, Marion and the house embraced him for a mid-week sleepover: seven-thirty Tuesday mornings until dinnertime on Wednesdays. Those nights the house was loudest with noise: rapid movement and huge belly-laughs. But after Jean's death, Stan seemed to need his son near him with great desperation—something Marion knew all too well—and she only got Orion to herself on Tuesday afternoons. There was noise then, but too much quiet after he'd gone. Too much quiet for the next seven days. But now he was back for an entire night and things were loud again. They were back on track. This was Orion's first sleepover since Jean's death and Marion could feel the pulse of her house beating, Digger's tail occasionally catching on.

At eight in the evening the wind was still making itself heard, but the birds were louder, bidding one another goodnight. Marion set her cup of tea next to the pile of applications for the Jean Harley Fellowship on the bedside table and crawled beneath the covers. Her body felt used, past its expiry date, and the bed was not firm enough to lend a hand in this most intricate maneuver. Her abdomen felt full of toxic pain so she had a quick puff from the marijuana pipe next to her teacup—more toxicity but less pain. She reached over to the pile, which had earlier been so menacing and now held such possibilities, and it was an awful stretch indeed. There were eleven applications; obviously not too many women over the age of fifty living in Australia were keen for a new career as a playwright. But at least there were eleven.

Marion closed her eyes. She was tired but she was fulfilled, her heart sighing in relief. The house was quietly snoring now, exhausted from the evening's action of Orion's bath, his chatter, his rediscovery of favorite toys and CDs, Digger's trotting down the hallway when a neighbor's dog barked. Exhausted and hypersensitive to the boy's young dreams and his nighttime breath, to Digger lying at the foot of the bed dreaming of seagulls or of the waves that kept coming and shouting *next* and *next* and *next*. Tomorrow the house would be whipped into action with morning and the breakfast table, more noise, more movement, more living. This was good, this giving back. This getting stuck back into life. Dying was so abhorrent.

Marion squinted then picked up her glasses. "Lesbian Mechanics." A young woman falls in love with her boss, the head mechanic, a confident and beautiful lesbian almost twenty years her senior. No romance, just strong friendship. It sounded OK. Another application read "The Long Road," and its synopsis was as generic as its title. Marion perused the applications, reading bits and pieces of the forms, getting familiar with the pool of candidates before she got up close and personal.

The tenth application listed "Untitled" as the play's title, striking Marion as sloppy. She herself had spent days, up to a week, getting a single application ready for a grant or a fellowship so that it would be just right, so that the panel knew she would not waste their time or their money; she expected as much from these applicants. She flipped through the proposal, grumbling that it was useless. Even the font seemed unprofessional—Comic Sans—unlike the other, more solid Times New Roman or Calibri. But this woman, this Rosalind Cox, wasn't a practicing writer waiting for her big chance, so she mightn't know that certain fonts were unacceptable in submissions and others were standard. She was an actress, had spent twenty-two years in various theatre companies in Perth. She said her favorite roles had been Desdemona and Lady Macbeth, and here was where Marion had another sip of her tea and sat up that little bit straighter.

Three years ago I was diagnosed with an aggressive form of MS and because of it I've had to stop acting. No one wants a cripple. As one might assume there was a period of mourning, as there always is with loss, but my creativity didn't dwindle with my legs, now resting in a wheelchair. My creativity shifted. I hope you enjoy the sample I've included of my first attempt as a playwright. It is called "Untitled" and it is about a writer who gets in a terrible accident, leaving her blind, but is determined to finish her novel. An old friend of mine, a playwright, recently told me to write what I know about what I don't know. Having followed his advice, I hope you think I'm onto something.

Marion set down "Untitled" and thought about time: Jean's time cut far too short; her own time persisting when it should be winding down; Rosalind Cox's time thrashing at borders, a lake dreaming of being an ocean, and this is what she wanted to do while there was still time. She loved the applicant's *confidence*, her *naivety* and her *optimism*. She took another sip of tea and held the cup for a very long time.

When she looked at the last application and saw that it was something redundant about an outback town, something having no punch in her gut, she picked up "Untitled" again, staring at it as if it held some answer. She read through the sample and it was good, so she whispered, "Yes," privately declaring "Untitled" her winner. She said, "Yes" that little bit louder, until tears relaxed in the cracks of her eyes, not wanting to go any further, just happy to be let out. Eventually Marion said a forceful "Yes" and Digger woke up, briefly howled. "Yes, Diggy! Yes!" Together they woke up the house, and Marion began clapping, Digger began thumping his tail to the rhythm of the house's chant, which sounded like *yes* and *yes* and *yes*, while Orion slept on, dreaming the dreams of a very young boy.

Very Viv

No breeze today, the sun simply holding up the sky and the ocean gently flirting with the sand where Viv walked this summer's morning. No sandals, no bra, her uterus emptying itself once again. Pregnancy scares did two things to Viv: brought back her past and shifted thoughts of her future. True, she'd never cared much for babies—she'd talk to them and hold them but never get *enthused*—and yes, she was always a smidgen resentful for being somewhat left out in a group of women when birthing stories sprang up from the well of bonding, but each time her period was late and she remembered a particular night with a particular lover and counted the days, did the math, she thought about a baby forming inside her, about what it might look like when it came out, and, for a short time, only flashes of moments, she experienced maternal longing. So on the packed sand of low tide, her footprints that little bit deeper because she was menstruating and therefore heavier in body and mind, Viv was as melancholy as the wind was still.

I wasn't meant to have his baby now, maybe never, but definitely not this time. It was a form of rationalization and it usually worked, relaxing all passageways and making room for air. But not this time. Not on the two-year anniversary of Jean Harley's death. Must've been the whole birth–death thing. Or the death–death thing, more likely. Viv whispered, "Fuck" and it had no less passion than had she yelled it.

She'd met Philip at the funeral, in that awkward space between the parlor and the parking lot, where people lingered, unsure of what to do. He'd passed by her and looked twice. "Sorry, but were you a friend of Jean's twenty years back, at Flinders University?"

"That's where we met. And you?"

"I'm Philip Cross. I was one of her lecturers back in the day."

"You're not the Philosophy one?"

"Oh dear. I'm afraid I might be."

Memories of conversations and confessions with Jean and Neddy regarding Philip were vague as so many years had passed, but how could she ever forget? Philip looked down at his shoes with what appeared to be embarrassment and pride, cementing for Viv that he was the lecturer Jean had slept with before she'd hooked up with Stan. He was Professor Sleazeman.

Jean had assured her friends that he was not sleazy. That, in fact, it had been she who'd seduced him, hungry for an experience with an older man and feeling like she could be anyone so long as she was in a foreign country, unaware at the time that Australia would become her home. "And an academic too," she'd sighed.

"You mean a sleaze," Neddy had said.

And forevermore he'd been referred to as Professor Sleazeman.

He'd escorted Viv to the wake, which was held in Neddy's backyard.

"Look at this spread. How did Ned have time to do this in between her children and her grief? How's she able to take all this on?" Viv had been finding it difficult to sleep at night, in a daze at work, apathetic toward the gym, so she was in awe, yet again, of Neddy's energy. The woman was a powerhouse, and a caring one at that.

"I'll be honest with you, this is a bit strange for me."

"For all of us." Children were playing in the grass. Two teenagers sat together on a bench. Middle-aged men and women tried to enjoy themselves in whichever way a wake allowed. The oldest of the bunch sat at tables, weary from yet another death.

"No," he'd said, "I guess you're right."

"It's good, though. Jean would've been happy with the turnout. She loved a party. We should dance before the wake ends." Viv smiled a sad smile, missing her friend, then imagined herself dancing with Philip in Neddy's backyard. What a kick Jean would've gotten out of the whole thing.

He seemed contemplative. She wanted to say shy but there was arrogance too. Serious-mysterious. She remembered thinking that Jean was lucky having bagged a lecturer and wondering if he'd be fair game when Jean and Stan got together. But Professor Sleazeman had disappeared and they'd never really talked about him again. Why would they have? But now he was here, so different from how she'd imagined him and yet also exactly the same: Professor Sleazeman. Professor Sexy, more like it.

She told him all of this that night as they lay in her bed, naked and sated, and he'd told her it had been a midlife crisis thing, his time with Jean, that it had led him to a life of near-celibacy and meditation. It had been intense for a while and it embarrassed him now, but he was trying to get back into the game.

"It appears to me that you're playing the game very well."

"Am I winning?"

"I'd say *I'm* winning." Viv'd had three orgasms in seven hours, unprecedented in her bedroom. Maybe it was due to the sex–death thing. Whatever the reason, he'd stayed another three nights and they called it a draw.

A long-distance relationship ensued: emails, sexy video calls, a rendezvous in the Hunter Valley she'd suggested, a visit to Thailand he'd suggested, then the week-long holiday to his old home in Katherine where Philip had hermitted after his affair with Jean, nothing to his life back then but a computer and a zafu and a two-person canoe. And it was in the gorge, in that same canoe, where Viv realized that she was in love.

Had she ever been in love before? When she told her therapist she didn't think she had, there was talk of her parents and their absence from Viv's life. She learned to blame them for all sorts of things and especially blamed them for this. They were her reason for feeling so vulnerable with Philip. One day he'd leave and devastate her completely and it would be their fault if she didn't survive.

When she finally told Stan about the affair, he'd asked if it made her feel better, knowing she could blame someone for something she was afraid of.

"It's easier than the alternative, isn't it?"

"Oh, yeah? And what's the alternative?"

"Leaving him. Being alone without him to love."

Stan had smiled and looked toward the sky. "Man, Viv. If Jean could only see you now."

Stan hadn't heard the names "Professor Sleazeman" or "Philip Cross" before, but he got an earful that afternoon. The story became the butt of many one-liners, an inside joke that set them both at ease, and when Orion had asked, "What's a 'Sleazeman'?" Viv told him, "It means 'funtastic.' Want to meet Funtastic Phil one day?" The boy's eyes grew wide and he nodded as if he'd just been asked if he wanted to meet Superman.

So Philip visited Viv, then Viv visited Philip, and it went on in this way until finally they were talking about living together, but where? He was a damaged man and protective of his space, afraid

to share for fear he'd ruin it like he had with his first and last partner, Rebecca. Viv was a selfish woman, also protective of space,
and wasn't leaving Adelaide. When home isn't about family, it
ends up being about place. Like it or not, Adelaide was hers.
"What would ground me if I left?"

"I could try to ground you."

Their last tryst had been three weeks ago, when Viv'd been
ovulating.

She walked along the beach, calf-deep in the water, the hem of
her dress wet and clinging, and she missed Philip, missed Jean,
wondered if Jean knew that she had brought the two of them
together and that the anniversary of her death, for Viv, would
always be mixed with deep thoughts of Philip, no matter what
happened now. She was forty-three, time almost up, and she
wondered if she should have his baby. Maybe Jean *wanted* her to
have his baby. The rebirth thing.

She felt her nerves turn in a point below her belly button and
deep, just there, where a commonplace miracle of nature was stir-
ring, where eggs were dying because they hadn't received her
lover's sperm.

She sat in the shallow water, letting the salty waves splash
against her thighs. A man and a woman passed with their toddler.
Viv watched them take turns carrying the little girl, setting her
down, the toddler walking and falling, walking and falling, the
parents picking her up again. Viv watched the family move forwards in this way, in this letting-go, this coming-back way that
they had, until she couldn't see them anymore.

After breakfast Viv put on an old T-shirt and skirt she'd had in a
bag by the door for an thrift shop drop. Never mind, today they
would be her painting clothes. She went to Bunnings and had
them mix an assortment of paints to give her three perfect shades

of pink: Scarlet Ribbons, Violet Orchid, Pompeian Pink. Her wooden chairs in the kitchen needed sprucing and she had it in her mind to paint a couple of random cabinet doors, too. Gaudy yet feminine. Seventies yet eighties. Viv's home was nothing like those she worked on for her job. Deep down she was a bit corny, and her apartment reflected it.

The regularity of the strokes, even the biting smell of toxic fumes, relaxed her body and got her mind moving. She interrogated her eggs, composed soliloquies to the child she was not having and addressed the fetus she'd long ago aborted. She'd never told the guy and now she could barely remember his name. *Jason Pan, Jason Pash, Jason Pink?*

Despite the synthetic Daft Punk rifts pumping through her speakers, she heard the phone on its first ring and knew it was Philip. Call it women's intuition, call it love, Viv answered the phone with a question: "Do you miss me?"

"Madly."

"Do you want me?"

"Always."

"I knew it was you."

"So it's not just how you've taken to answering the phone, hoping one of these days the right man will be on the other end of the line?"

"I'm pretty sure you're it."

"Pretty sure?"

She was sure. "How about me?"

"How about you what?"

"Am I the right person? On the end of the line?"

Sometimes the way they communicated was nothing but a game. Like catch or charades. What she wanted to say was that she was bluer than the ocean outside her window because she was bleeding the red, heavy discard of her what-if.

They continued to back-and-forth, the sort of foreplay telephone calls allowed them, then they worked out some details for their next rendezvous. Griffith, New South Wales. The Acacia Motel. Would they be able to keep quiet during sex and not wake Orion?

"I'm not doing it with him in the room, sorry."

"Are you sure he needs to come?"

"He's coming, Philip. We've already talked about this. I'm helping Stan out and I'm really looking forward to it."

Since Jean's death, Viv had made Orion a major priority. She wanted the child to grow up knowing he'd always have her to talk to because shouldn't every boy have a woman's gentle ear and soft-breasted hug? They were getting closer. They were beginning to need one another. At Marion's wake, such an awful day, Orion had clung to Viv's neck, resting his head on her shoulder, ignoring everyone's kind words and gentle touches. He'd been six, not too light, but she carried him around, never setting him down for a full two hours. In the end she'd carried him to bed.

"I don't know, Viv. Is it so wrong for me to just want you? What if I told you I don't ever want to share you with anyone?"

"I'd tell you to piss off." And that was the end of the playful banter.

"You OK, babe?"

"No, I'm grumpy. Menstrual. I'm just in the middle of something I should get back to."

"Yeah?"

"Yeah."

"Well, I'll let you go then. I'll call you later, though. Happy hour."

"Sounds perfect. I'll be better with a wine in my hand."

They said they loved each other, and so they did, no doubt about it, but was it love because Viv was a childless woman who, on the surface, wanted to remain as such and Philip wanted exactly that in a partner? A love of convenience. Uncomplicated. If things changed, if she changed, if he ever had to share her with a little someone else, would he stay?

What if she lied and told him she was pregnant just to see what he'd do? She'd never told Jason whatever-his-name-was when she was pregnant with his child—could it be any worse? She wondered what that old flame might say today if she found him and told him she'd been pregnant then, way back when, after they'd met at some pub near North Terrace. Had it been an old church converted to a drinking spot? Inside there had been blue lights. Everything had been blue, she remembered this. She had drunk a bottle of wine to his four bourbon and sodas and he had told her she was sexy, very sexy, a jungle candy so sweet he wanted to roll her around on his tongue, leave bits of her in the crevices of his teeth for later, when she had gone and the smell of her had disappeared. It had been an impressive pick-up line and she'd allowed him to spend the night with her in the one-bedroom house she shared with a budgie.

She'd been only twenty-three at the time, and the question of what choice did she have was very simple to answer. They hadn't been in love. To have the baby and move back home with her parents was out of the question because her parents were living in Tanzania while her dad was knee-deep in writing his first script, a career change that would never see the light of day. What kind of role models were they anyway? Viv didn't know how parents were supposed to act and she wasn't about to figure it out herself. To stop her pursuit of oils, prints, clothes, jewelry, all that she created, to care for a baby? It had been unthinkable.

She'd made the decision the moment she found out and sealed it over fire-hot sake with her two best friends.

"What if you regret it later in life? What if you found yourself childless at forty and you realized that this had been your only chance?" Neddy, always the optimist. Even then she'd wanted so badly for them all to have children who would play together in their backyards for birthday parties and random barbecues and surprise pop-ins. Neddy had had this way of insisting that normal was natural.

Then Jean said, "We'll have children for her."

Viv finished the chairs and two cupboards and laid them outside to dry. Only one-thirty—too early for happy hour? She poured herself a sav blanc and opened her laptop to have a look at what Griffith had to offer. Her cat jumped onto her lap, and for a moment she was lost in the warmth of his purr. *I know. I know.* She breathed him in, then got back to all the restaurants and the cellar doors for a romantic couple's getaway. But Orion would be there, so she looked at the wildlife park, the hill with a lookout, the farm tour with tastings and the pool at the motel. The boy deserved to have fun and hopefully this would suffice. He'd just turned seven, was struggling with his dad's first girlfriend after Jean's death, but not as much as Stan was.

"Orion's got to come first."

Viv got it but knew it to be more multifaceted than that. "So can't she come second and still be an important part of your life?"

"I'm not sure if it'd work anyway. She uses those flush things that stick inside your toilet. Drives me batty. When would I ever find the time or the energy to make it work? I'm so tired, Viv. Probably too tired for a girlfriend. Ugh—that *word*. It's so adolescent. I'm beyond that now, aren't I?"

A girlfriend? No, Viv didn't think he was, so she'd offered to take Orion with her for the week she and Philip were to meet halfway between their homes. She hadn't thought of consulting with Philip, only thought it was something she really wanted: for Stan, for Orion, for herself.

So now they were leaving in five days, Friday, after school. They'd make a road trip out of it, stay overnight in Renmark, maybe some little place on the Murray. And the next day, would she look at Orion in the rearview mirror as they passed over the New South Wales border, and would her heart ache for what the boy had been through and for what he'd have to go through for the rest of his life, and would she think about Jean, once again, *We'll have children for her*? Yes, she would.

Maybe she was ready. "It's only hormones talking," she told her cat. But why now? In her mind, she played out an imagined conversation with Jason what's-his-name:

"I was pregnant with your baby and I aborted it without telling you." She envisioned an old wheelchair with pin-striped canvas and scratched metal. One that Jason found stylish, particularly in its refusal to be a motorized scooter. By all counts it was practical, transporting him around his house, across the street to the local shops, down the corner to the train station. And she knew its backstory, too: it was his first wheelchair. Mornings, it sat next to his bed, awaiting the curve of his arse, the weight of his upper body, the drooping of his legs. His trusted old friend and nemesis. It reminded him always of the car crash that had taken away his wife and unborn daughter.

Viv imagined meeting him at the café for her overdue confession. *"I was pregnant with your baby and I aborted it without telling you."* He would tell her he could no longer father children, the irony of the situation not lost on either of them, the sadness heavy and encompassing. And then Jason would cry. And then Viv would cry. And then the story, as she saw it, would end tragically with Jason going back home on the train, waiting for the conductor to lay down the ramp while some teenage boys looked almost sick watching him struggle to position himself for departure, as if the idea that one day they could be in wheelchairs had suddenly hit them, as if they finally realized the transience of "invincible." There were Jason's muscles working the handles on the wheels. There were Jason's hands, calloused. Jason's legs, dangling. Jason's phone, vibrating with Viv's message of "I'm so sorry," because she had told him, *"I was pregnant with your baby and I aborted it without telling you,"* and she imagined him not answering because he needed to get back to his lonely home so he could let go of his piss in the catheter.

"I should've been a screenwriter," she told her cat. "Taught my dad how to do it properly. Or a playwright like Marion." But she was the interior designer. And when Viv had known Jason it was Neddy who could write, Jean who could dance and Viv who could paint. Then it hit her, and the tears streamed quickly down her face. Neddy didn't write anymore, Jean was no longer alive, and his name was Jason Prant.

In the loo, looking despondently at the blood on her pad, Viv asked herself again, *What if I'd been pregnant this time?* She didn't play the whole scene out with this one. She only imagined the ending, which would be happy. Very Hollywood. Very Julia Roberts. She and Philip would have a baby girl, who they would dote upon, who they would travel the world *with*, who would have seriously incredible talents. A girl who would make them better people and make the world a better place. She and Philip would be the couple with the toddler on the beach.

It all seemed so simple, so easy, but would Philip make a good father? What made any man a good father? Stan was a good father, but he'd told her he doubted it nearly every day. He'd once said that a teacher at school had called him in because Orion had bullied a younger child as initiation into a gang, and Stan had seen pity for the Single Father in her eyes and he'd felt like screaming at her not to pity him, just tell him what to do.

"It's the not-knowing-what-to-do that makes me think I'm not doing it right."

"What the hell is right?" Philip had asked, reaching for Viv's hand, and Stan had responded, "If I knew, we wouldn't be having this conversation."

On the way home Philip had said, "It's good Bec never got pregnant. I'd have been a terrible dad."

After Viv had dealt with her past and her hypothetical future and come to realize that the present is simply what it is, she returned to the four chairs and two unhinged cabinets sitting on her balcony and brought them in. They looked good. A job well done. Inside, three small blocks of wood sat on the drop sheet on the living room floor. She would cut them into the shape of love hearts and paint them with the leftover pinks. Later, she would attach one to Orion's ceiling—he'd told her he still had trouble sleeping at night. Said he looked up at the ceiling most of the time, feeling lonely. She would give one to Philip too, because she wanted to give him all of her heart and somehow that little bit more. The last heart would go to Jean, though she'd hang it in her own bedroom. What a curious and glorious trio of hearts.

Riding Bikes

Stan and Jean were like two tires on a tandem bicycle, the road they traveled upon being their love. The purpose of their journey was evident: move forward. Their motto was a given: enjoy the ride, even the bumps. If one went flat, the other would carry the load and ride them to a safe place where they would find air and fill themselves so that they may begin anew. Like two tires on a tandem bicycle, Stan and Jean were one, and Stan and Jean were separate.

★

The afternoon before Jean's accident, the sparkling cider had been going down a treat, the scent of lamb smelling of good things to come. They'd been celebrating all right, their son climbing a jungle gym, enjoying the surprising burst of sunlight after an afternoon of rain. They hadn't told Orion the news yet. They were only trying to process it themselves. They'd told Stan's mum on the phone; it hadn't gone down too well.

"What if I die? What if I die and you are in America, in *Jean's* home, and can't say goodbye to me?"

"Mum, you survived cancer, for chrissake. And besides, you could get hit by a car tomorrow. You can't live your life thinking about death and you can't expect others to." In the silence Stan had imagined his mum swallowing with some difficulty and preparing her voice to drop a few levels. Which it did.

"Stan, I'm nearing eighty. What do you bloody expect?"

"You're years away from eighty, Mum."

"The cancer could come back. What if the cancer comes back?"

And Stan knew this. Stan felt this. "Mum, why don't you come over? Help us celebrate?"

"Why would I want to celebrate you leaving me for a year? It's my worst nightmare come true."

"Because Jean's glowing, because there's a double rainbow in the sky, because Orion said he's getting his kit off when it starts raining again, because we need a reason to open up the next bottle of sparkling. Should I go on?"

"Perhaps. I'm not sure I'm convinced."

"Because we can be together *now*."

Stan knew she hadn't needed any more convincing and that it was probably icing on the cake that Jean would be going to the pub with her friends for more celebrations later that night, so he'd be alone with Orion and wouldn't she want to spend the night with them?

"Only if you promise to get out the backgammon."

So he'd appeased his mother, if only temporarily, but her words had hit him and hit him good. Did he want to do this? He was thrilled Jean had won a fellowship at a university only hours away from her hometown and her mother, only hours away from her brother and her niece. She'd been living in Australia for twenty-two years now; didn't she deserve to go home for longer than a three-week holiday? She deserved to share the northern night sky with her son, where Orion's Belt was upside down, where she would say, "See, it's right-side-up!" Yes, he wanted this because she deserved it and because he loved the woman endlessly. They were a good fit. At night, curled on the couch, their arms the most comforting of limbs, no one reached for the remote; television was agreed upon with the same type of regularity as choosing which side of the bed to sleep on. Jean's taste in music might have leaned more toward the bluegrass of her upbringing while Stan never shied from Aussie glam rock, but they both sang boldly when Paul Kelly played from their stereo and they went to WOMAD every year, always coming home with a few CDs. Give these two their own bikes loaded with panniers and ask them where they wanted to go, however, and Stan and Jean would kiss each other a long farewell and point in two different directions.

At the outdoor table on the undercover deck, they were looking at a map, hypothetically and half-seriously planning The Great Bike Tour of Missouri. The rain started up again and Orion got naked, as planned, but Jean was able to talk him into a raincoat—they were practical parents when push came to shove. Jean's fellowship was at the University of Indiana, not far from the state where she'd grown up. Surely they'd have time to show Orion his mum's hometown from the best vantage point possible. A family bike trip. It seemed entirely possible.

They'd never done a major bike ride together. History had proven that Jean stuck to the long road of bitumen. Many a time she thanked Stan for introducing her to bike travel, then paid him back by leaving for weeks with a single-person tent strapped to the back of her bike. She did it every April, as a rule, though missed the year following Orion's birth. Still, that April, when Orion had been only three months, Jean had kissed her little boy on his eyelids and disappeared on her bike for a little over an hour.

Stan went bush and he went with friends. Every few years he spent thousands of dollars to dissemble his bike and stick it on a plane and land somewhere remote. He liked the hard road, the off-road, the fear and confidence it took to master it, which might explain why he didn't even mind the occasional stack. They reminded him that he was alive. They reminded him he was mortal.

When Jean had brought out the atlas and said, "We could do this," and Stan had popped the sparkling and said, "Yeah, we could," the year away became real. They could ride together, Orion on a tagalong attached to a tandem bike.

★

After Jean had died, Stan's bicycle gathered cobwebs. A film of plaster and dust rested on the sleek black seat while both tires lost air and settled in for a lengthy rest. Jean's road bike had been demolished, of course, but her touring bicycle had been given to the neighbors' teenage boy, along with one of her old helmets. It was almost ghostly when that kid rode up and down the street. Now there was the blue and red Avalanche—absent of its training wheels—and a little boy hopping on.

Without being aware of it, Stan had been preparing for this day since Orion was a baby. He hadn't imagined it would be on this footpath running diagonally through this nearly forgotten park and he hadn't imagined their dog Digger would be there but Orion's mum wouldn't, twenty-eight months dead. How could he ever have imagined it?

"OK, just look ahead on the path. Look where you want to go and pedal."

He could tell how nervous the boy was, clearly working on balancing his fear with some greater sense of confidence but coming up short on the confidence. Stan could see it in the way his son's eyes wouldn't rest on his own but scoured the track ahead of him, already looking where he wanted to go, yet needing a little security.

"Don't let go, Dad."

"I won't," he lied, knowing he would have to if he wanted his son to succeed. And just as Orion moved his foot to the pedal, Stan wondered if in any way his son connected with the absurdity of the moment: he was about to learn how to ride a bike, and it was a bike accident that had killed his mother.

But then he was off, the bike occasionally leaning to one side and Stan correcting it with his wrist, keeping the boy straight. "Good job, Orion, good job." But it was difficult to run with the bike while bending over so far, and eventually Orion fell.

"You OK, mate?"

"Why did you let go?"

"I didn't let go. I lost my balance as much as you did. I've never done this before, just like you. It's hard work. But it's pretty fun. And once you're riding this thing on your own, it'll be heaps fun. I promise."

"OK." It was a grumble but it was a good sign. This was going to happen and it was going to happen today.

Orion stood up and looked at his knees and hands while Stan pulled up the bike. He was a brave lad, so much like his mum: a risk-taker who had the good sense to be practical. Orion used to love that his mum rode her bike to work, but, after having ridden on the bus with her one rainy day to the city, he'd told his mum that she shouldn't ride her bike on rainy days. He'd told her that the day of the accident too. Even though she had her wet-weather gear on and assured him she wouldn't get too wet, he told her he didn't want her to "ride next to the big busses where all the people look out the windows and see you get splashed." Stan had laughed at his son's practicality and said, "You should listen to him," then kissed

Jean on the cheek, gently squeezed her arse and said, "See you later."

Some people would say, "At least she was doing something she loved," while others would say, "Rubbish—it's shit to be killed by something you love." More than two years later and Stan still didn't know what to make of it.

Orion took hold of the bike and swung his leg over it. "Are you ready, Dad?"

Stan laughed, wanting to say no, but yelled to his son, "Let's do it to it," something Jean used to say. "This time pedal a little faster. Sometimes the faster you go the easier it is to ride straight."

"But don't let me go."

"I won't."

Orion's foot left the ground and Stan held the bike firm, determined to give the boy a solid start. Then they were moving more assuredly than before. Stan felt the boy's equilibrium. Seconds must've passed before he took the firmness of his grip away from the bike seat. "That's it, that's it, that's it!" But then Orion stopped pedaling, looked down to the left, and fell accordingly.

"Dad, why did you let go?" This time there were tears.

"I didn't, mate. You were doing so well I just eased back, and then you got away from me. Sorry, Orion. Come on. Stand up and catch your breath."

Stan reached for the bicycle to hand to his son once he'd got some control of his breathing. Jean would've given him a hug before standing up the bike.

"OK, close your eyes."

Orion did as he was told.

"I want you to imagine the tires on your bike, right? See how they're rolling on the footpath? They're moving together, aren't they, the two wheels? Can you see them moving on the footpath?"

"Yes."

"They're going to go exactly where you want them to go if you just keep pedaling and looking straight ahead. Now, can you see yourself riding?"

"Yes."

"OK. Don't look down. Don't look back. Can you see yourself looking ahead to where you want to go?"

"Yes."

"Can you see yourself pedaling?"

"Yes."

"Are you having fun?"

Orion giggled, as if catching onto a joke. "Yes."

"OK, let's ride."

Orion swung his leg over his bike again, this time with great enthusiasm. The memory of his tears was as distant as their starting point 100 feet back.

"Don't let go, Dad."

"I won't."

This time Stan started pushing as soon as Orion's foot left the ground. "Pedal," he said, pushing him just that little bit more, and he didn't notice Digger taking a shit in the bushes, he didn't notice the strain forming in his back that would later force him to seek out a chiropractor for the first time in his nearly fifty years, he didn't notice that he'd made a firm decision to not yell out anything encouraging to his son so as not to disturb his concentration—all he noticed was that the boy felt safe, balanced and confident, so Stan let go, in so many ways.

★

A couple more years without Jean passed, the ghostly neighbor having gone off to live with some friends and so there were no more sightings of Jean's old helmet or bike. Orion had a new bicycle, one big enough for a nine-year-old boy and rough enough for the occasional homemade ramp and a little off-roading. Stan's bike came out of its corner rarely and only for short rides to the shops or around the neighborhood with his son. His bike was not happy being relegated to intermittent use when it knew it had once been a mighty mountain bike that'd seen the world. In fact it had had enough, so one day it yelled out to him, *Hey, fool, she might be gone, but I'm still here!* because bicycles do not understand the love shared between humans, only the love humans share with them.

Stan was surprised to hear from Neddy's husband Rodd as they only ever saw each other on social occasions with their families and friends, never one-on-one, and they'd only spoken to one another on the phone maybe twice before in all the years they'd known each other.

"A friend of mine is going to Far North Queensland for a two-week mountain bike trek, some organized group thing. I'm thinking about going. Never done anything like it before, but I reckon by May I'll be ready for a break. The house is crazy. Thought you might want to come along."

Did Stan want to go along? The thought of it sent a fright through him, but it was one full of adrenaline. "Oh, man, Rodd. I'll have to think about that one. How long can you give me to make a decision?"

"End of the week? He's got a few other guys in mind who might want the slot."

Seeing as it was Sunday, this sounded fair. Stan hung up the phone and went into the garage to sort through some hard rubbish for Monday's pick-up. That's when his bike called to him. He didn't hear any harsh tones, any name-calling, as it were. He heard a silent pleading, and wasn't sure if it had come from his bike or from deep within himself.

Damn, but he wanted back on! The thrill of the downhills and the barely marked paths; the slip of the gears going up an incline in the dirt or mud; the unremitting yet welcomed ache in his muscles when the day was over. But what to do with Orion? There was no family support because there was no family. Jean was obviously gone and so was his mother. She'd outlasted the doctor's estimation by almost a year but, in the end, the cancer had won. Painful as it was to her and painful as it was to watch, especially near the end when she'd moved in with them, Stan had known his mother was ready and, because of that, he had been too. Now the closest thing to family he and Orion had was Very Viv and Funtastic Phil. They were always willing, but they were busy people with interiors to design and students to teach. There was Neddy, who had taken Orion for three days when Stan had chaperoned a school camp the previous year. Orion had loved that time with Juniper. But there was a third child now, only four weeks old. Surely Orion would tip them over if the house, as Rodd put it, was crazy. Orion had his own friends from school, of course, and Stan was friendly enough with the parents to ask them for a favor. They always said, "Anything we can do. . . ." their faces so obviously full of compassion; but still, what if something happened to him on the trip? It wouldn't be the first time someone had broken a neck on a particularly tricky descent and become a paraplegic. It wouldn't be the first time an airplane had crashed. It wouldn't be the first time someone had been hit by a van on the way to the airport. Stan knew he couldn't live his life thinking about death, but he was a single parent. He couldn't help it. What would become of Orion?

Stan looked at his bike. There would be no going away with Rodd, but there was a serious need to start riding again. If he was going to go on an extended bike trip with anyone, it would be with Orion.

The night was hot, and Stan had moved the mattress into the lounge room to keep cool under the air-conditioning when he slept. He'd move Orion in to join him later, when he was ready to turn off the lights. For now, he'd sprawled himself on the mattress and welcomed Digger into his arms. "Too hot for this, boy," but he couldn't stop himself from petting and rubbing and feeling the warmth of his dog. Digger was getting old. He could never leave Digger now, either. He only had a handful of months left in him, if he was lucky. There was a chance Stan would have to put him down before the dog died on his own. Digger gave a dog-purr, as Orion called it. It was a satisfied low-pitched sound in a high-pitched octave from the back of his throat.

"Love you too, Digger."

He opened up the atlas of America, turned to the page that showed Missouri. The last time he'd looked at it was the afternoon before Jean's accident, when they'd been talking about their family bike ride. "What do you think about this, huh? You think Orion and I should go there one day when he's old enough?" But what was "old enough" when bicycling accidents plagued his dreams and, even worse, his consciousness?

Digger dog-purred again.

"You do? Fly into St. Louis, travel down to Lesterville, see Grandma Pearl?" They could even cycle over to Illinois, where Orion's Uncle John lived. Coraleen lived somewhere in Illinois too. They could make a summer of it. Hell, they could make a year of it. It would take a lot of planning, a lot of patient planning, but they could do it. "What do you think, boy?"

Digger's dog-purr was longer than usual, just a smidgen lower in tone as well, as if he was saying, "Go. Go as soon as you can. Life doesn't always wait."

To Jean Harley

Neddy felt she could not rise to the winter sun, sensed she might put her five-month-old son in his cot for another hour until he fell back asleep, try to wring more rest out of her worn-out body. He'd been fed. He'd been changed. There was a mobile to look at in the cot. An activity toy clipped to the side bars. He'd be fine. She couldn't be expected to hold it together every day.

Rodd was dressing, the curls of his hair still dripping onto his shirt. He never fully dried himself. He was either impatient or ambivalent, either way, at that moment, nearly shitting her to tears.

"You getting up?"

"No."

He bent over to kiss her forehead. "Try to have a good day, Ned. Do something fun with Leo."

As if it was easy. As if showering was simple. As if going somewhere fun wouldn't be complicated by filling up the car with gas. As if babies Leo's age didn't need at least two naps a day. As if she didn't need at least two naps a day. "I'm just tired, Rodd."

Juniper ran in to give kisses goodbye and left singing a pop song: a tween at nearly eleven years old. Willow was more tentative, waiting by the door until her mum patted the bed. She hugged longer. She kissed her baby brother too.

"Bye-bye, sweetie," Neddy said to her. "Have fun at school."

Rodd picked up his baby boy and hugged him as if there were music playing on the radio, something slower than what Juniper had been singing, then placed him next to Neddy on the bed. Leo squirmed into his mother's arms and breasts in a tussle of mirth, only causing the slightest upturn of one side of Neddy's mouth. Her aim was not to get caught up in playing. She discarded the cot idea, decided to let Leo fall back asleep in her arms. He was, after all, a lovely baby.

No, Rodd and Neddy hadn't planned on falling pregnant so soon after Willow. In fact, she and Rodd had been talking about vasectomies when Neddy felt the first ache in her breasts and the initial cravings for milk straight from the carton. The verdict was out for the first few days on whether or not it had been good news, but the idea of another baby grew on them as it grew in Neddy's belly, and before they'd even realized, they were preparing for a third child: web searches for a bigger car, measuring the office to make way for baby furniture. She'd felt the first flutters in her stomach very early, though Rodd could never feel them, and she compared them to those of her other children. Maybe this one would be a boy. Then she stopped feeling them. Neddy had told Rodd as she held the dead twenty-five-week-old baby girl in her hands that she had wanted to give her the middle name of Jean. And now, on the four-year anniversary of that little baby's birth and death, Neddy couldn't mourn for her without mourning for Jean too.

After the stillbirth, the decision to have a third child had made itself. Of course they wanted a baby and of course they wanted it before it was too late. Neddy had been forty-one at the time of the stillbirth and she didn't know how many more years she had left in her. Turned out she had at least three more.

He was a needy baby, cried a lot, but he seemed to like to cuddle the most of all of her children. "This one feels the love," she'd said on their first day back home after his birth.

Now he wouldn't fall asleep in Neddy's arms. He was cranky and confused by the scent of her milk at odds with his full tummy. Neddy gave up and carried him to the kitchen, where she strapped him into a reclining chair that sat on the table. It had squeaky soft bugs that dangled into his eyes, which mesmerized him until he finally fell asleep. Neddy, now over the idea of resting her own body, got to work.

With the dishes done and then veggies chopped well ahead of dinner, and somewhere in between these chores a few more pages of a book she'd borrowed so long ago from Jean, before the accident, which, now that she'd finally started reading it, felt like something of an addictive and guilty obligation, she'd somehow managed a shower too, so even if it was a sad day for Neddy, once it got started it had promise. Not the kind that makes you happy for birds and love and the miracle of life, but the kind that moves toward night, bit by bit, and does so without any disasters. She then attempted the garden.

In retaliation to the unseasonable rain in the middle of the December when Jean's bike went down, that February had brought with it the worst heatwave in Neddy's memory. A quick one, but harsh—three days over 109 degrees. Neddy's idea had been to get them all out of the house and into a cool environment every day. The first afternoon she'd taken the girls to the shopping center for things they needed but hadn't needed. They'd enjoyed an extended lunch of Hokkien noodles, which they all shared, however sloppily, with two pairs of wooden chopsticks. Four hours had melted away; a marvelous outing sprung from a shitty situation.

Another day they'd gone swimming. The place had been packed with children and mothers. Loud. Humid. Neddy had sweated into the water that buoyed her body as she walked Willow in big circles, singing to her to kick, paddle, paddle, kick, the baby squealing every so often.

The day at the museum had not been so good. Neddy had been tired from the heat and still grieving over Jean; she'd been tired of all the action, of all the trying to stay out of their hot tin house with the inefficient air-conditioning unit over the front door. They'd all become tired, got cranky. In the corridor to the restroom, where people had passed them and stared, they ended up crying and cuddling for their lives.

That night Rodd and Neddy had lit candles, sat outside and finished off a bottle of sav blanc, breast milk be stuffed. They'd talked about Jean and the family she'd left behind, Stan and their little boy Orion. They'd talked about death and how they lived life. They'd laid out a blanket and touched one another while looking at the stars. Their legs bent into one another. Things became frantic, flawless, like falling in love and the early days, before children. Neddy knew that it was partly the wine, partly the heat, but more so a reaction to the still painful loss of Jean mixed with the fact that she loved her husband very much. Mourning, releasing, magically conceiving. Neddy just knew that that had been the night they'd made their third baby girl.

When the heatwave had broken the next morning the wind blew passionately, opening the heavens and releasing a short burst of intensive rain. Neddy had stood outside in the garden, her body, the ground, the plants, everything cleansed. It'd seemed so unfair to be happy when Jean was gone, even the rain a reminder of the day Jean had been hit by the van, yet how could she not have been thankful? This was still life. She was still living. Time kept moving and plants kept growing, their sole watermelon big as Juniper's head.

Now, more than four years later, with her focus on a different baby, a little boy, it was a different garden.

Ned heard the postman and knew it would wake Leo. It always did. She walked around to the mailbox, knowing this would be the end of her own quiet time. She was reluctant to begin hands-on parenting again but knew, too, that she needed Leo to lift her out of her melancholic reverie.

Having a sign up on their mailbox that read No Junk Mail, Please was the right thing to do by the environment but it sometimes led Neddy to feelings of despondency. What was there to look forward to but bills? Where was the color in bills? Where were the surprises? This post, however, was different in that it brought a yellow envelope, handwritten to the five of them by none other than Stan. *Welcoming Day . . . long time coming . . . our backyard . . . welcome "Very Viv" and "Funtastic Phil" to the family.*

"Really." It wasn't a question but a statement. Not only a statement but a recrimination. This was a godparent-thing. Neddy was well versed in Baptisms, Naming Days and Welcoming Days and they all amounted to the same thing: an elder is chosen to help mold a child. Why the hell was Stan doing this when Orion was nine years old? And why the hell had he chosen Viv?

The emptiness Neddy felt did not ache nor smart from the adjoining pain of memory; it just sank, and sank endlessly, and still it endlessly sank, forcing Neddy to put down the invitation and make her way back to the kitchen, where Leo was beginning to stir. She made noise now, wanting the baby to waken, desperately needing him. What was happening here? Since when was Viv fit for playing a semi-maternal role? As far as Neddy knew, Viv didn't even like children. Neddy wiped something uncomfortable from her thigh: Weet-Bix. She'd yet to clean up Juni's and Willow's breakfasts, and now she had to sit on what was left of them.

Neddy's lungs were huge and her thigh muscles felt each long stride. Wasn't it good to don the Going-Out Boots? Wasn't she feeling sexy in the purple dress? It was her first night out since Leo was born and she was on a mission.

She thought every pub experience should be fun. There should be flashes of uncontrollable laughter, laughter that's sly, nervous laughter, laughter from outlandish confessionals, giggles, snorts, harrumphs. Such was the case before Jean's accident when Neddy and Viv were in the same room, but things had changed.

After the funeral Neddy couldn't get her head around the inappropriateness of Viv sleeping with Professor Sleazeman. Had it been Viv's slutty way of holding onto Jean? An if-I-can't-have-you-I'll-take-some-man-you-fucked thing? Neddy held onto that anger for months, avoiding the issue with Viv, so afraid she might explode. She avoided Viv too because it was the easiest way of ensuring that she didn't explode. And avoiding Viv had been so simple. Since Neddy had been the assumed organizer of all luncheons, dinners and drinks with Viv and Jean before the accident, after the accident she had a reason to stop organizing. As unfair as she knew it sounded, Jean was that reason. And when she'd stopped organizing, Viv hadn't taken over.

"She takes me for granted!" she'd yelled to Rodd. "She always has."

"You think that about everyone who loves you, Ned."

Trite emails had been exchanged saying, "We should catch up," but they didn't. Neddy had found herself stalking Viv's Facebook page, enraged all over again to find happy photos of Viv and Professor Sleazeman. But when Ned had lost the baby, she wanted to see Viv. She'd needed a woman to talk to. A woman's ear. A woman's touch. Unfortunately, she'd forgotten that Viv had never been that woman, and when it had taken Viv three days to surprise her with flowers after she'd let her know through a short email, Neddy hadn't been impressed. Jean had taken three *hours* to book a plane ticket to America after she'd been told about her sister-in-law's depression. She'd gotten on that plane and flown halfway around the world to help in any way she could, while Viv couldn't even listen to Neddy for more than a few hours, saying she needed to go back to work. *Fucking work!*

What Ned had resented most about Viv visiting with lavender and daisies was that it had not been Jean visiting with soup.

After she'd given herself time to grieve, Neddy had come to the decision that Viv was not to blame and the whole issue was to be chalked up to people moving on. There would never be any hard feelings, there would never be any animosity. What Neddy had told Rodd was: "We have great memories, though, and that will never go away." Now, walking toward the Crown & Sceptre (because the Cellar was certainly out of the question), Neddy hoped it would be enough.

She saw her first at the crossing. Actually she saw Viv's Going-Out Boots in their bright lime vinyl glory first, suddenly feeling hers were incomparable. She stood back for a moment, taking in her old friend, who seemed to have aged far less than Neddy had in the last couple of years. But, as far as she knew, Viv wasn't dealing with a new baby in her mid-forties. She wasn't sleepless and frantic with two other children, a husband and a dog. What could possibly age her but the sweet passage of time?

Vivian was stunning, Neddy had to admit, if slightly discombobulated after searching in her bag for something and coming up empty-handed when the lights changed. And though Neddy thought she might have even flinched when she saw her, there was genuine warmth. So Neddy came up to Viv and linked arms. As Viv looked up, Neddy felt the cold of an Antarctic wind on her cheeks. She squinted and smiled and tried to forget about jealousy and her yearly blues brought on by the raw memory of the stillbirth, but neither is something a person can squelch and, truthfully, Viv irked her. Now, adding kindling to the fire, Viv and her boots had become the perfect catalyst for Neddy's insecurity. *Just let us be able to laugh*, she told herself.

They hugged briskly, in that surprised sort of way, commented on the horrid weather, each other's boots. They huddled into one another as they made their way into the pub.

The Crown & Sceptre was warm with all of the bodies giving off energy and an open fire in the corner. "My shout," Viv said. "Red OK?"

Neddy nodded, becoming lost in a moment of *don't-I-know-you?* with a man sitting at the end of the bar. She nudged Viv. "Hey, does that guy look familiar to you?" He was a very large man with a long, pointed beard.

"Goodness, no, why would he?" Viv put the change from the bottle of wine in her purse and began scouting the room for a place to sit.

"Oh my god." Neddy grabbed her arm.

"Shit, Ned, you made me spill! What?"

And then they were off, Neddy pulling Viv toward Charles Cromwell II.

"Excuse me, but I think I remember you. From the hospital. You were writing and you stared at us a lot. Then I saw you at Jean Harley's funeral standing all alone, like you didn't know anyone. Did you know our friend Jean?" It was him, all right. The beard, bald head, the soft and sad eyes. Neddy wondered if this was the ex-con her old friend Lisa had told her about. What was his name again?

The women stared at him, waiting for him to say something. He stared back, as if trying to say something too. Then he said it: "I ran over her." Charley looked down at his hands and began picking at skin while Viv gasped and Neddy said, "Jesus fuck," because the strangest things leave our mouths in moments this intense.

Still looking down, he began mumbling how sorry he was, how sorry he was, and when he looked up, Neddy could see he was holding in more than just tears. There was a lifetime of hurt in this man's eyes and he couldn't stop scratching his neck. As she stood there, unsure of how to react to his apology, she remembered hearing about him from her old friend Lisa at Jean's funeral, who knew this man, and probably had come to the funeral with him, now that she was putting it together. Lisa had taught him to read in prison and she still received letters from him. She'd said he was a gentle and kind man, and that the accident had torn him apart.

"Why don't we all sit down for a drink? There's a quiet room over there." Viv pointed with the bottle of wine to the two empty couches at the back, and though Neddy had momentarily wanted to comfort the man, she now cringed inside her woolen coat, thinking how many times they'd gone to a pub like this with Jean, and thinking, *Jean should still be here. Not this man.*

The three found space on two couches, where Neddy and Viv sat closely together, touching not because they physically had to but because emotionally they did.

"What's your name?" Viv poured the wine out in equal measure for her and her old friend, cool as always—Charley had a whiskey. Neddy was a mess of knots, wondering what they were doing having a drink with this man whose name was on the tip of her tongue.

"Charley."

Holding up her glass, Viv solemnly said, "Well then, to Jean Harley."

"To Jean Harley." They clinked. No one was smiling. There was no pub laughter from their small table.

Neddy took a sip and said, "I can only have one. Maybe two. I'm breastfeeding."

"I've seen photos of him. He's gorgeous, Ned."

"I got your flowers at the hospital. Gorgeous, too." Neddy inhaled deeply, stiffening all over. She'd have liked her reaction to be an obvious one of sarcastic proportions but Charley's presence superseded all that. Here was a man who'd not only taken Jean's life but now took her place at the table. Neddy couldn't hold her breath forever and when she let it out, she lost her composure. "I'm sorry, why did you go to the funeral? Weren't you in prison for murder or something?"

"Ned!"

"I don't care, Viv. I'll say what I want. I'm not going to pretend he's our *friend*." She stopped short of saying, "or that *we're* even friends." Their moment had passed. This was now about Jean.

"It's OK," he said, then he tried to tell them what the accident was like but it was difficult; he seemed to have so few words. They egged him on and he tried to describe the state of the woman who'd opened her car door and how the woman's baby cried bloody murder until somehow the light rain had lulled it to sleep. They wanted details and he had them, though it was hard to understand him through the mumbles but he managed a story about cars passing him and how he'd felt guilty and ashamed and wished he could've hidden. Neddy, despite her breasts, drank from her third glass while they asked more questions, becoming apologetic themselves as he tried to tell them where he'd been going, how he had remembered thinking Jean was crazy cycling on a morning like that, and what it had felt like when he found out she'd had a son. His stilted language meant they only got snippets of each story but it was, however, enough. So often Neddy came in charging like a bull then bowed her head in submission. She was submitting to Charley now. He was only human. Someone else's child.

But then she felt the beast in her rising again when Charley asked how Jean's family was.

"Have you seen much of Stan and Orion, Viv?" Neddy stuck the heels of her Going-Out Boots into the floor, bracing herself as an ex-girlfriend might when asking the boy who broke her heart if he was happy with his new girlfriend. Maybe their moment was going to surface after all. Maybe it couldn't be helped.

"They're getting on. Stan's mainly focused on work and being a single dad to Orion. Hasn't met anyone else. I don't think he's trying too hard. A few dates here and there, nothing serious, though I wish it could be otherwise. He's a good man. He deserves to be happy. And Orion, you know, he's doing well at school. He's a lovely boy, just so lovely. He's started playing the guitar. You know he's only nine and he's writing his own songs? Can you imagine?"

"I was writing poetry at nine, so why not? Kids are just little people, Viv. They each seem so amazing and unique, but they're just little people." Neddy should have left it at that but she couldn't suppress her laughter. It was sarcastic, not an ingredient for a good night at the pub.

Viv's look at Neddy seemed one half confusion and the other half caution. She turned to Charley and said, "I don't have children of my own, but I love Orion. We're very close. I'm glad he's in my life."

"We all love Orion." What should have been gentle words of Neddy's had a sting in them and were meant as a challenge for Viv.

"Of course we do." And from the sound of her voice, Viv appeared to have flicked away the stinger and accepted the challenge.

Whether Charley had caught on as well was not on Neddy's mind; she was that focused on how annoyed she was at the Welcoming Day invitation. She knew it was inappropriate given the unique circumstances presented to them tonight, but she couldn't help it. "I feel like I don't know who you are, Viv."

"Why would you? You haven't wanted anything to do with me since Jean died."

Neddy felt the need to roll up her sleeves and get down to business, this being The Moment, such a long time coming. "Sorry, Charley, I just can't . . ." Neddy looked up to the ceiling and shook her head. "If you hadn't taken Jean out just so you could sleep with that *boy* at the pub, she'd be here now. With us. Have you ever even thought of that?" She'd said it. She wasn't sure if she really believed it—the trite old saying of "accidents happen" had lasting merit and Neddy held true to the chaos of life and randomness of days—but she'd stewed over the theory for years now. How much of what she'd said was grounds for ending their friendship and how much was simply reaching for a reason?

"How dare you." It was quiet and measured, but Neddy saw that it easily could've bubbled over. "How dare you say that. Jean was Jean that night. She was dancing, she was celebrating, so don't you dare say I made her do a thing. She *wanted* to be out and I am *so* happy I got to dance with her on the last night of her life." Viv was staring Neddy down, leaning forward, her muscles taut, a statue.

Charley signaled the bartender with a lift of the chin and a whiskey on the rocks was brought to him. "I take it you need one of these, mate?"

"Ta."

The girls didn't miss a beat.

"If you're so sure it was all my fault, then why didn't you ever say anything? Why didn't we ever talk about it? You never contacted me. You dumped me like we'd never even mattered after Jean died."

"So if I don't contact you then we're not friends? It's completely up to me? You could've called me. I'm pretty fucking busy too, Viv. I don't just go to work then knock off at five and wait for people to invite me out. I've got a family. I've got a very full life."

"Whoa, Ned, slow down. What's—"

But Neddy didn't slow down. "Remember uni, Viv? You, me and Jean putting on plays, making art, meeting guys, traveling. We were all new to life then. It was all so equal and easy. It's not now, is it? You're perfect and Jean's dead and I'm just . . ." She used both of her hands to motion to her body.

"Equal?" Viv scoffed. Another laugh for the list. "You and Jean got all the good guys."

"Me? I had no guys. It was you and Jean. Jean had the accent and you had the charm."

"Jean had the amazing body and you had this way of making boys want to be men."

"What?" Neddy turned to Charley, who was tugging on the point of his beard. "Excuse us, Charley," she said, then turned back to Viv. "That's bullshit, Viv. Jean was good at conversation. You had sophistication. I can't believe we're even talking about this."

"No, Jean was the most adventurous. Guys loved that about her." Viv looked at Charley, still tugging away. "She used to suggest rock climbing for a first date." She looked back at Neddy. "You were the most caring. When a guy needed sympathy, he went with you."

"What, like when he broke up with his girlfriend?"

"Yeah, you were always there!" It was a good-hearted joke that they both smiled at, tentatively.

Viv poured more wine. Neddy put her hand over her glass. "Enough for me. I need water."

The uncomfortable man, and rightly so, got up uneasily from the table and offered to get the water. "I could use another whiskey, eh." He looked around the room and Neddy wondered if once he'd made it to the bar he might keep on walking out the door. She felt sorry for him for what they were doing. She felt sorry for Viv, for their damaged friendship. She wondered, if the two of them had gotten it all wrong, had gotten *each other* completely wrong, what about Jean? If she'd been here, with them, instead of the man who'd caused her death, what would she have said?

Neddy realized that her Moment had shifted. She began again, this time without accusation. "You were always so successful, Viv. Things seemed to just fall into your lap and you'd take them and grow them into bigger things. I'm a jealous bitch, I know, but I have the upper hand on children. It's just what it is. And I can't bear for you to take that away from me."

"Welcoming Day, right? Ned, I'm not going to be his mother. His mother is Jean. His mother will always be Jean. I only want to be his friend. Stan's just doing this because he wants Orion to be taken care of if anything happens to him. He's making it official in his will and we decided to celebrate because of Jean. Jean loved a party and would've wanted to celebrate too."

"What, celebrate you and Professor *Sleaze*man? Oh, sorry: Funtastic Phil, wherever that came from."

"Ned, stop. I love Orion and so does Philip. We both want what's best for him. We both want to be happy for him when he's thrilled to bits with a song he's written, you know? The little things and the big things."

"I know. I'm sorry. I'm screwed up, I'm sad, I'm hormonal, tired, scared, drunk, what have you."

"Jean was the dancer, you were the writer. Have you written anything lately? Do you ever write about Jean?"

"I haven't written in years."

Charley returned with a small jug of water and three glasses, one filled with whiskey. "I write letters." He looked no one in the eye.

"I know Lisa. She said you write beautiful letters."

"Can't spell worth shit. Me mum used to write me letters."

"So she passed that onto you?"

"Guess. Guess it'll stop with me cause I don't have anybody to pass it onto. Don't have me own kids."

"Does that make you sad? Not having children?"

"Never thought it was something I'd do, but I reckon so."

"What about you, Viv? Are you still glad you never had children?"

"I'm not so sure I'd use the word 'glad.'"

"Every kid could use more love, eh." Charley poured out the waters and drank from his whiskey. "Coming from a man who never had a dad and misses his mum like hell."

A long silence ensued. Somehow, between this new trio, it was a very comfortable silence. Neddy looked at Charley. She was glad he was with them. And she was glad she was with Viv again. And though this trio would never meet in any pub or anywhere else ever again, and though Neddy would return to considering Charley the man who ran over her old friend Jean and Viv an old friend she used to know like a sister but didn't see anymore, it felt right in the Crown & Sceptre. So right that Neddy picked up her water glass and said, "To Jean Harley."

"To Jean Harley."

And though it was another somber cheers, this time they all managed to smile. Before the night was over, they would laugh too.

How to Fill an Empty Space

He'd finished the letter to Orion. It took years of starting then crumpling up then discarding the idea entirely but, after meeting Neddy and Viv in the pub four-and-a-half years after Jean Harley's funeral, he knew the time was now. He couldn't let what happened with his mum happen again. When he'd finally sat down to write her his first letter from prison, she'd been dead for two years. Orion was only a kid and would probably live for another seventy years, but accidents happen.

He took the envelope off his fridge, leaving a space he'd never fill again. No electricity or water bill, no calendar telling him what week was the yellow bin and what week was the green, no coupon for a six-inch sub would ever fill the space where Orion's envelope had hung for years. He'd even thought about putting it back and hand-delivering the letter because once he put the letter in the envelope, sealed it up and mailed it off, Orion would be gone from his life, and Orion had shared every meal with him, more than a thousand packs of cigarettes, gallons and gallons of coffee and highballs and shots of whiskey. Could his life get any lonelier? Placing the letter into the envelope, sealing it up and walking down the street to the mailbox where he dropped it into the slot, he was about to find out.

~

It was a fairly long walk on a narrow road without a footpath, past a few houses set back in the bush, past two cyclists in their Lycra and clip-on shoes. *They'd better be careful,* he said to himself. He always said that to himself. Charley breathed heavily and sweated around his neck and the backs of his ears, under his arms, where his belt held up his pants, between his legs and inside his socks. He wasn't in good shape and was resigned to the fact that he never would be, so what was the point? Maybe the day he couldn't do this walk was the day he'd decide things needed to change. Or the day he packed it in. For now, stuff it. A little exercise wasn't going to kill him. A lot might, though.

It was like slow motion putting the letter through the slot, saying hello and goodbye at the same time to a little boy he'd known for years though only ever met once, at Jean Harley's funeral. This was it. *This* was *it*.

Back at home there was a letter waiting for him. *What are the bloody chances?* No, not a letter. Not quite. A postcard. His first too. Seeing it was from Lisa (who else could it be?), he smiled.

On the front was a photograph of the MacDonnell Ranges. Maybe at sunset, maybe sunrise. Pink either way. Long ranges, ones he couldn't have imagined without seeing them on the front of this card even though Lisa had described them many times before. "You lucky dog," he said, meaning Lisa, such a funny turn of phrase, but seeing those ranges on the glossy postcard, he definitely thought her lucky.

Dear Charley,
I hope you like the look of Alice Springs because I'm inviting you up
for a Christmas holiday. It's high time you met the family. No need
to bring presents, just say yes!
Your friend,
Lisa

Charley walked around the back of his house and lit a smoke, inhaling deeply and looking at the sun reflecting off the leaves, mist in the air from the morning's rain, still dripping from the trees. So different from where Lisa lived. Could he afford the trip? He wasn't thinking about money because all he ever bought were a few tins of soups, some fresh eggs, cheap sausages, milk, coffee, whiskey and secondhand books and lots and lots of smokes, so he had plenty of money in the bank; could he afford the experience?

Wasn't life simple in this open prison space of his where he could go days without saying anything? Wasn't their friendship simple, just the two of them and with only pieces of paper between them? *Coward*, he thought and shook his head as if shaking off his very cowardice and making an easy decision.

He'd have to go to the thrift store and buy a suitcase. Nothing big. Something for a few shirts and an extra pair of jeans. Something with a pocket for his toiletries. Did he need a toiletries bag too? The suitcase would have to be big enough to carry some presents, even though she'd said not to bring any. But what would he bring for a family of people he'd never met? Her children weren't children anymore. Maybe he didn't need to bring them anything after all.

Charley focused on a single leaf and it came to him.

The salvage yard had just what he needed: a large slab of gray cement.

"Nice to see you, Charley."

"You too, Don."

"See you next time."

"See you, Don."

A friendly little place.

At home he took his tools out from the shed he'd built himself when he first moved in after getting out of prison. He smashed the slab into smaller pieces, then picked the right one to chip away, smoothed out the corners of edges, leaving only dust to be taken by the wind. It took him one weekend and three nights to get it right, almost thirty hours, he reckoned, and it was just right, fitting perfectly into his new but old suitcase, adding quite a bit of weight but fitting in flat among his few shirts and extra pair of jeans. He stuffed socks and jocks into the corners, probably more than he needed, so the piece wouldn't move around too much. He had no idea how they'd handle his luggage on the bus. He'd never been on a bus with luggage. He'd just have to ask if he could load it himself and he'd have to be there when they unloaded it too. It was precious cargo, this first present he'd ever given anyone other than his mum. A carving of a stack of ten books, piled high, with *YOUR FRIEND, CHARLEY* engraved on top.

The bus ride was long and all the way to Coober Pedy he sat behind a rank-smelling man, though he himself was no flower. The city turned to suburbia, then spread to the open space of the mid-north, then to complete desolation: Aboriginal communities, gas stations at pubs, the old all-in-one where the bus driver would stop and pick up and drop off packages while the passengers hurried toward toilets and meat pies and the longed-for cigarette.

Sleep was a bitch because here was a man who enjoyed sleeping on his side with a duvet to his chin and now he had to sit up straight and tilt his head back and, if it fell to the side, be very aware of the passenger next to him but not so aware that he couldn't sleep, so here was a man who didn't get much sleep and felt cold without a blanket.

More than twenty hours later and the bus pulled into Alice Springs, the MacDonnell Ranges welcoming him. As were Lisa and one of her kids. The back of Charley's neck ached from the sleep and now itched from nerves. Lisa began waving to him before the bus even stopped. Already he was preparing for the hug that would come, for Lisa's tears that would fall because she'd always been a bit of a wimp, for the introduction to the kid. And would the kid know her mother had taught him to read in prison? That he was a murderer, guilty as charged? That she used to call him Rascal because he'd been too afraid of his own name? That Lisa had come down to visit him once, years ago, to take him to the funeral of a woman he'd run over with his van on a rainy morning and left a young child to grieve for the rest of his life? What would he do, hold out his hand and say g'day, pretending not to notice that the kid couldn't close her mouth from the shock of taking in the size of him? His ugly mug? The tattoos and scars?

Charley walked down the steps of the bus to a dry heat and bevvy of flies, looking at Lisa nearly jumping up and down and her kid standing there nonplussed. He looked to the left at the bus driver opening the luggage compartment where his second-hand suitcase held the present for Lisa to place in her backyard, near the veranda, so she could see it when she read his letters and so her kids and her husband, too, could say, "That's from that strange man called Charley," then think about what it might feel like to be the reason for not one but two people losing their lives. And here was Lisa and the kid, walking to meet him, the bus driver hefting the suitcase carefully to the ground. And here was Charley, thinking to himself, *This is it.* This *is* it.

Downhill

Comfort comes in many ways and this one came in the slice of a pizza: the way the heat bubbled on the pepperoni and the pepperoni crunched when he bit in, the way the cheese stretched over his tongue then settled warm in his belly. Orion looked up at his dad, who was too busy for words—they both were—too hungry to do anything but eat, and this was comfort. On this tremendous bike trip through Missouri, the boy was learning that there is life and there is death, and in between there is great hunger and thirst. His dad took a long swig from his beer and Orion took one from his milk, then they both went back to eating. How good life could be.

Orion knew adults had it tough. His dad had to get up early and go to work and when he was at home he had to do so many chores. He had to take care of the garden and mow the lawn and chop the wood, and he had to buy food and cook food and do dishes, and he had to go to the hardware store and Big W and, when their car kept breaking down, the mechanic as well. And he had to drop him off at school and pick him up and take him to soccer on the weekends and swimming on Thursdays, and that was tough, Orion knew, but Orion refused to believe that he, a twelve-year-old boy, had it any easier. He had friends to worry about. Sometimes they seemed to like him and sometimes they didn't. Sometimes he felt like one of the cool and happy kids and sometimes he didn't. He made up songs and played his guitar. The songs were about being lonely.

"I'm not like them, Dad. They've all got mums. It's different in our house. They don't understand."

"No, they probably don't understand. And yeah, it's very different in our house."

They'd been slurping up pasta, a plate of buttered bread between them. The house had been quiet. Orion drank from a glass of milk. His dad drank from a glass of beer.

"I mean, their mums do stuff at school, like they help with reading or canteen or breakfast club, and at home they probably do heaps of stuff with them."

"I know. It's not fair. But we have fun, right? We've got a pretty good life."

Orion nodded yes and smiled, not looking at his dad. He wasn't so sure his dad understood either, but it was OK, because that was the night his dad had told him they were going on a bike ride. A big bike ride. And now they were on holiday: no issues with friends, no work or school or sport, no chores, no errands: just holiday. By day they rode and at night they camped. At first it felt impossible. No way were they going to cover 383 miles on bicycles. Orion was just a kid and cycling was tough. Sometimes he ached. Sometimes he fought through the ache and was left with pure annoyance. Sometimes there was pain. From exhaustion. From a fall. Sometimes he cried. But then there were daily feelings of joy and pride, like he'd never felt before, where small mountains became big triumphs and fast creeks and surprise waterfalls screamed at him that he was lucky, that he and his dad had it good, that life was actually great.

Today was a day of strong wind; even the blockade of hardwood trees couldn't lessen its impact. Orion and his dad had debated over their morning tea of Nutella, banana and honey sandwiches whether a headwind or an uphill was worse. Unlike his dad, Orion said an uphill. His dad had said it might seem harder because his body was smaller and his muscles not so strong, but that it could also have to do with his outlook. He'd said when you can't see the top of the hill, it seems like you're never going to get there and that's when it's really hard, but you've just got to remember that there *is* a peak and, when you get to it, it's an easy ride from then on, it's all downhill from there. Orion only knew that he'd struggled so much going through the Ozark Mountains that he'd forgotten what his dad had said and had a breakdown on the side of the road. Tears. He'd said he was not going to ride any further.

"You're the strongest boy I know, Orion. If anyone can do this it's you."

"I can't. I've got no muscles."

"They're there; you just can't see them yet. But you know what I can see?"

"What?"

"Your determination. Remember, it's downhill once the climb is over. I know you, mate. You can conquer anything."

So he did. They did. Together. And now there was pizza.

"That was good," his dad said after tucking into the first slice, then taking another drink from his beer and looking around at the giant vats that had brewed it. He was calling the trip The Great Bike Tour of Missouri, but Orion was calling it The Great Brewery Tour of Missouri because they seemed to dine at one whenever they could. His dad thought pizza and beer was the perfect combination after a day of cycling (unless he'd ordered a burger) and Orion thought it was pizza and milk (unless he'd ordered pulled pork). He was a seventh grader now, and his grow-ing bones craved milk like nobody's business. He could match his dad's two pints of beer every time.

Stan slid an envelope across the table, landing it right by the milk. It had Orion's name on it. The stamp was from Australia. According to the lettering around the stamp, whoever had mailed the letter to him had done so over two years earlier.

"What's this?"

"It's another letter about Mum."

Orion had once been accustomed to letters about his mum. They came at a pretty steady pace the year she died. They were supposed to help him remember her, even though the stories written in them weren't his memories. He kept them in a box under his bed and sometimes pulled them out when he missed her. He tried to imagine her catching crayfish in the creek with Uncle John when they were kids living in Missouri. They called them crawdads; he liked that word and he was going to call them that as soon as he and his dad finally got to that creek. He tried to imagine his mum laughing so hard in the library that she got kicked out. He tried to imagine her in dance school when she was his age, and again when she was older, and again when she'd come to Australia and taught it to little girls. He tried to imagine *her*, but the image was vague, only solid when found in a photo-graph. He hadn't gotten a letter about his mum since he was little: five or six, some when he was seven. Why in the world was he getting one now and who in the world was Charley Cromwell?

Orion flipped the envelope around. It had already been opened.

"Why didn't you give it to me when it came?"

"The time wasn't right."

"And you think it's right now?"

"I've got no idea, mate. How about after you read it, you let me know if I've done the right thing?"

Orion nodded, wanting nothing more than to read it straight-away. He looked at his dad with his eyebrows raised.

"You want to read it now?"

"Yeah."

"Why don't you wait till you're alone? When we get back to the tent you can take the torch in with you."

"OK, Dad."

"OK, son."

Both took a drink from their glasses and reached for another slice of pizza.

They'd made their campsite in a small clearing in the woods. At the end of every hard ride—and they were all hard rides, just some harder than others—Orion and his dad would veer off the road, take the non-traveled path, which wasn't a path at all, and find a spot just big enough for their two-man tent and a small fire. Sometimes the remnants of an older fire made their campsite an obvious choice, but sometimes the spot looked as if it hadn't been discovered by any other human being, let alone two travelers from South Australia.

This one was perfect for the two of them. They'd have to maneuver around a small dogwood when going from tent to fire and a decent-sized redbud when going from fire to bikes, but it looked like the kind of spot they wanted to call home for a night. The ground was clear of large roots and clumps of long grass, and it was soft, a bed of leaves and rich black dirt. Squirrels climbed up and down trees.

When they got back from dinner, Orion's dad busied himself with the fire while Orion oiled their bike chains. It had become his regular job and he could do it almost without thinking. Tonight, as he spun the pedal, he thought about his mum when she'd been alive. He had plenty of memories, but he was old enough to know that some of them might not be his own, that some of them came from the letters people sent to him or, most likely, from his dad. The one he thought of now was of his mum and him playing the animal game, where they had to name an animal then cross the yard being that animal, and he always remembered her as a squirrel, making herself small and running in little bursts, jolting her neck at every noise and puffing up her cheeks as if they were filled with acorns. Most Australian four-year-olds didn't know what squirrels were, but thanks to his mum Orion had not only known what they were, he'd known how they moved, what they ate and how they ate. He knew his mum should be here in this clearing with them right now, pointing at the squirrels in the trees, with Orion saying, "Remember that animal game? Remember when you were a squirrel?" The memory of his mum as a squirrel was his and his alone.

"I'm done, Dad."

"OK. Torch is on the picnic table."

There was still light but it would be dark in the tent. Normally Orion was asleep before the sun had gone down but tonight he was mentally energized, ready for the letter from Charley Cromwell.

"Night, Dad." He kissed his dad goodnight as he did every night, still young enough to not be embarrassed yet old enough to know that his dad felt privileged.

"Night, Orion."

As he unzipped the tent, his dad said, "Great riding today."

"Yeah, it was."

DEAR ORION,
I NEVER GOT A LETTER FROM A STRANGER
BEFORE BUT I AM GESSING ITS PRETTY WEERD.
IF YOU COULD SEE ME YOU WOULD THINK I WAS

*REALLY WEERD. I GOT A GRAY BEERD THAT
GOES DOWN TO MY BELLY AND I GOT A RELLY
BIG BELLY. I AM VERY TALL. I GOT ME BUILD
FROM DEAR OLD MUM WHO WAS A STRONG
WOMON. I AM BALD AND I AM MISSING 3 TEETH
THO YOU PROBLY WOULD NOT NOTIS THE
MISSING TEETH IF I DID NOT TELL YOU. I HAVE 2
TATOOS I WISH WERE NOT THERE AND 1 I LIKE. I
GOT A SCAR BY MY EAR I HATE EVEN MORE
THAN THE BAD TATOOS. WOW WHAT AN
UNLUCKY BUGGER I AM! I HAVE DISLEXIA SO I DO
NOT SPELL GOOD BUT I AM NOT STUPID. IT TOOK
ME A LONG TIME TO REELIS I AM NOT STUPID. I
HOPE YOU CAN READ THIS LETTER OK.*

Orion was glad Charley told him about the dyslexia because he
was thinking the guy might be a bit slow since he misspelled so
many words and he'd actually been thinking it was strange that
his mum had even known somebody who couldn't spell.

*NOW I HAVE TO BE ONEST AND SAY I DID NOT
KNOW YOUR MUM SO WHY WAS I AT THE
FUNREL? GOOD QUESION. I MUST HAVE ASKED
MESELF THAT 12 TIMES AT THE FUNREL. ITS BEN
A LONG TIME NOW AND I AM STILL ASKING IT.
SOMTIMES THINGS HAPEN AND THEY ARE RELLY
BIG THINGS AND THEY MITE NOT HAPEN TO YOU
OR EVEN SOMONE YOU KNOW BUT THEY ARE SO
BIG THAT YOUR LIFE CHANGES. I CULD SAY I AM
WRITING YOU THIS LETTER BECAUSE I WAS AT
THE FUNREL AND THEY TOLD US TO BUT ITS
MORE THAN THAT. ITS BECOS I WANTED TO TELL*

YOU THIS IN PERSEN BUT I AM NO GOOD WITH
WORDS WHEN I HAVE TO SPEEK THEM.

YOU PROBLY HERD THE STORY BY NOW ABOUT
YOUR MUMS ACCIDINT. SOMONE OPENED A CAR
DOOR WICH NOCKED YOUR MUM OFF HER BIKE
AND THEN SOMONE RAN OVER HER. I AM SORRY
TO SAY THAT WAS ME. I AM THE ONE WHO RAN
OVER HER.

The tears came immediately. Orion didn't know if he was angry with this man for running over his mum or shocked from having just read about it or sad because now the vision of the accident was somehow clearer simply because the driver had been given an identity or horrified that the man had the guts to send him this letter, but he was crying. A private cry, and he didn't want his dad to hear and he didn't want to hear it himself. So he stopped and listened for the sound of the creek, where they had rinsed off the long ride after their tent was up, where they would rinse away their long sleep the next morning. He calmed then and sniffled slowly, afraid to make any noise. He breathed through his mouth until he felt better.

I DID NOT KNOW YOUR MUM BUT I THINK OF HER
EVERDAY. JUST LIKE I DO NOT KNOW YOU BUT I
THINK OF YOU EVERYDAY TO. SOMTIMES THE
WIND PICKS UP AND I THINK OF HER LIKE HER
SPIRITS BEN CARRIED BY THE WIND AND IT
BRUSHES PAST ME JUST TO REMIND ME THAT I
AM SPOSED TO BE HAPPY FOR LIFE. IT IS A HARD
THING TO DO. ALL WAYS HAS BEN. ITS BECOS I

WAS A LONLY KID AND I GREW UP TO BE A LONLY MAN. I DO NOT KNOW WHY THAT WAS. I USE TO THINK IT WAS BECOS I DID NOT GROW UP WITH A DAD. HE DIED WHEN I WAS LITTLE LIKE YOU WERE LITTLE WHEN YOUR MUM DIED. THAT CAN MAKE A PERSEN MAD. BUT NOW I AM PRETTY MAD AT MESELF BECOS I SHUD HAVE BEN OK WITH ONLY HAVING MUM AROUND. SHE WAS A GRATE MUM. SHE FED ME AND KEPT ME IN CLOSE AND TOOK ME PLACES AND TALKED TO ME. SHE LOVED ME. AND I LOVED HER TO BUT I WAS TO ANGRY TO SHOW IT AND YOU KNOW WHAT? ITS TO LATE NOW. SHE DIED TO AND NOW I GOT NO MUM BUT I WANT TO TELL YOU THAT SHES NOT GONE. TO THE OUTSIDE WURLD SHE IS BUT NOT TO THE INSIDE OF ME AND HAVING YOUR MUM ON THE INSIDE IS A BEUTIFUL THING MATE. ORION I AM RELLY SORRY ABOUT YOUR MUM. IF I COULD CHANGE ANTHING ABOUT MY LIFE IT WOUD BE THAT DAY. I COULD HAVE LEFT 10 MINITS ERLIER OR 10 MINETS LATER. I COUD HAVE DRIVEN IN A DIFRENT LANE BUT I CANT CHANGE IT AND I HAVE TO LIVE WITH IT. ITS HARD BECOS I MISS MY DAD. I MISS ME MUM AND NOW I MISS YOUR MUM TO AND I NEVER EVEN NEW HER. SOMTIMES I EVEN MISS YOU. I AM PROBLY SCAREING YOU NOW BUT I AM NOT SCARY. JUST SORRY. ANY WAY THANKS FOR READING.
YOUR FRIEND,
CHARLEY

Orion put the letter back in its envelope and put it under his pillow. His body was sinking heavily into his sleeping bag, but his mind was racing as fast as his bike on a downhill ride. He'd just read a letter from the man who'd killed his mum; now everything was different. It had to be, right? He turned off the flashlight and listened to the fire sparking the air outside the tent, his dad making small swishing sounds and thumping about when he moved. The boy could see Orion's Belt when he looked up because they hadn't put the tarp up tonight, wanting to wake up with the sun, and there was a mesh opening above him which let him see the stars. The constellation was upside down here, though his mum would've said it was right-side up as it had been from the beginning of time. Maybe things weren't different.

He was confused. He didn't know how he was supposed to feel so he just let sadness wash over him. It was so sad that he only had his mum on the inside because he wanted her on the outside too, and it was so sad that Charley didn't have his mum on the outside either, and not only that but he didn't even have a dad. Orion had the best dad in the world who was taking him off-roading tomorrow, which made Orion nervous but really excited too. He had a dad who told him that he was strong, even though he was skinny and short. And he had his Grandma Pearl and his Uncle John and his cousin Coco, who he was going to see in a few days when they got to Lesterville. And he had his Very Viv and Funtastic Phil, who were going to meet them in California at the end of their trip. They were all going to go to Disneyland and swim in the ocean. And he missed his nan too, but she was on the inside, right? That's what he'd tell himself from now on. Like Digger. Digger would always be on the inside. Best dog ever. Even better than Juni's new pup. And he had his friends at school, so many friends at school, who he sometimes talked to about his mum, but not much because she was just on the inside, right? And they couldn't understand that. Charley Cromwell understood.

He switched the flashlight back on and turned it to his pannier, which he brought into the tent every night. His dad carried all the camping gear and clothes while Orion carried things one might find in an adventurer's junk drawer, things like maps, a pocketknife, a compass, bike tools and a patch kit. He carried his dad's phone, an address book, a journal and some pens. In his mind, he could hear his dad saying, "Big day tomorrow. Best to get a good night's sleep." But how could he do that now? He got out the journal and a pen and, without a plan as to what he was going to write, he began writing.

Dear Charley.

Acknowledgments

It's well near impossible to express my gratitude to Cal Barksdale at Arcade Publishing for taking on this book and publishing an American-Australian in her home country, but I'll give it a go: thank you, Cal, and thanks to everyone else at Arcade and Skyhorse who worked on it.

This book was a wonderful collaboration between myself and the four women I've come to call the Extremely Nice Ladies Club, in which there is no president because all of the women are equally nice and intelligent and passionate: my agent and friend and favorite reader, Jo Butler; my Australian publisher, Madonna Duffy, for life-changing encouragement; and my two editors, Clara Finlay and Cathy Vallance, both of whom have taught me so much. Greatest respect to you all.

To other women like Tessie Delaney and Nancy Koreen, like Alison Flett and Rachael Mead, for inspiring such love between a trio of friends. Women need women and I'm so lucky to have you. To the Archetiers—Katherine Arguile, Rebekah Clarkson, Rachael Mead and Anna Solding—for early reads, useful feedback and practical conversation like, "Just turn it into a novel!" Thanks to Brian Castro and Matthew Lamb, for reassuring an emerging writer and including the chapter "Apricots" in the *Review of Australian Fiction*. Thank you to Sharon Holmes, for all the work you do with dyslexic children, mine especially. Thanks to Penny Strickland, for lending me your beautiful home in Far North Queensland so I could finish the first draft of this book. And thanks to Mike Hopkins, for joining me on an epic bike ride with a midway break in a cottage in the Yorkshire Dales, where I finished the final draft of this book. The cycling was as important as the writing.

To Mom and Dad, for always asking how my writing's going and listening when I carry on for far too long. Thanks to my dog, Tom, the inspiration for Digger the dog, who gave me such joy when writing about the animal–human relationship. And thanks—enormous thanks—to my children, Guthrow, Sunny and Matilda, who've indulged me by becoming regulars at book launches, and especially to my partner, Dash, who understands the value of a literary culture and loves me for my contribution to it (among other things). I love you, too—the entire clan—so much.